"Open the envelope. It could be a juicy lead on a new story that'll land you in the office next to mine," Brody teased.

"You *are* trying hard to butter me up." Hallie laughed.

"Not at all. I recognize a woman with a destiny when I see her."

A tiny smile curved her mouth, and Brody's pulse did a little cha-cha.

"Get out of here, Jordan. I've got work to do." She turned away, and he left, chuckling.

A scream halted him midstride. He whirled and raced back to her carrel. Hallie stood in the aisle between work stations, hands to her chest, wide stare fixed toward the floor. He followed the direction of her gaze and spotted the manila envelope on the carpet. Next to the packet lay a braided gold rope.

Hallie pointed a trembling finger toward the dropped items. "Somebody sent me the cord that strangled Alicia. And this, too." She thrust a piece of plain white paper at him.

Plain block letters in bold black marker said YOU COULD BE NEXT.

Books by Jill Elizabeth Nelson

Love Inspired Suspense

Evidence of Murder
Witness to Murder

JILL ELIZABETH NELSON

writes what she likes to read—faith-based tales of adventure seasoned with romance. By day she operates as housing manager for a seniors' apartment complex. By night she turns into a wild and crazy writer who can hardly wait to jot down all the exciting things her characters are telling her, so she can share them with her readers. More about Jill and her books can be found at www.jillelizabethnelson.com. She and her husband live in rural Minnesota, surrounded by the woods and prairie and their four grown children who have settled nearby.

WITNESS TO MURDER

JILL ELIZABETH NELSON

Steeple
Hill®

Published by Steeple Hill Books™

STEEPLE HILL BOOKS

Steeple Hill®

Recycling programs
for this product may
not exist in your area.

ISBN-13: 978-0-373-44345-1

WITNESS TO MURDER

www.SteepleHill.com

Printed in U.S.A.

And you will know the truth,
and the truth will set you free.
—*John* 8:32

To those whose lives have been stunted by fear. (Isn't that all of us at times?) May the truth spoken in love—to ourselves, to others—make us free to live in the joy and peace God intends for His children.

ONE

Channel Six television news reporter Hallie Berglund put her right foot on the bottom step of the swaybacked porch, then stopped cold. The hairs on her arms prickled. What was that awful noise coming from inside the house? Some kind of music? This century-old Victorian was rented by four University of Minnesota coeds, but even if they liked punk rock they wouldn't listen to this. And why was the front door several inches ajar?

Careful to keep the heels of her pumps from clacking against the wood, she walked carefully up the remaining two steps, but angry creaks from the porch boards announced her arrival. Whoever—whatever—was inside gave no indication her approach had been heard. The noise progressed in decibels.

Hallie frowned. There had to be a logical explanation. On the telephone, Alicia Drayton had sounded eager, almost desperate, to do the interview as soon as possible. The part-time fashion model and full-time student had said her roommates would be out all afternoon—a perfect opportunity for the two of them to talk privately.

The sound continued—long, drawn out. Like something a person would hear on a dark and moonless night, not in the balmy afternoon of a cloudless June day. She doused the impulse to back away and wait for her cameraman to catch up with her. She was a reporter, and she needed to find out what was going on. Sooner rather than later.

Her rap on the warped door panel widened the opening, revealing a foyer done in dark wood and last decade's wallpaper. She stepped inside onto a scatter rug and was greeted by lingering scents of mingled women's perfumes. To her left a set of stairs led upward. Ahead and to her right lay an opening framed in old-fashioned wide wood.

"Alicia?" Hallie's voice sounded hollow in the open space.

The noise stopped, and silence fell like a skipped heartbeat. Then a loud sniffle announced a fresh round of wails, this time in words spoken in a masculine tenor. "No, no, no. This isn't real. Allie, baby, wake uuuuuup!"

Hallie's breath caught. Was Alicia hurt? Hallie hurried forward, heels tapping the faded floorboards. She stepped through the opening, and a squawk escaped her throat.

What whirlwind had trashed this living room? The couch was tipped onto its back, an easy chair lay on its side, and the entertainment center had fallen face down, scattering shattered electronic equipment. And who lay sprawled on the floor near the heavily curtained picture window? The head and torso were concealed from view by a lean man with spiked blond hair who crouched over the inert body. His bare, muscular shoulders quaked beneath a sweat-streaked tank top the same shade of tan as his running shorts.

"Who? Wh-what?" The words stuttered between Hallie's lips. "Should we call 9-1-1?"

The man eased to his feet, all six feet six inches of him. He swiveled toward her like a man in a trance, slate-blue eyes staring blankly. Wetness glistened on drawn cheeks in a face all sharp planes and angles. In his fist he clutched a braided gold cord. "She's…dead."

Hallie's gaze fell to the head and shoulders on the floor behind the man's feet. She gulped. Whoever had trashed this room had also done a number on the woman's face…and her neck. Raw cord marks dug into her pale throat.

Alicia? The glossy auburn hair splayed around her head matched the publicity photos that had been sent over to the station, but the facial features were too puffy to be identified.

The giveaway was the man with what appeared to be the murder weapon in his hand—Alicia's boyfriend, Minnesota Golden Gophers' bad boy, Damon Lange. The college basketball player's famous temper had finally turned him into a killer.

Hallie's gaze locked with his. Ice encased her muscles, and her heart slammed against her rib cage. A change melted over Lange's face. Pinched sorrow fell away, relaxed into openmouthed awareness, and then red-faced fear—and fury. Lange raised the fist that held the cord and charged toward Hallie.

She shrieked and whirled away, racing toward the open door. The scatter rug on the floor slid beneath her heels. Hallie's cameraman, Stan Fisher, stepped into the house, exclaiming, as Lange's body struck Hallie from behind. She careened into the cameraman, and the two of them went down in a heap at the foot of the stairs. Hallie's knees hit the floor—hard—and her suit pants did little to protect them. Pain speared up her legs. Damon disappeared out the door. His boat-sized feet struck a hollow tattoo on the porch.

Gasping for air, Hallie rolled away from Stan, who lay on his back spluttering and clutching his precious camera to his bony chest. Heedless of her aching knees, she scrambled on all fours toward the doorway and gripped the doorpost. Out on the sun-soaked street, Damon charged into the street, arms pumping, the braided cord no longer in hand. A green-and-blue Papa Morelli's Pizza delivery car whizzed up the road, and the ball player dodged barely in time to avoid being hit. Then he raced onward and out of view between the houses.

"What was that all about?" Stan's footfalls came up behind her.

Dazed, Hallie stared up into his wide-eyed face. "Call 9-1-1. Damon killed Alicia. I saw." Her voice came out in a rasp. She struggled to her feet, leg muscles jittering. "At least, I think she's dead. I'd better…I need to check." She forced a lump down her throat.

Stan gaped at her, freckles standing out like punctuation marks on his pale cheeks.

"Just call." Her voice rose an octave.

She brushed past him and wobbled into the living room. Debris crunched under her pumps as she approached the body. To one side lay the cord she'd seen in Damon's hand. He must have dropped it when he fled. In the background, Stan's excited voice reported the emergency.

Gaze averted from Alicia's face, Hallie watched the body's chest for some sign of rising and falling, but she spotted no movement beneath the gauzy, long-sleeved tunic top swirled in psychedelic 1970s colors. She crouched beside Alicia and pressed two fingers to the inside of her wrist. She held her breath while she counted to ten. Not a flicker of life.

Groaning, Hallie closed her eyes and bowed her head. *Not again, Lord.* Why did women stay with men who abused them? She'd asked that unanswerable question over and over in the nine years since Teresa's senseless death. Back then, as a college sophomore, she had been powerless to gain justice, but this time she was in prime position to make certain the guilty party didn't get away with murder just because he was a popular athlete.

Jaw clenched, Hallie opened her eyes, and her gaze fell on the edge of a band of metal on Alicia's wrist that she'd nudged aside in order to feel for a pulse. The etching on the band looked familiar. Hallie pulled the featherweight shirtsleeve away from the inch-wide bracelet and took a closer look. Every muscle went rigid.

She knew the unique markings on that brass and copper armband. The Nigerian artisan had been dead for over two decades, since Hallie was eight years old. But the woman had never in her life sold her work commercially—only given it to people she regarded as special.

Why was Alicia Drayton wearing a bracelet fashioned by Hallie's mother?

Hallie sucked in a deep breath, and then let the air seep from her lungs. Her hand dug for the camera phone in her purse's outside pocket. This was going to be the most distasteful thing she'd ever done in her life. But she couldn't step away without a clear record of her mother's work, and she couldn't make off with the bracelet. Blanking her mind and moving quickly, she snapped several shots of the dead woman's arm.

"The cops and the paramedics are on their way." Stan's voice came from the doorway.

She glanced over her shoulder and spotted an eight-by-ten photograph lying face-up on the floor. The glass inside the cherry-wood frame was cracked in a crazy pattern that suggested someone had stepped on it, but she could still make out a man's smiling face. No taller than average, with hair touched by gray and a middle displaying a small paunch, his confident presence overshadowed the women in the photo. He stood between them with an arm around each of their shoulders.

One of them could only be Alicia, just a few years younger. Her full lips pouted beneath a bored green gaze. Typical teenager. The other woman, Alicia's decades older mirror image, stood stiffly and a bit glassy-eyes, as if the camera made her nervous. The man—Alicia's father?—grinned like he'd won the lottery. And why not? His wife was stunning and his daughter even more so. Correction. The daughter *had been* stunning. These parents now had horrible news coming to them. A whimper squeaked out Hallie's tight throat.

Nausea squeezing her stomach, she stood and picked her way toward Stan. How could he hover there, calmly panning his video camera over the room?

"Remind me," she said as she brushed past him into the foyer, "never, ever to volunteer for the police beat."

"You couldn't guess in a million years the trouble Hallie walked into this afternoon."

The tense words brought Brody Jordan's head around from the sports highlights he was editing in the video room. Vince Graham, the crime reporter, stood in the doorway, craggy face drawn into those taut planes that made his mug so compelling on the air. Brody clicked off the video and waved Vince in.

The crime reporter shook his head. "No time for a chat. Stan called the story in, and I'm headed for Alicia Drayton's house. The woman's been beaten and strangled, and Hallie caught Damon Lange in the act."

Brody stiffened, nostrils flaring. "I don't believe it."

Vince frowned. "Hallie's not given to hallucinations, Jordan. The cops and the medical examiner are already on the scene, and they're taking the whole thing very seriously."

"No, I didn't mean Hallie imagined a murder, but there's no way Damon hurt Alicia."

The ends of the crime reporter's mouth twisted upward. "Enjoy your illusions, buddy. One thing I've learned on this beat is anyone's capable of anything."

"Have they got Damon in custody?"

"Naw. He skedaddled. There's an APB out on him."

"I'm coming with you." Brody rose.

"Aren't you forgetting something?"

Brody narrowed his eyes at his smirking coworker.

"The six o'clock news broadcast? You can't be in two places at once."

Brody checked his watch. "It's later than I thought. This is one time in a million I could do without being the evening sportscaster. Just let me know if Damon is arrested, okay?"

"You got it." Vince strode away.

Brody grabbed his suit coat from the back of the chair and headed up the tile-floored hallway toward his office. Should he call Hallie and get the story firsthand? He could find her cell number on the interoffice list. Arriving at his desk, he opened the top drawer then froze, hand on the internal directory.

No, getting her on the phone was a bad move. Not only would she be up to her neck in police questions right now, but he didn't want to have this conversation long distance. He had to look her in the eye and make her repeat the claim that Damon killed Alicia. Even then he wouldn't buy it. He knew the young basketball player too well. In his experience, Hallie told the news with integrity and enthusiasm, but maybe her crusading nature got things exaggerated or misconstrued this time.

Brody frowned. Then again it was kind of hard to mis-understand a dead body. He sank into his desk chair, tugged at his left earlobe, and ruffled his fingers through his coarse brown hair.

A few months ago, Brody hosted the Golden Gophers star basketball player for a live interview, and the young man had brought Alicia along to watch. Yes, she sometimes treated Damon like gum under her shoe, but that day she'd been in a good mood, playful even. She teased the ball player about his "camera presence," green eyes sparkling in that cameo-perfect face. Damon adored her. He would have given his life for her, not snuffed hers out.

Brody bent and pulled his trash can from under his desk. If he could get Hallie to himself for a few minutes and ask his questions, maybe he could start to understand. Fishing amongst crumpled papers, he came up with an invitation he'd chucked a couple of days ago. The rectangle of card stock showed a multi-colored cake with many candles on top and read: *Guess Who's 29. For Real!*

The decision not to attend the surprise party thrown by Hallie's two best friends had been a no-brainer—even though everyone at Channel Six was invited. Hallie and he hadn't exactly hit it off in the three years since she'd joined the staff. Not that he didn't find her attractive. Who wouldn't? The camera loved that glossy, raven hair, those big, brown eyes and the gleaming, white smile against her smooth caramel complexion. She was all grace and wit. She was also openly disdainful of sports figures she considered "arrogant jocks." And according to the cameraman who'd quit the station before Stan came on, she expected the moon from herself and everyone who worked with her.

Exactly the kind of high-maintenance trouble this thirty-five-year-old divorcé needed to avoid. After his experience with Deborah, only God's unexpected grace saved him from becoming a bum on skid row rather than a man with a career he loved.

Brody flipped the invitation over and read the details about when and where. He'd really rather stick his hand into a piranha tank, but it looked like he was going to a party after all.

TWO

"Vince is here to do the story."

Stan's voice brought Hallie's head up from the backrest on the news van's passenger seat. A metallic blue sports coupe glided into a spot at the curb in front of the van. The crime reporter thrived on drama, even in his choice of vehicle. She flipped down the sun visor and used the attached mirror to help her readjust the enameled pins that partially tamed her mop of black waves, and then refreshed her Perfectly Plum lipstick. She frowned. Her eyes were almost as red as they were brown.

Giving a statement to the police had about turned Hallie into blubbering mush. In her head, Teresa's dead white face kept popping up alongside Alicia's battered features. Could she get through this TV interview with the tiniest shred of dignity? *I'm going to need a boatload of strength, Lord.* Grimacing, she climbed out of the van and smoothed her mocha colored pantsuit.

The sun shone just as warmly as it had when she and Stan first arrived at the house, so why did a quiver shoot through her stomach. Maybe it was the sight of a white-sheeted gurney being wheeled out the front door. The outline of the human form beneath the covers betrayed its grizzly burden. Stan was busy capturing the moment on film.

Hallie turned away toward the WDJN crime reporter.

"Busy afternoon for the cops in the Twin Cities metro

area," Vince said. "Three-car pileup on I-94, a convenience store robbery on Highway 100, a gang shooting near Hennepin Avenue in Minneapolis, and an apparent suicide in south St. Paul. But our top story—Golden Gophers star strangles girlfriend." He let out a low whistle. "You ready to give Channel Six the scoop before every media hound with a police scanner descends on us?"

Hallie's manicured fingernails jabbed her palms. "I need to do whatever I can to make sure Alicia Drayton's killer gets what he deserves."

Vince winked then motioned toward Stan, who took up a place in front of them, headphones on and camera ready. The crime reporter looked at his watch. "This'll be live feed as the lead news story for the six o'clock broadcast."

Hallie gasped. "Is it that late already?"

"Why? You got someplace else to be?" He shot her a one-sided grin.

"I do, but I'll just have to be late, as usual."

Stan began counting off seconds with his fingers. Vince squared his shoulders, and Hallie cleared her throat. Stan signaled they were on.

Iron-faced, the crime reporter introduced the location and the situation then turned toward Hallie. "When you came here today to interview Alicia Drayton for a story on Minnesota fashion models, you hardly expected to find yourself in the midst of a murder."

"That's very true, Vince." Hallie's voice cracked, and she swallowed. "Today was supposed to be a good publicity break for a young woman with talent, intelligence and a life of endless prospects before her, not her last day on earth."

Vince's hazel eyes glinted approval of her dramatic answer. "Tell us what you saw."

Hallie opened her mouth, closed it, and then licked dry lips, tasking her lipstick. She could do this. The soft whir of the camera, the familiar microphone near her mouth, Stan's homely, expectant face—this was her life, her career, and a fresh chance to use it to right a wrong, just as she'd intended when she became a reporter. A knot unraveled in the core of her being, and she lifted her chin.

"I'll share with our viewers the same information I gave the police. When I approached the house, I heard strange noises from inside. I thought maybe someone was hurt and needed help. Since the front door was ajar, I hurried inside. Alicia lay on the living room floor, dead, and Damon Lange stood over her with a braided rope in his hand. A curtain tie, I think. The police will probably discover it was the murder weapon."

Vince pulled the mic away from Hallie's mouth and put it to his own. "There you have the testimony of Channel Six's own feature reporter, Hallie Berglund, who this afternoon was an eye witness to murder. Golden Gophers player Damon Lange is currently being sought in connection with the death of his girlfriend, college student and fashion model Alicia Drayton. Anyone with information as to his whereabouts should call the number on your screen." Vince turned toward Hallie again. "What went through your mind when you walked in on such a tragic situation?"

"Disbelief… Horror… Fear for myself." Hallie crossed her arms, barely containing a shudder. "Lange chased me, but Stan, my cameraman, came into the house so Mr. Lange only shoved us down and escaped. I don't know what he would have done if Stan hadn't been there." She paused and took a deep breath. "Ever since I confirmed Alicia was dead, I've been furious and…and just sick. I despise abusers. It looks like another life has been lost to one today." Hallie blinked against a prickle behind her eyelids.

"Thank you for so candidly sharing your traumatic confrontation. I suspect you could use a little R & R right now." A sympathetic smile crossed his face.

"That's right, Vince. I plan to spend a quiet evening with friends, but I won't rest easy until Damon Lange is in custody."

"Understandable, Hallie." He turned his face toward the camera. "This is Vince Graham of WDJN News reporting live from the scene of the crime."

The red light flashed on Stan's camera, and they were off the air. Weariness flowed through Hallie's limbs. "I've got to get out of here," she told the guys.

"Let's boogie." Stan lowered the camera from his shoulder.

The crime reporter leaned close to Hallie's ear. "Brody's on the warpath over Damon."

Hallie suppressed a snort. Of course, that man would be. What was this? Some kind of sick jocks-must-stick-together thing?

Vince waved and headed toward the perimeter of crime scene tape where forensic technicians and police officers worked. The screech of brakes and the slam of doors announced the arrival of three news vehicles, adding to congestion on the road. Slipping away in the WDJN van was going to be tricky. Hallie recognized logos from two newspapers and a rival television station. In seconds, she was swarmed by microphones and questions shouted from eager faces.

Hallie lifted a hand for silence. "I saw Damon Lange holding what I believe to be the murder weapon and Alicia Drayton lying dead on the floor. Mr. Lange is currently on the loose. Anyone who knows where to find this man should contact their local police department. That's all I have to say. Exclusive details have already been given to Channel Six news."

She barged between the microphones and lunged through the van door that Stan had thoughtfully opened. They eased away from the scene, the cameraman threading the van between vehicles with inches to spare.

Hallie slumped. "Now I know what it feels like to be the media entrée du jour."

Stan chuckled. "Things have just started to get interesting. Wait until the case goes to trial, and you're the main witness."

"They have to catch Damon Lange first. The world will be a safer place when he's behind bars."

Twenty minutes later, they pulled into the parking lot behind WDJN's headquarters in downtown St. Paul. The four-story building blended in with other early 1800s brick structures in the renovated neighborhood of restaurants, condominiums and businesses a few blocks from the Mississippi riverfront. The granite and glass face of the bank up the street announced that time had marched into the twenty-first century, but few would guess that the Channel Six building from a bygone era housed the latest gizmos and gadgets for electronic communication.

"You coming in?" Stan shut off the engine.

Hallie shook her head. "Places to go and people to see."

"Oh, yeah, that 'quiet evening with friends.'" He snickered.

She punched his shoulder. "I'll have you know I'll be addressing wedding invitations. Wonderful, boring job, and that's about all I can handle right now."

Stan's eyes widened. "You're getting married?"

"Not me, goof. One of my best girlfriends, Samantha Reid, is tying the knot with a great guy in five weeks. I'm the maid of honor…well, one of them. You see, Sam couldn't possibly pick between Jenna and me so—"

"Spare me." Stan presented his hand, palm out. "Wedding stuff gives me the willies."

"How come? You've never been married."

"My point exactly."

A tiny laugh seeped between Hallie's lips. "Well, when the love bug bites, you'll make a beeline for the altar."

"Don't count on it."

"Uh-oh!" Hallie's gaze narrowed on the dark head that had popped out the back door of the WDJN building. Brody was looking for something…or, more likely, someone.

"What?" Stan looked around.

"I so cannot handle a grilling by the champion of all things jock and jockette. See you tomorrow." She slipped out of the van and hurried across the lot, keeping vehicles between her and the hunter sniffing her trail.

Every once in a while, Brody's wry humor at a staff meeting surprised a laugh out of her, but most of the time he seemed to make a project out of establishing fresh roots as a nettle in the garden of her life. Female viewers might go gaga over those storm-gray eyes and the trademark one-sided dimple, but the charming facade didn't work on her.

She never forgot what she overheard him say to the station manager about her the day she started at WDJN. Cheerleader type, indeed! He might as well have pasted a couple of pom-poms to her hands, because she'd been doing mostly feature fluff ever since—such as the Minnesota model story she was working on today. She had become so well-known for that type of reporting that the modeling agent who had intrigued the station with the story idea had asked for her by name to do the coverage.

Scowling, she continued up the sidewalk toward the corner of the block, heels clickety-clacking against the cement. A year ago she'd landed a big story about labor union corruption, but she'd had to freelance that one on her own time. She got the scoop, all right. Then Brody had the gall to seem mad at her about it. Okay, so maybe he'd been a little right. She should have arranged backup for herself when she went undercover, but everything had turned out great anyway. She'd do it differently now if the station would give her more hard-hitting stories. Not likely if Brody kept using his influence against her with his buddy Wayne Billings, the station manager.

Hallie joined a group of people at the crosswalk. A few of them glanced at her and sidled away. She probably looked ready to take a bite out of someone. Smoothing out her expression, she nodded to several who lived in her building. The signal changed, and the group surged across the street in a tight little herd that dispersed as soon as their feet touched the sidewalk. Hallie trailed a pair of chatting women carrying briefcases and a man with an iPod in his hand up a set of stairs onto a wide, cement landing shaded by a canopy. They skirted a cast-iron sculpture of a boy and a girl playing leapfrog. The man pulled out his building key, opened the front door, and they all filtered inside, Hallie bringing up the rear.

The still coolness of the lobby welcomed her. The rent rate insured that she drove an economy car, but living across the street from work was priceless in her business when time often counted in getting the scoop. Right now, she'd just as soon close the blinds and take the phone off the hook for about the next decade. Maybe she should forget about addressing invitations tonight. Jenna and Sam would understand better than anyone why today's tragedy turned her inside out. Then again, maybe she should be with close friends.

The elevator door whispered open in front of the little group just as Hallie's cell phone vibrated inside her blazer pocket. She checked the caller ID and smiled. Letting the others board the elevator, she turned away and sat in a lobby chair.

"Hi, Jenna. No, I haven't forgotten. It's been a day like you wouldn't believe."

A laugh trilled from the other end of the connection. "What's new in the life of Hallie Berglund?" The clatter of dishes in the background entered Hallie's ear. Jenna must be calling from the kitchen of her restaurant.

"You haven't seen the news tonight?"

"No way in this mad house. You'll have to fill us in. But I wanted to let you know that we're set up in the private dining room, and Sam's here already, chomping at the bit."

Hallie worked the high-heeled pump off her right foot and massaged her instep. A soft groan left her lips. "You'll have to get started without me."

"Pleeease don't tell me you're not coming. It's so important to—"

"What? You want me to break tradition and be on time? I just need to change clothes and freshen up."

"No problem. If it seals the deal, I made tomato and por-tabella quiche in pepper pots."

"Woman, don't bother to bar the door, I'm busting in."

They broke the connection, laughing. Hallie pocketed her phone. Maybe getting out would do her good.

She rode the elevator up to the third floor. Her hallway was empty but the muted strings and woodwinds of classical music drifted out from her neighbor's apartment. Stepping inside her unit, the scent from her blooming frangipani plant greeted her. The fluffy throw pillows on her tan-and-olive couch beckoned, but she breezed past into her small bedroom, where she changed into jeans and a blouse and comfy cross-trainers for her feet. In the bathroom, she took out the enameled pins that kept her dark hair away from her face for work and ran a comb through the thick strands. The shag cut feathered around her forehead, cheeks and jaw, before falling in tousled waves below her shoulders. Good enough. Teasing with the brush, curling iron and hair spray sounded like too much work. After all, it was just the girls tonight.

Twenty minutes later, she was on the interstate heading south toward Jenna's restaurant in Lakeville. She turned up the CD player. Belting out a few praise songs with Point of Grace should keep images of death out of her head. The Highway 42 exit came up as the third song was finishing. She glided off the freeway with a deep green Impala in her wake.

Her gaze narrowed on the rearview mirror. Hadn't that car been behind her when she left St. Paul? The temporary dealer plates were distinctive. It had to be the same car. Somebody was driving new wheels. Her heart rate quickened. She must have been in la-la land during the trip not to notice the green car had stuck with her. Of course, with several lanes of freeway traffic going in the same direction, the tail might not have been too noticeable until now.

The Impala hung back several car lengths, making it impossible to see the driver's face. Could Damon Lange be hunting her? She swallowed a bitter taste. No, that was silly. The college ball player couldn't afford a new car. He was squeaking through school on a sports scholarship. Her grip on the steering wheel eased, then tensed until her knuckles were white. If a man could commit murder, he could steal a car!

Ahead, a traffic light turned amber, and Hallie gunned through the intersection, heedless of a possible ticket. The green car was caught by the red light. Pulse washing in her ears, Hallie took the next turn, and then zigzagged around the area until she was sure the Impala hadn't found her again. The dashboard clock told her she was very late, rather than just sort of late by the time she pulled into a space at The Meridian, but at least she wasn't about to be accosted by a killer in a restaurant parking lot. She slumped and let out a breath.

Maybe she was making too much out of an innocent co-incidence of two people from the same place headed for the same area at the same time, but better to be paranoid than sorry. She'd have to report this incident to the police tomorrow, and see if any green Impalas had been stolen recently. Maybe by then they'd have Lange in custody, and she could relax.

Scrounging up her last scrap of energy, Hallie got out of the car and trod into the stucco and half-timbered restaurant. Laughter, the hum of voices, the clink of silverware and a mingling of divine food odors greeted her senses. People sat around cloth-covered tables under the mellow light of chandeliers hanging from exposed roof beams. Some patrons wore jeans, others suits or dresses. At The Meridian, no one felt out of place and everyone was pampered. Jenna and her business partners had a great thing going here.

Carla, a hostess Hallie recognized, rustled toward her, dressed in a modest, yet form-fitting black dress. "They're waiting for you in the back. Dr. Pepper, right?"

"Thanks, but no caffeine and sugar tonight. I've had enough stimulation for one day. Ice-water with lemon would be a life-saver."

"I'll send a tall glass your way." Carla smiled and glided toward the server's station.

Hallie threaded between full tables and busy wait staff on a circuitous route toward the private dining room. Peace and quiet in sympathetic company beckoned. She opened the door…and stepped into a carnival.

Balloons. Brightly colored banners. Flashing cameras.

"Surprise! Happy Birthday!"

The joyful din assaulted Hallie from dozens of grinning people. Her feet rooted to the spot, and her mouth fell open. A steel band wound around her chest, and pressure flooded behind her cheekbones. Tears burst their banks.

THREE

Whoa! The birthday girl was about to fly apart. Brody shot up from his chair while everyone else still cheered and laughed. He put his wide shoulders between Hallie and her well-wishers. "Hang in there, trooper. You can handle this." He dabbed at her cheeks with a linen napkin.

She sniffed a long breath, gazing at him with teary sable eyes. The air stalled in his lungs. She curled her fingers around his. He took in the contrast between their skin—his lightly tanned, her deeper tone natural and exotic. She slipped the napkin from his hand and finished wiping her eyes. Then she stuffed the piece of cloth into his suit coat pocket and stepped around him, a brilliant smile on her face.

"I'm—" Her voice cracked and she cleared her throat. "I'm overwhelmed."

Hallie's friends who were throwing the party, slender Samantha and full-figured Jenna, hustled forward and gathered her in hugs then whisked her into the crowd, chattering away. So much for "Thanks for the quick thinking, Brody."

A chuckle next to him drew his attention. It was Ryan Davidson, the tall guy who had introduced himself as Samantha's fiancé when Brody arrived.

"Quite the trio, eh?" Ryan jerked his chin toward the three women who stood practically joined at the hip as guests greeted the birthday girl. "I never know what they're going to come up with next. Hallie thought this was going to be a work night, stuffing and addressing wedding invitations. It's not really her birthday until tomorrow." He tucked a hand in a jeans pocket. "Sam and Jenna did the invites yesterday, but saved a couple for Hallie to do tonight so they can claim they didn't lie to her."

Brody laughed. "Clever. I take it the ladies have known each other for a while."

"Since forever. They went to high school together and belonged to the same youth group in Hallie's uncle's church."

Brody stared at Samantha's fiancé. "I didn't know Hallie was a Christian."

"I don't suppose faith is a common topic of conversation where you work."

"You mean amongst the liberal media?"

The man opened his mouth, shut it, and then shook his head. "I guess that's what I was thinking when I said it. Sorry if I was out of line."

"Don't worry about it." Brody let Ryan off the hook with a grin. "I'm a believer myself."

"No kidding! There's at least two at Channel Six then. Must be why WDJN is my preferred station for the news."

Brody studied his loafers to hide his frown. If he and Hallie were on the same page spiritually, how come they'd never sensed the connection? Maybe because they went out of their way to avoid one another. He needed to alter that habit if he expected her to be open to a discussion with him about what happened today. "Come to think of it, I don't know much about Hallie. What do her folks do?"

Ryan's brows lifted. "I guess you *are* in the dark. Her parents were killed on the mission field a long time ago."

"Oh, man, that's tough."

"Sam says Hallie was a little girl when she came to the States to live with her father's brother's family. I don't suppose she remembers much about Nigeria. Sam and I are having our wedding ceremony in Hallie's uncle's church." The blond man rocked back and forth on his heels, grinning like his face would split.

Brody looked away. Here was one guy charging gleefully into matrimony. He'd been a starry-eyed groom himself once. Hopefully, Samantha and Ryan would make a better job of it than he and Deborah had. They could hardly do worse.

Ryan slapped him on the shoulder. "Let's grab some of that awesome buffet spread before the rest of this bunch gobbles it up."

"I'm right on your heels, buddy." Brody smiled. He could sure like Hallie's friends. Too bad she was such a prickly rose.

As he piled fresh fruit and veggies, cold canapés and steaming gourmet concoctions onto his plate, he studied her. She stood flushed and laughing amidst faces he knew from work and many he'd never seen before. Hallie stood half a head taller than most of the women and at least as tall as some of the men. Brody only topped her by a couple of inches himself. With her brand of class, she could walk the runway as easily as Alicia had done.

By the unclouded expressions on everyone's faces, she was keeping mum about her experience this afternoon. A movement by the door caught his eye. Uh-oh, peaceful ignorance wasn't going to last long now. Stan sauntered into the festivities. The lanky cameraman was never one to hang onto juicy information, at least not after it had already been reported.

Brody looked around. Vince Graham wasn't here at all. Probably wouldn't make it since he'd be haunting the police for breaking developments on the Drayton case. And none of the other evening news staff was present. Since the rest of the guests seemed to be ignorant of events, there was no reason for Hallie's party to be darkened by murder talk, unless…Stan's gaze stopped on Hallie's group, and he headed that direction like a man on a mission.

Brody intercepted him. "Here you go, Stan the Man." He held his brimming plate toward his coworker. "Chow down."

"Helloooo delicious sustenance." The cameraman took the plate. "Thanks. How did you know the smells were already driving me crazy? I haven't eaten in at least…" He glanced at the wall clock…"four hours."

Brody chuckled. "That's forever to you."

"I'm hypoglycemic." He bit into a seafood and veggie wrap. His freckled face went slack and he moaned. "Whoever made this must be a five-star chef. Believe me, I know good eats."

"Around here, a food aficionado should have no problem satisfying the beast. Though the way you eat, you should be a heavyweight not a welterweight."

"Don't begrudge me my great metabolism." Stan looked up from the plate. "Maybe I'd better say happy birthday to Hallie before I get lost in gourmet-land. It practically killed me to keep quiet about the party when I was working with her today."

"Between you and me, I think she's more than a little shook up about her experience this afternoon. We'd probably be doing her a favor to let her enjoy the party without any nasty reminders."

Stan bobbed his head. "Gotcha! You can count on me to zip my lips—especially when I'm filling them with stuff like this."

"Hi, guys." Jenna wandered up to them. "Are you finding everything to your satisfaction?"

"Stan here fell in love at first bite," Brody said. He performed introductions between the cameraman and one of Hallie's best friends. "I'm told that Jenna's the lead chef and part owner of The Meridian."

"You made this ambrosia?" Stan gestured with the piece of seafood wrap between his fingers. "The touch of cumin draws out the natural sweetness of the crab meat. Perfecto!"

"Spot on." Color tinted the woman's cheeks. "What an amazing palate you have."

Stan's face lit like she'd handed him an award. She gazed back, a tiny, bemused smile playing around her mouth.

Okay, third wheel here. Brody turned away, shaking his head. Did Hallie notice how he ran interference for her? He looked her direction and found her staring at him, the corners of her lips turned down. She might as well have shouted at him—*what are you up to?* Brody sighed. He'd known thawing the Queen of Sheba would be a tough task.

He kept his distance through the birthday song, the cake and the cards, but as people began to leave, he edged closer to his target. At last, with only a couple of die-hard guests left, he noticed Hallie stifling a yawn.

Nearby, Jenna laughed, Stan at her elbow, where he'd hovered most of the evening.

"Tough day?" Jenna asked.

"And then some." Hallie's gaze met Brody's then darted away.

That determined smile materialized. Was he the only one who picked up on the shadows in her eyes? Or maybe he only imagined the hovering hurt because of his own concerns. He should wait until another time to ask his questions… No, he couldn't. Damon was out there, a fugitive, and this woman's testimony could end his freedom and his career.

"This was great." Hallie swept a hand around the room. "I can't believe you guys went to all this trouble."

Samantha walked up, and threaded her arm through Ryan's. "Just wait and see what we do for the big three-oh."

Hallie planted a hand on her hip. "You have a death wish?" Everyone laughed, but Hallie's chuckle cut off short. "Methinks it's this old woman's bedtime."

"That statement coming from the night owl?" Samantha shook her head, grinning.

"We'll walk you to your car," Ryan said. "It's dark now."

"No need." Brody stepped forward. "I'm heading out anyway."

Hallie blinked like he'd snapped his fingers in front of her face, but didn't object when he took her elbow and guided her to the door amidst a chorus of goodbyes. Outside the private room, she disengaged herself from his grasp and walked ahead of him through the restaurant. Male heads turned as she went past. Brody drew himself up taller and stayed close on her heels.

They exited into the halogen-lit parking lot, and Hallie glanced over her shoulder at him. "Thank you." The words came out pinched, but at least she said them.

Questions pooled behind his lips as they crossed the asphalt, but he held them in. The darkness smelled of car exhaust, cooking fumes and cooling tar.

She walked around to the driver's side of her coupe and gazed over the car roof at him. "I'll see you tomorrow."

"Cruise me around to my car. It's on the other side of the lot."

She grimaced, but the sound of electronic locks releasing met his ears. He hopped in on the passenger side before she could change her mind.

"Don't start it," he said as she inserted the key into the ignition. "We need to talk. Damon didn't kill Alicia."

"So that's what this was about. Attending the party. The emergency napkin. Walking me to the car. You want a private interview with the witness to a crime involving a sports figure."

Her cynical snort sent his nostrils flaring. The woman could rile a sleeping turtle. "Sure, I came to the party to talk to you, but I don't care about an interview. Vince is handling the story."

Her brows disappeared beneath groomed bangs. "Then what's your interest?"

"The police are looking for the wrong man. Damon's no murderer. I need to know exactly what you saw in that house." Did he sound as frustrated as he felt? Why had he thought Hallie might spill her guts to him, of all people?

Hallie's shoulders slumped. "I keep replaying that scene in my head." Her gaze was fixed straight ahead. Weariness hung on her like an old coat.

Brody's conscience stirred, but now was not a good time to go soft.

She turned her face in his direction, chin jutting out. "I walked in on Damon crouched over Alicia's sprawled body. He was moaning and carrying on like someone who's done something terrible and can never take it back. When he heard me, he leaped up with a braided cord in his hand. Alicia was strangled, so don't tell me Damon didn't kill her."

"You didn't actually see him put that cord around her throat and pull it tight."

She shuddered visibly. "If I had, I would have clobbered him."

"I can believe that." Brody let out a dry chuckle. "But I still don't believe Damon killed Alicia. Did you notice anything about the scene that didn't add up?"

"We-e-ell." Hallie frowned and looked way. "I don't suppose these things are ever neat little slam dunks, but there were a couple of things."

Silence fell for several heartbeats. "What things?" Brody prompted.

She met his gaze. "I did wonder why bits of glass were scattered on top of the body. If there was a struggle *before* the murder, why wasn't all the debris under the body? And why didn't she have defensive bruises on her hands, which she would have used to shield her face? I think somebody stronger than she was sat on her, beat her and strangled her, and then they trashed the room in an excess of fury. Anger followed by regret is Damon's modus operandi, considering the numerous times he's blown up and apologized later on the basketball court."

"Impressive. Even the assumptions about Damon are detective level observations."

"More than you expected out of someone like me?" Her tone had an edge he couldn't define.

"I'm not sure I know what you mean by that question, but Vince would probably tell you it's amazing for anyone unused to dealing with crime scenes to keep so much presence of mind."

Her eyes widened. "Thank you."

Brody's insides warmed. Mark this one down in the history books. Hallie Berglund expressed sincere gratitude to Brody Jordan. He opened his mouth to ask what more she'd noticed, but his cell phone began to play. He popped the phone open and answered. Heavy breathing came over the line, and his belly muscles tensed.

"You've got to help me," a familiar voice whispered. "I don't know what to do."

"Damon?"

Hallie gasped and her huge, dark eyes riveted on him.

FOUR

How could Brody sit and talk so calmly to a brutal murderer? Oh, that's right. Hallie curled a lip. He didn't think a talented basketball star could also be a supreme creep.

"That's not an option, Damon." Brody's fingers drummed against the console between the driver's and passenger seat. "You can't run from this. You've got to—" Paused. "I know it, and you know it, but now we need to convince the police."

Shouted curses from the opposite end of the connection carried to Hallie. She winced. Creep, all right. Kills a woman and then only cares about saving his own skin.

"Get a grip!" Brody's icy tone sliced through the heated explosion. "There's only one right alternative at this moment, and you'd better take it." Pause. "When and where?" Pause. "I'll be there." Brody snapped his phone shut then turned toward Hallie. "I've got to go. We'll have to finish our chat later. Can you swing around to my car?"

"Don't tell me you're going to meet with a wanted fugitive. You could get in big-time trouble. Not to mention, since he's capable of murder, you're risking your life."

One side of his mouth lifted, and the trademark dimple flickered. "Thanks for your concern. I appreciate it, but this is something I have to do."

Hallie shrugged, bitter protest burning on her tongue, but what was the point of wrangling with this stubborn man? "I hope it's not your funeral…literally."

Brody laughed. "I think you're doomed to see me in the office tomorrow, not a casket."

Gritting her teeth, Hallie started the car and backed out of her space. She should boot him out and make him walk, but she was raised to be Minnesota nice, a code of courtesy that had trickled over the border to her Eau Claire, Wisconsin family address. "Where's your vehicle?" She guided the compact around The Meridian.

"It's the Impala right there."

Her gaze followed the direction of his finger, and she punched her brakes. They lurched forward against their seatbelts. "You're the one who was following me in a new car." She skewered him with a glare.

Brody's storm-cloud eyes studied her like she must've fallen off the turnip truck. "Is there something criminal about trading fresh every couple of years? Lots of people do it."

"That's not the point. You scared—I mean I thought…" She trailed away on a huff. Nothing like making an idiot of herself in front of a guy who already considered her little better than window dressing at the station.

"Ahhhh." That viewer-popular dimple took up residence in his right cheek.

Would Aunt Michelle approve if she slapped it off? She looked away and scowled out her window toward a young couple leaving the restaurant hand-in-hand.

"Given what you believe about Damon," Brody said, "you thought my car might contain the killer looking for the only witness."

She turned a hard gaze on him. "So I'm a little skittish after what I saw this afternoon."

"Actually, I don't blame you. Under the circumstances, that was sharp thinking and a good reaction to ditch me. Though I did wonder where you disappeared to when I arrived at the party, and you weren't here yet." He laughed.

The tension in Hallie's muscles eased. The guy could be charming. Not that she cared about that, but maybe he was starting to get that she wasn't a total airhead. "I had intended to report the incident to the police tomorrow. Guess I won't have to now."

Nodding, Brody climbed out of the car, then bent and poked his head inside. "Rain check on our conversation."

"You're not the only one with questions to ask. I want to know what makes you so sure your golden boy's not a killer. And it better be good."

He smacked the top of her vehicle with his palm. "Deal. And it is."

Her car door thunked shut, and the sportscaster strode into the dusk. She'd find those broad shoulders appealing if they didn't bear that "I'm all it" swagger she'd detested in Teresa's fatal tormenter. Hallie shook her head. She thought she'd come so far in erasing those images from her mind—getting on with her life—but they'd only been hiding. Lurking for an opportunity to pounce. She had to put the memories back in their cage. How would she cope if she started having those nightmares again? A shudder rippled up her spine.

She needed to make sure today's monster was taken off the streets as quickly as possible. No way could she trust Brody to do the hard thing with his Wunderkind. She slipped her vehicle into an empty spot near the restaurant exit but behind the cover of an SUV. A few seconds later, Brody's new car cruised past and turned onto the road. Hallie maneuvered out of the parking lot and crept up behind him, allowing a car between them. Shortly, all three of the vehicles glided onto the interstate going north. Hallie took a different lane than Brody and stayed behind the other car as a buffer.

Minutes ticked past. Was it stifling in here, or was she just nervous? She turned up the air conditioning and repositioned her sweaty hands around the wheel. Find out where Brody was meeting Damon and call 9-1-1, that's all she had to do.

But what if the killer spotted her? He'd know for sure she wasn't going to back off from her testimony. Did that matter? He'd be behind bars. Unless, of course, they let him out on bail. They wouldn't do that, would they—not after he'd already run once?

Hallie slid her cell phone from her purse and placed it at the ready in the cup holder on her console. Doubts and fears made no difference. She had to do this.

For Alicia. For Teresa.

What did that woman think she was doing? Brody checked the driver's side mirror again. It wasn't so pitch dark he couldn't make out the shape of her little car a couple of lanes to his left. When she'd followed him from the restaurant onto the interstate, he hadn't thought much about it since their routes coincided for the moment, but she should have veered off on 35E toward St. Paul instead of tailing him on 35W toward Minneapolis.

One thing he'd observed from afar during their time together at WDJN, Hallie Berglund chose the high road toward whatever she perceived as truth and justice, regardless of personal risk. He'd admired her more than once for putting action to her convictions—and wanted to shake her more than twice for the chances she took. Like the time she didn't tell a soul at the station before she posed as a waitress and sneaked into a backroom meeting between high-level management of a major corporation and top union representatives. Her story had exposed corruption on both sides of the table, and big heads had rolled. If she'd been caught pulling that stunt, she'd probably be wearing a cement straightjacket at the bottom of the Mississippi River.

A familiar chill flowed through Brody's veins. Yes, a reporter sometimes needed to take chances to get a story, but they also needed to make sure their backside was covered if things went south—not go freelancing after a dangerous scoop without someone in the know.

Tonight, she no doubt figured on catching herself a murderer. He'd have to disappoint her. He was going to see Damon alone and without interruption. What happened after that was up to Damon. If Brody had done half the job he hoped with the kid, the young man would make the right choice.

The exit to France Avenue came up, and he took it. Hallie's car lurked behind a Lexus sports coupe that would have had his ex shooting him eyeball daggers because they couldn't afford one on a sportscaster's salary. Like she couldn't get a job? Brody shrugged off the residual resentment. Deborah was no doubt driving whatever she liked ever since she'd snagged the sort of sports idol she craved. The guy was rich and famous…and headed either for a breakdown or the hoosegow, from the inside information that had come to Brody's ears.

He glanced at his rearview. Yep, Hallie was still back there. Now she'd put a Papa Morelli's Pizza delivery car between them. If she could lose him on the mildly busy road in suburbia on the way to the restaurant, then turnabout was more than fair play. She didn't stand a chance of staying with him in the downtown Minneapolis maze of stoplights and one-way streets. Brody grinned and pointed his vehicle into the heart of the city.

Forty-five minutes and one phone call later, he pulled the Impala over to the crumbling curb in front of a seedy stucco home in a rundown neighborhood. A single light glowed in a front window. Brody stepped out of his car. Garbage smells assaulted his nostrils. He looked upward and stars sparkled back at him, visible only because most of the streetlights were out. From a house across the street, rap music thumped through quality speakers. A car belched smoke and screeched away from in front, leaving two junkers at the curb and a low-slung sedan in the driveway. Drug house.

Brody headed up the walk toward the stucco dwelling. The doorway eased open several inches, and a narrow pillar of light spilled onto the tiny ragweed lawn.

"That you, bro?" Damon's voice quavered toward him.

"In the flesh."

The door opened wide, and Brody stepped into a musty-smelling foyer that barely contained the two of them. The towering basketball player wrapped him in a bear grip and dropped his head to Brody's shoulder. Sobs shook Damon's whipcord frame.

"I shouldn't have done it…" Gulp. "But that woman, she—"

"What are you talking about?" Brody shoved Damon against the wall. "Don't tell me—"

"You didn't see Alicia. You don't know *anything!*" Damon's muscled shoulders drooped. If despair had a face, Brody was looking at it. "That other woman," Damon continued. "The way she looked at me made me want to hurt her, but I just—"

"Brody Jordan." The hoarse words brought both of their heads around. In an interior doorway stood a rail of a woman dressed in a stained T-shirt and dirty jeans that sagged around bony hips. Thin lips stretched away from yellowed teeth, and the acrid taint of cigarette smoke, mingled with a harsher kind, wafted from her body. But Brody's stare riveted on the .45 pistol she clutched in white-knuckled hands. "I never thought I'd say this to you, but get out of my house. You're not taking my boy to jail. They'll never let him out."

Brody gazed into Meghan Lange's dilated pupils. Here stood the reason that Damon was born and raised an emotional yo-yo, but the woman loved him the best she could. There was no doubt about that. And right now, there was no more dangerous creature in the world than a terrified mother on drugs.

Hallie stopped her car behind Brody's and sat squeezing the steering wheel. Did she dare step foot outside in this neighborhood? She glanced around the area. Had Brody gone inside the house where the music blasted or this other one where the door stood open? Under her rearview mirror light, she checked the address Vince had given her over the phone after she'd lost Brody. She looked at both homes, but couldn't read the house numbers in this darkness.

Well, she was always one to take a chance on the open door. She tucked her cell phone into her jeans pocket. As soon as she confirmed Damon was present, she'd make her call and scoot. Gripping her car keys in her fist, one key poked outward for a quick jab into an eye if necessary, she hustled up the chipped and weed-ridden sidewalk. Somewhere in the shadows to her left, a snap sounded. Hallie froze, muscles wired for flight. For long seconds, all she heard was her own pulse. Then a woman's voice grated from beyond the doorway ahead. Brody's tones answered, smooth as butter. Placating.

"Mom, put that thing away," a third voice rasped. Damon? "You're so wasted, you're as likely to shoot me or yourself as anyone."

Shoot? Hallie's heart fluttered. Brody was in danger, just like she'd warned him, but not from the source she'd anticipated. What could she do about it?

Her hand closed around the phone in her pocket, but that wasn't the whole answer. The police couldn't get here fast enough to stop the tragedy that could occur at any second. Maybe there was a rear entrance. If she could sneak inside and create a distraction, Brody might get the gun away without anyone being hurt. That was a big "if," but better than walking inside and giving the crazed woman another target.

Hallie darted across the lawn toward the left side of the house. Her peripheral vision caught Brody backing out the front door with his hands in the air. She reached the narrow strip of ground between houses and plunged into darkness. A low growl ahead stopped her in her tracks. Then a hiss and rustle indicated a retreating feline. Who knew what else lay ahead of her? What was she thinking trying to creep around the dark in this neighborhood? She needed to call the police right now! Hallie yanked the cell phone from her pocket, and her fingers found the keys. 9-1—

Crash!

That was no gunshot. Male voices shouted, one of them Brody's, and a woman started crying. Hallie backpedaled and poked her head around the corner of the house.

A scarecrow woman stood on the front lawn, wringing her hands. "My window!"

The front window sported a jagged hole, Brody now clutched the gun, and the lanky Damon wrapped his mother in his arms. No one else was in sight, but from somewhere nearby, tires screeched on pavement.

Gaze darting from side to side, Hallie hustled up to Brody. "What happened?"

"What are you doing here?" He glared at her.

"I was trying to save your bacon, but then this." She gestured toward the shattered pane.

"You didn't throw a rock?"

"No, I was sneaking around back."

Brody scowled. "You win the Girl Scout badge for tracking me, but you need to get out of here. Now!" He turned toward the noisy house across the street.

Her gaze followed his. A pair of dark figures lurked by the fancy car in the driveway. Their unseen stares crawled beneath her skin. "What about you?"

"I'm not a beautiful woman, and besides, Damon and I are leaving, too. I called and got police blessing for me to bring him in, rather than them coming for him. Now go!"

Hallie glanced across the street and gulped. The watchers had moved to the end of their driveway. Brody took her elbow and steered her to her car. She hopped in, slammed the door and locked it, then lowered the window a crack. "Aren't you leaving now, too?"

Brody stood on the street with his back to her, eyeing the observers, Damon's mother's gun in plain sight. "You're the spark that could set this situation off. I'll be fine. Trust me, please, and get moving."

Hallie started her car. A hasty retreat could be a wise thing once in a while. She peeled out. The rearview mirror showed Brody walking back toward the mother and son on the lawn. The other two men were retreating to their own domain as well.

Invisible clamps loosened from Hallie's chest, and she took in a deep breath. Was Brody really going to bring Damon in, or was he playing her?

"Trust me," he'd said. That was a novel idea where the WDJN sportscaster was concerned. Still, Brody *had* called her beautiful a few minutes ago. Her skin warmed. *Humph!* Like that compliment meant anything. In the breath before that, he'd equated her with a Girl Scout. He might as well have patted her on the head and offered to buy a box of cookies. But then, he had looked pretty impressive standing there with a gun between her and those thugs across the street. Of course, he was thinking about his own hide at the same time, not to mention looking out for that slime Damon and his wigged out mother.

Reaching a main thoroughfare well away from the shady neighborhood, Hallie popped open her cell phone and dialed. "Hello, Vince? Remember that favor I owe you?"

"What? I'm about to collect already?" The crime reporter chuckled.

"Brody says he's going to bring Damon in. If you get down to police headquarters with a cameraman, you could get footage that'll scoop the other media again."

A low whistle sounded in her ears. "That tidbit is worth another favor back at ya."

"I warn you, I don't forget things like that." She laughed.

They ended the call. Now Brody had better come through.

A little while later, Hallie let herself into her apartment and pulled off her shoes near the hallway closet. In socks, she padded into her living room and touched the button to boot up her laptop sitting on the coffee table. Then she went to the kitchen and put the teakettle on to boil. Some folks nuked their tea in the microwave, but her mother had taught her from a little girl that the old-fashioned way is best. Of course, Yewande Berglund's tea had been made with native roots and barks. Tonight called for double chamomile. The natural relaxant had a way of warding off bad dreams. She didn't need those after today. Hallie put two scoops of crushed leaves into the strainer.

While the water heated, she went to her bedroom and changed into pajamas. Then she opened the lacquered wood jewelry case on her mirrored dresser and took out a shiny child-sized bracelet. The solid circlet of copper fit on her palm. Engraved elephants, linked trunk to tail, marched around the circumference. On the right rear foot of the hindmost elephant stood the Yoruba tribe's symbol for blessing, Hallie's mother's signature.

The same symbol she'd seen on the bracelet that adorned a dead woman's wrist.

The teakettle screamed, and Hallie jumped. Man, she was keyed up. Time for that tea…and a little research while she sipped. She checked the bedside clock. Too late to call home and ask Uncle Reese and Aunt Michelle a few questions about the time in her life they rarely discussed—her Africa years. That conversation would have to wait until tomorrow evening after her full day of interviews for her modeling story, which would include plenty of questions about Alicia while she was at it.

"I'm coming," she called to the whining teakettle as she headed back to the kitchen.

Soon she carried a steaming mug into her living room and perched on the edge of her couch. Savoring the pleasantly pungent taste of chamomile, she transferred her cell phone photos to her computer. Alicia's bracelet filled the screen. This circlet also featured elephants, but these stood nose-to-nose. Hallie zoomed in until she came to the pivotal part.

The Yoruba symbol for blessing on one of the elephant's hind feet was clearly visible. Hallie's mother *had* made this bracelet. The confirmation raised a million more questions, each more puzzling than the last.

How and when did Alicia get the armband? Had she purchased it by chance at a flea market, a rummage sale, a pawn shop? If so, how had the piece come to be on the market? Yewande Berglund had never sold her work, only gave it to those who would treasure the items. So who had passed the bracelet to Alicia? The model couldn't have been a year old when Hallie's parents were killed. Had that person known her mother and father? How? Why?

Was there some mysterious connection between her and the woman she'd found murdered only hours ago? Could more than publicity have been on Alicia's mind when she requested that Hallie do the interview? What would she have told her if they'd had the chance to talk?

Hallie surged to her feet and marched her empty mug into

the kitchen. Those were questions that demanded answers, and as a reporter she was equipped to find them—for herself not the station.

Only one question remained. Hallie leaned on her palms against the countertop. Did she have the courage to face the shadowed fears in her own mind that those answers might disturb?

FIVE

Hallie awoke with an ache throbbing behind her eyes. She shut her alarm clock off before it could shriek at her. At least, she hadn't been pursued by nightmares. Probably because she'd tossed and turned most of the night, despite the chamomile. Impressions from family life in Africa had haunted her mind. Her mother's dusky smiling face, displaying the little gap between her top front teeth Hallie'd all but forgotten. The cozy warmth of sitting in her father's lap while he read her a story. The images were welcome, not frightening, but so fleeting they brought frustration instead of satisfaction.

And questions piled on questions. Why did Uncle R and Auntie M so seldom speak of her parents? Their words were positive—almost reverent—but they were few, careful. Why had she never insisted they discuss her family and Africa…and even that last tragic day? How come she had allowed herself to assimilate so quickly into American life and lose the Nigerian part of her heritage? Was that neglect the source of the confusion she sometimes felt about who she was and where she was headed in life?

Hallie slammed the side of her fist onto her mattress and flung off the covers. Way too many deep questions for a fuzzy-headed morning when she had tons to accomplish. She rolled out of bed and plodded to the shower.

A half hour later, she flipped on the television to catch the morning news. Her hand, bearing a strawberry cream cheese bagel, froze halfway to her open mouth.

There he was! Brody Jordan in the flesh, following a slump-shouldered Damon Lange into the police station. The clip had been filmed late last night. Vince got his scoop, Brody kept his word, Lange was off the streets. This day might not turn out to be such a trial after all.

Humming, Hallie got ready for work. She'd have to compliment Brody on his accomplishment. He'd taken the tough route and seen it through. It'd be even tougher on him when the ball player was found guilty. Note to self: Cut Brody a little slack at the office. Of course, she wouldn't be able to implement her new benevolence plan until late this afternoon. Brody's hours didn't start until midmorning because he worked into the evening, and she had interviews to conduct all day. Hopefully, nice meaty ones, with lots of good dope on Alicia and maybe even Damon Lange—anything she could get to help insure a killer went away forever.

As was her habit on sunny summer days, she ignored the enclosed skyway route to the WDJN building and went out the front door of her apartment complex for the short walk to the station. A tall, solidly built man in a rumpled suit loitered near the sculpture of the leapfrogging boy and girl. His gray gaze lit when she appeared.

"Brody, what are you doing here?" She stopped in front of him. "I thought you'd still be catching some zs after your late night." She looked him up and down. "Have you been to bed at all? You're still wearing what you had on yesterday."

"Haven't even been home yet." He fingered his chin and grimaced. "I suppose you can tell I haven't shaved, either."

"I wasn't going to mention it, though 8:00 a.m. shadow doesn't look half bad on you."

He grinned, and Hallie glanced away, sobering. She didn't need to get carried away with the be-nice-to-Brody project. Comments on his personal appeal might give him the wrong idea.

She cleared her throat. "You haven't answered my original question."

He shifted his weight from foot to foot. "What am I doing here? Waiting for you. I have a favor to ask."

"What is it?" *Uh-oh.* This didn't sound good. Not when she and Brody were on opposite sides of the Damon issue. She wrapped a hand around the shoulder strap of her purse and narrowed her eyes.

"Please don't look at me in that tone of voice." A thready chuckle punctuated his lame attempt at humor. "You and I both want the same thing—the truth. Wayne tells me you're going to interview Alicia's modeling agent this morning. I'd like to tag along."

The purse strap dug into Hallie's tightened fist. "So you've been to the station manager about this, and I'm being ordered to cooperate in your quest to clear a killer." Why had she ever for one second entertained the notion that she should warm up to Brody Jordan? He was just as arrogant and manipulative as she'd always thought.

He lifted placating hands. "There's no mandate here. I went to see Wayne at his house early this morning to arrange for the next couple of days off. As a side note, he said it would be okay for me to *ask* you for permission to go with this morning, but it was up to you if you wanted me underfoot."

Hallie let out a soft huff, and her shoulder tension eased. "Not looking like yesterday's leftovers, you're not."

The dimple ghosted across Brody's cheek. "I'll clean up at the station. Be ready in twenty minutes."

"Give it half an hour. I need to check my e-mail and organize my notes before we leave. We're not due at the agency until nine-thirty." She led the way down the steps and to the intersection, Brody trailing.

"I really appreciate this," he said as he came up beside her in the crosswalk.

Hallie focused her gaze straight ahead. "Don't thank me too soon. I suspect you're headed for a world of hurt when your protégé gets convicted."

"I'm willing to take that chance, if you're willing to hear evidence that suggests he's innocent."

Hallie humphed. "That'll be quite a trick to come up with evidence that convinces the witness not to believe her own eyes."

"I'm a man of faith, not sight. I hear tell you're of the same persuasion. A miracle could still happen."

"Isn't that just like you to play the faith card like some quarterback sneak."

Brody chuckled. "You never fail to surprise me. Quarterback sneak? You know more about sports than I would have guessed."

Hallie gritted her teeth. Maddening jock!

Brody hustled through his shower and shave in the men's room set up for busy reporters needing to get presentable at a moment's notice. Then he changed into the suit he kept at the station for emergencies.

Gazing into the bathroom mirror, he rubbed his smooth chin. So Hallie didn't find him utterly unattractive after all. What a surprise! A pleasant one. He grinned at himself, then sobered, thick brows drawn together. *Watch it, buster.* No way could he allow himself to enjoy that woman too much.

"She's poison to you, man, and don't you forget it." He spoke aloud and then left the men's room in search of Arsenic Hallie. Too bad he was looking forward to his next dose.

He rounded a corner then did a two-step dodge. "Oops! Didn't mean to almost bowl you over."

Vince stopped and laughed. "We need traffic lights around here."

Brody scowled and poked the man's thick chest. "I've got a major bone to pick with you. You told Hallie how to get to Damon's mom's house."

"So?" Vince shrugged. "She'd have found out some other way if I didn't cough up. Besides, her return favor got me to the police station in time to catch you escorting the prize of the day into the slammer. You know how these favor things work in this business."

"Yes, I know how things work, and yes, she would have found the address on her own eventually, but not in time to drive into that neighborhood after me in the dead of night. Do you have any idea how badly that could have turned out for her?"

"She didn't!"

"Next time you carelessly give her the means to put herself in danger, I will personally wring your neck."

Vince leveled an assessing gaze on Brody. A sly grin crept over his rugged mug.

"What?" Brody crossed his arms.

"You got it bad for our lovely feature reporter. Can't say I blame you. If I wasn't happily married—"

Brody stalked off, trailed by a spurt of hyena laughter from that off-base crime reporter.

He didn't find Hallie in her cubicle and wandered the halls until he came upon her in the lobby, talking to Daria, the receptionist. As he approached the tall reception counter, Rick, the security guard, looked up from his kiosk opposite the front desk and nodded. Brody returned the gesture and kept going. The hushed conversation between Hallie and Daria seemed animated, with the receptionist gesturing so that the many bangles on her wrist flashed under the fluorescent lights. Other than the raised hand, the flame-topped head was the only part of the woman visible behind the high counter with the huge letters *WDJN* embossed across the outside. Hallie leaned toward her, elbows on the desktop, as if hanging on every word. Brody came within hearing range and caught a few words from Daria.

"We're already getting phone calls from irate basketball fans." The woman looked up, spotted him, and shrank back against her seat.

"Hey, don't worry about me," Brody said. "I want to hear whatever you know."

Hallie glanced over her shoulder, and her darkened gaze speared through him. "People don't want to admit that their sports idols could be lousy human beings."

He pressed his lips together against a sharp retort. Hallie was doing him a favor today. He didn't need to screw it up with his big mouth.

"Oh, most of them aren't defending Lange." Daria fluttered red-painted fingernails. "They feel betrayed by him. Folks do care about their Golden Gophers. Hits 'em hard when one of their heroes goes down." She pursed a rouged mouth in Brody's direction. "I'm not too surprised tragedy happened between Damon Lange and Alicia Drayton, considering what I saw."

Hallie leaned closer. "You knew them?"

"No, not personally. Lange brought her with him when he came in to tape a segment a while back. The lovebirds were going at it tooth and nail when they left here."

Brody groaned. "They were so good together during the session. Must not have lasted much past the studio door."

"They were fighting?" Hallie asked.

"Raised voices, nasty words, threatening gestures. My heart galloped sixty miles an hour." Daria pressed a hand against her chest. "I thought things might get physical. Rick started coming toward them, but they charged right through and took it outside. Isn't that right, Rick?"

The security guard looked up from his screen. "Just about got me my first collar in this tame joint." He grinned and went back to his monitor.

Hallie frowned toward Brody. He kept his expression non-committal, but on the inside, his heart sank. *Oh, Damon, when will you ever learn to rein in your temper?* Of course, Alicia could be quite the piece of work, but neither of these ladies had any way to know that yet.

"What was the fight about?" Hallie nodded toward Daria.

"From what little I could make out," she glanced from Hallie to Brody and back again, "Damon was steamed that Alicia was late for his championship game because she was 'too busy batting her eyes at runway groupies.'"

"Runway groupies? Hmm." Hallie tapped a manicured nail against the marble counter. "Jealousy. That's a powerful motive for murder. Maybe this Minnesota model story has more to do with the killing than I expected." Her glance grazed Brody and continued toward the wall clock. "We need to leave soon if we're not going to be late for our appointment." She returned her attention to the receptionist. "Has Stan come in?"

"Bright and early. He went off to polish up Norman." Daria snickered. "He should break down and adopt that camera. The way he babies it and even has the thing named, no judge in the world would deny his request."

Brody chuckled and Hallie laughed. "He should get hitched and have a human baby," she said. "Life would get into perspective awfully quickly."

"Says the pot to the kettle, Miss Workaholic. Happy birthday, by the way. Time turns backward for no one."

Brody smacked his forehead. "I should have been the first one to say that to you today."

Hallie shot him a lopsided smirk. "You're excused. You've had a few things on your mind."

"There you are." Stan stepped into the reception area, camera case in one hand and accessories bag hanging from a shoulder. "Thought maybe you'd sleep in after yesterday's excitement, Hallie."

"Not hardly." Hallie shook her head. "Places to go, people to see. Remember?"

"Always! We keeping on with that Minnesota model story? Norman sure won't mind filming a few beautiful women." He grinned and patted his camera.

"We are, and we've got company coming along." She jerked a thumb at Brody.

Stan's eyes widened. "Well, well, there's a new team at WDJN."

Brody frowned, and Hallie's expression mimicked his. At least they were in agreement that there was no agreement.

SIX

"Thank you for showing us around the training center." Hallie followed Monique Rimes, head of Monique Modeling Agency into her thickly carpeted office. Brody and Stan followed behind. "The career of a model looks fascinating and challenging."

If one liked being poked, prodded, contorted, barked at, dressed and undressed like a fashion doll, and starved half to death. Not that she'd voice that personal opinion. Ms. Monique, as she invited them to call her, had been all that was gracious in showing them around the academy and agency headquarters located in Plymouth, a western suburb of Minneapolis. Stan had gotten some nice footage of models in training.

"My pleasure. I'm glad you enjoyed yourselves." The silver-haired agent executed a model-style pivot and rested the pads of long fingers against the top of her desk. "Is there anything more I can do for you?" The print on her silk, button-up dress consisted of swatches of wide charcoal-gray-and-white stripes traveling in opposing directions, set off by an oversized collar and cuffs. The getup might have looked ridiculous on another figure, but the style added softness and curves to an angular body. The woman did know fashion.

"Just a few words with you. Perhaps we could stand over there." Hallie pointed toward a case containing trophies and plaques.

Ms. Monique's smile bloomed around impossibly white teeth. "Excellent idea."

They took up positions that allowed the camera to catch most of the awards as well as the two of them. Brody stood back next to Stan, arms crossed. Hallie couldn't fault the man's behavior this morning. He'd been quiet and unobtrusive throughout the interview, even though he must be bursting with questions he'd been hoping to ask the agent.

Hallie faced Ms. Monique, and the camera rolled. She asked about the contents of the case. Ms. Monique gestured extravagantly and gushed on for ten minutes about the agency's accomplishments over the years.

Hallie inserted appropriate exclamations then touched Ms. Monique's animated arm. "Before we wrap this up, I think we'd be out of line if we didn't address the pink elephant that's been following us around all morning."

A delicate moue flitted over the agent's narrow mouth. "You mean about the untimely—er—loss of one of our models?"

"Exactly. How will Alicia's sudden absence affect your schedule?"

A slight frown hinted at wrinkles lurking beneath the artfully applied makeup. "Those who knew her and worked with her are very saddened by her death. She was a tremendous asset to this agency and to the modeling profession."

"So she will be difficult to replace."

Ms. Monique huffed and met Hallie's gaze beneath lowered brows. "Could we take this conversation off the record?"

Hallie hesitated. Maybe cooperation would yield surprising dividends. "Certainly." She turned toward her cameraman. "Stan, could you stop the film?"

"Sure thing." Stan lowered his camera.

Brody dropped his arms to his side and straightened. Hallie met his gaze, and he nodded in support of her decision.

Ms. Monique issued a pained grimace in Hallie's direction. "You must understand that this is a very fluid business. Highly competitive. Many talented individuals are after the limited slots offered for television and movie spots, catalogs and runway models. Any individual, even one as gifted as Alicia, is only a drop in the sea. Remove that drop, and others instantly rush in to fill the void."

Brody took a step forward, and Hallie moved aside. Might as well see where this new direction was going.

"Did she have any enemies that would want to hurry that process along?" he said.

The agent's nostrils flared. "No more than anyone else who naturally excels at what they do in a competitive field. And certainly no one who would have beaten and strangled her merely to wear her outfits at the next fashion revue."

"So you're implying there was rivalry," Hallie said, "but not deadly rivalry."

"Who felt the most threatened by her talents?" Brody added.

Ms. Monique curled her upper lip and glared first at Brody and then at Hallie. "I am not going to dignify either of those questions with an answer. The point is that a beautiful young woman is dead." Her mouth drooped and she sighed. "I can hardly believe she's gone. And that her young man—" The woman shook her head. "Inconceivable that such a thing could have happened."

"Inconceivable?" Hallie said. "I thought everyone knew Damon and Alicia had a troubled relationship."

"What I mean is a person never thinks that someone they know is going to be *murdered*. And I'm not sure I would have characterized the relationship between those two as 'troubled.' More like…unusual."

Brody nodded like he knew exactly what the agent meant.

Swallowing irritation, she smiled at Ms. Monique. "How so?"

The agent went to her desk and settled into her leather chair. At the woman's gesture, Hallie took a seat opposite the desk, and Brody appropriated the other guest chair.

Ms. Monique cleared her throat and steepled her fingers in front of her. "Alicia was a highly disciplined young woman, as you need to be in order to last long in this business. A model must pay constant attention to diet and exercise and training. She was scrupulously punctual for every appointment, analyzed each paycheck to the last decimal point and gave a hundred and ten percent to every client. If Alicia had a fault…"

She pulled off her glasses and tapped the frames against her desktop. "See, I don't care to criticize the dead, at least not for public consumption." Her gaze swept toward the dormant camera and back to Hallie and Brody. "Other than a few freckles on her nose that we covered with makeup, our biggest issue with Alicia was getting passion out of her. If anything, she was too cool, too controlled. When we wanted an ice queen look, she was our go-to model. If we needed heat, we…well, perhaps an illustration might tell the most compelling story." The agent reached for a portfolio on the corner of her desk, opened it, and pulled out a short stack of eight-by-ten photos. She selected two from among them and laid them out on the desk.

Alicia filled both pictures. Her rich, auburn hair floated around her exquisite face. Her smooth skin glowed fresh and peachy. The sleek lines of her neck and arms flowed gracefully in differing poses against dissimilar backgrounds. But that wasn't the contrast that arrested Hallie.

In the shot on the left, every elegant plane of Alicia's face, the form of her full lips, and the expression in those vivid emerald eyes screamed, "Do not touch!" In the photo on the right, the mouth softened, pouted, sassed, and her eyes sparkled like every facet of a finely cut gem exposed to light. Both photos were arresting, but only one exuded zest for life.

Hallie looked up at the modeling agent. "What made the difference?"

Brody made a humming sound. "I may have a glimmer what it was."

Hallie frowned at him and returned her attention to Ms. Monique.

The agent smiled. "Whenever we needed fire out of Alicia,

we invited Damon to the shoot. He'd walk in and—" She spread her hands toward the picture on Hallie's right. "Sometimes, when he wasn't available to come in person, we'd just get her started talking about him, and the same effect would happen. Sure, they fought epic battles, but without him, Alicia was a masterpiece carved in stone. With him, she softened into flesh and fire. Amazing, isn't it?"

Brody chuckled. "I was only around Alicia when she was with Damon, so I guess all I ever saw was the fire."

Hallie touched the picture on the right. "It almost looks like Damon was good for her. How can that be when there was something so sick about the relationship that he turned around and killed her?"

"I don't believe he did," Brody said. "But I would have to admit that the fire wasn't always to the good. She could be a real dragon-lady."

Ms. Monique chuckled as she gathered up the photos. "Seems like you two have a major difference of opinion about who did what." The agent lifted penciled brows in Hallie's direction. "You're the eye witness. Do you have any doubt about what happened?"

Hallie lifted her chin. "No. No, I don't. I know what I saw." Of course she did. Why did her stomach give that little flutter? Brody's assertions about Damon's innocence must have gotten to her more than she'd realized. She smiled at Ms. Monique, smirked at a tight-faced Brody, and crossed her legs. "I have a couple more questions, but these are of personal interest, so they need to remain off the record, too."

"You'd like to become a model?" Ms. Monique beamed. "You're starting late in life. I like to get them going in their teens or even younger, but nowadays there are more and more opportunities for the *mature* models. With that stunning complexion and the way you carry yourself, you certainly have po—"

"Nothing like that." Hallie bit back a laugh. Out of the corner of her eye, she caught a telltale tremble at the corners of Brody's lips. *Mature?* She hadn't planned on hearing those words spoken about herself in that tone of voice until she was ready for Social Security.

The agent sniffed.

Hallie laughed. "I'm flattered right down to my pinky toe, Ms. Monique." *I think*. "But I already know I haven't got what it takes to be a model."

"I don't agree with that statement." Brody's teeth gleamed. He'd lost his fight against the grin. "I was just thinking yesterday that she'd be fabulous on the runway."

Hallie wrinkled her nose at him. "Are you fishing for ways to get on my good side?"

The older woman laughed. "So if I can't turn you into a runway goddess, then what can I do for you?"

Hallie hesitated. Now she'd have to air her private issue in front of Brody. She cast him a sidelong glance. He gazed at her intently. What difference did it make if he knew about the bracelet? None, really. She shrugged. "I didn't see it in those photos, so I don't guess Alicia kept it on during shoots, but do you remember her showing up for work wearing a particular bracelet? This one would have been a couple of inches wide, made of contrasting shades of copper and brass, and engraved with—"

"Elephants?"

"That's the one!" She leaned forward and gripped the edge of the desk. "Did she ever talk about it? Tell you why she wore the armband, where she got it?"

Ms. Monique cocked her head. "We never discussed any details about the piece. I admired it one day. She said thank you—it was special to her. Then she sort of hid it under her other hand and walked away. Why do you want to know?"

Hallie rubbed her hands against her beige suit pants. "I know I must seem deranged about this, but my mother made the bracelet. She's been dead for years, and there's no earthly reason I can think of that a stranger would have had the handcrafted ornament."

"Ah, that *is* a puzzle." The agent went back to steepling her fingers in front of her.

"Anyway." Hallie stood up, and Brody rose beside her. She felt his speculative gaze on her but kept her focus on Ms. Monique. "Thank you for your time. This afternoon we'll take in some of the actual shoots from the list you gave us."

"Very good. Perhaps one of Alicia's fellow models will know something about her jewelry." The woman rose and extended her hand. Hallie took it, then the bony member clamped tight around Hallie's. "I would appreciate it if you wouldn't upset the girls by hinting that someone here had anything to do with Alicia's tragic death. They didn't, and they don't need the distraction."

Hallie tugged her hand away from Ms. Monique's. "I thought we were already clear on the identity of the murderer."

"And so we were." The agent nodded coolly toward her and Brody. "Goodbye, Ms. Berglund. I look forward to seeing the modeling segment on television soon."

On the way out of the building, Stan strode ahead, whistling under his breath. Hallie peeked over her shoulder to find Brody trailing a few steps behind, head down, both hands in his pockets like a man deep in thought. When they reached the van, Hallie grabbed shotgun position, and Brody climbed into the rear seat, still without a word. She shook the kinks out of the hand the agent had pulverized. "The woman has a grip!"

From the driver's perch, Stan chuckled. "Good enough to strangle someone? I mean, it wouldn't be the first time a person's boss killed them."

She shot him a narrow-eyed look as they drove away. "You're lucky I know you're joking around. Not that it's appropriate humor, by the way. But for your information, it's usually the disgruntled employee who offs the boss. Besides, we know who killed Alicia."

"*You* know. I'm still holding out for another suspect. Any other suspect."

Brody's deep chuckle interrupted their conversation, and Hallie raised her brows at him then returned her attention to

Stan. "So you're a Golden Gophers fan. Don't you feel 'betrayed' by Damon's crime?"

Stan shrugged. "Not unless he's found guilty. I'd just as soon he turn out to be a guy who was in the wrong place at the wrong time, and we keep on winning ball games."

She glared at her cameraman. "That reason for wanting Damon innocent is about as deep as a rain puddle. I would have expected as much from the jocks among us." She refused to spare Brody a glance. "But I'd hoped for more from you."

Stan let out an easy-going chuckle. "I'm an honest puddle, anyway. Now Madame Monique—" he drawled the syllables "—was about as genuine as a three dollar bill with her proclamation that 'all who knew her' were saddened by Alicia's death. Didn't you notice how uptight the over-the-hill babe got when you and Brody started poking around with questions about Alicia's relationship to her coworkers?"

"Duh! What was your first clue? My last one was crushed fingers." She rubbed her knuckles. "I thought I might take skin off getting my hand loose."

"Soooo," Brody drawled, "you do intend to make a few probing inquiries about intra-agency relations during the interviews this afternoon."

She gave him a disgusted look. "Am I a reporter or chopped liver?"

Brody answered her exaggerated Bronx accent with a full-dimple grin that sent a tingle straight to Hallie's toes. *What's the deal? He's not that cute!* Well, maybe he was, but who was telling?

"All riiight." The cameraman patted Norman, resting in the space between the captains' chairs. "What was this about a bracelet your mother made? Had to be a chill and a half, seeing it on a murdered woman's wrist."

"Not much to tell. My mom was a skilled craftsman in several arts, but she specialized in metallurgy. She and my father were killed in an accident when I was eight years old."

"Samantha's fiancé, Ryan, told me you were a missionary brat." Brody's tone was gently teasing. "Did they die overseas?"

"Nigeria. I lived there through the first half of my childhood, and then my father's family took me in after the accident."

"Do you see your mother's family at all?"

Hallie rolled her shoulders. "Not hardly. My last name should tell you my dad came from hardy Scandinavian stock. Pale as a piece of paper." A smile flickered across her lips. "He left Wisconsin to run an orphanage near Lagos, Nigeria. That's where he met and married my mom, the daughter of a regional *Oba* in the Yoruba tribe."

"Is that something like a chief?"

"Along that line. But her family had disowned her because she stopped worshipping ancestors and became a Christian."

Stan glanced her way, eyes wide. "How come you never let on you're some kind of displaced African princess?"

A tiny laugh bubbled from her throat. "A princess? Come on! I'm just an all-American girl doing the best she can."

"If you say so." Stan grinned. "You must have a bazillion stories to tell. Your whole formative years were spent in a different culture. Maybe you could do a segment for the station on—"

"Put a hold on the enthusiasm, buddy." Unease prickled across Hallie's skin, and she shifted in her seat. "That was a long time ago. Too outdated to be newsworthy."

"Right." Brody chuckled. "Even our Ms. Monique noticed Hallie's *maturity*."

Laughter filled the van. Then Brody got Stan going on the prospects for a winning Minnesota Twins baseball season.

Hallie pulled a small case from her purse, flipped it open to expose a mirror, and went to work on putting strands of hair back in order. She halted with a tuft between her fingers. Why didn't she want to talk about Nigeria? Maybe because she didn't have much to say.

How pitifully little she could tell anyone about the first eight years of her life. Her memories of family life in an African village, friends, the mission church had faded to sepia tones, shrouded under the horror of that final night. She pressed a palm to her stomach. Best not go there in her thoughts. She hadn't dreamed about those terrifying hours in a long time, and she didn't want to invite a rerun. Those dreams were worse than the ones about Teresa. If anything could be.

They got back to Channel Six around noon, just in time for Stan to race across the street to the food court for lunch.

"Don't you want to go with him?" Brody asked as he held the back door of the station open for Hallie. As pale as she'd turned in the van when Stan started probing about her early years in Africa had him wondering if she was either hypoglycemic, too, or hiding something. What secrets lurked behind that earnest brown gaze that seemed to take in the whole world and remain aloof at the same time?

She shook her head and preceded him inside. "I want to throw some notes into the computer about this morning's interview before we have to take off for live model shoots this afternoon. Are you coming along to those, too?"

"No, but I surely wouldn't mind seeing the footage later." He fell into step with her. "You probably don't want to know what I'm doing this afternoon."

She curled that lovely, full lower lip. "Something to do with getting Damon out of jail."

"A meeting with him and his lawyer. The arraignment is tomorrow."

"You have to know I'll be praying for no bail to be granted."

"And you have to know that bail or no bail, Damon Lange is no threat to you."

She snorted. "What? You're going to babysit the guy every minute of every day?" They arrived at her cubicle in the general worker's bull pen. She turned to face him, brushing an escaped tendril of hair from her cheek. "You still haven't gotten around to explaining your mysterious connection to Damon that makes you so sure of his innocence."

"I have to touch base with my substitute sportscaster for tonight and then head out for my meeting, but I promise to take care of that oversight soon. If I hadn't had a bazillion things on my mind during our drive time this morning, I might have remembered to mention it." He tilted his head to the side and tugged his left earlobe. "You seemed a little pre-occupied yourself."

She looked away and picked up a puffy manila envelope that sat on her desk alongside a stack of other mail. "Funny. It's marked overnight mail and there's no return address."

So she wanted to change the subject. He'd let her…for now. "Well, at least you can know Rick passed it through the detector for anything suspicious before it got to you. Could be a juicy lead on a new story that'll land you in the office next to mine with a daily anchor spot."

She barked a laugh. "You are trying hard to butter me up."

"Not at all. I recognize a woman with a destiny when I see her."

A tiny smile curved her mouth, and Brody's pulse did a little cha-cha.

"Get out of here, Jordan. I've got work to do." She turned away, and he left, chuckling.

A scream halted him mid-stride. He whirled and raced back to her desk. Hallie stood in the aisle between work stations, hands to her chest, wide stare fixed toward the floor. He followed the direction of her gaze and spotted the manila envelope on the carpet. Next to the packet lay a braided gold rope.

Hallie pointed a trembling finger toward the dropped items. "Somebody sent me the cord that strangled Alicia. And this, too." She thrust a piece of white paper at him.

Plain block letters in bold black marker said: YOU COULD BE NEXT.

SEVEN

Squatting beside the evidence, the police detective pursed her lips. Then she scooped up the braided rope from the floor with the end of a pen and dangled it in front of her like a limp snake. A deadly one.

Hallie shivered despite Brody's warm presence next to her. The man hadn't left her side even though he must be late for his meeting with Damon and the lawyer. He shifted his weight closer to her ever so slightly. If she turned toward him, would he hold her? She stifled the impulse and hugged herself instead.

"I can assure you of one thing," said the detective who had introduced herself as Millette. "This is not the cord that killed Alicia Drayton. Our lab has that one." She rose to her feet.

The woman couldn't have stood over five-foot-three and probably didn't tip the scale much over a hundred pounds. Shouldn't a police officer be more solid?

Hallie dropped her arms to her sides, fists balled. "But it *is* the mate to the murder weapon. Both sides of the living room curtain hung loose at the crime scene, and I didn't see the other tie. I think we've found it."

Millette frowned without a word and slid the cord into the torn envelope, which she held in a gloved hand.

"And I also think Damon Lange sent it to me as a warning not to testify," Hallie continued.

Millette's head snapped up, and she narrowed her eyes.

"You've got to be kidding!" Brody stepped between Hallie and the detective, glaring from one to the other. "Damon is in jail."

Hallie jabbed a finger at him. "He could have mailed it yesterday when he was at-large."

Brody shook his head. "Cold and calculating is simply not Damon's style. He's a blow-up-now-and-apologize-later guy. You said you didn't see the second tie at Alicia's house, so I have to assume he didn't have it in his hand when he fled."

"Maybe he stuffed it into the pocket of his shorts. Did you think of that?"

"His shorts didn't *have* pockets. I know. I got stuck with his things after they issued him the jail jumpsuit."

Hallie bit her lip and looked away, heart hammering. Damon sending this nasty surprise to her was the only explanation that made sense. Why couldn't the blind man see that? Surely, the detective would agree with her.

"Could be a prank," Millette said. "Don't you sometimes get that stuff after you air a story. You did tell the public about the cord, you know."

Hallie lifted her chin. "But I didn't say what color the thing was."

"Maybe the prankster made a lucky guess. This is a pretty common type of curtain tie."

"Right," Hallie snorted.

"I thought you law enforcement types weren't big on co-incidences," Brody said. "It could be the mate to the murder weapon, all right, and sent by someone else who was there that afternoon. The real killer."

The detective studied him with cool hazel eyes. "If someone other than Lange murdered Alicia, why would he want to betray his presence at the scene by sending the matching cord to a reporter? Why not lay low and let the boyfriend take the rap? Ms. Berglund's theory actually works better, if not for the logistics of how Lange concealed the cord on his body during his escape and why he would do that at all."

Brody scowled. "So you're saying your prankster theory is better than either of ours."

Millette released a vague smile. "I'm saying that I'll take this back to the lab, and we'll visit with Lange about the matter." She took a card from her shirt pocket and held it toward Hallie. "If anything else unusual occurs, however slight, please notify me immediately, night or day. My emergency cell number's on there, so keep the card with you at all times."

Hallie accepted the offering. "Should I be grateful you're trusting me with your twenty-four-hour access number, or worried that you think something else might happen?"

"I'm not predicting anything, only preparing for contingencies."

Hallie swallowed. Contingencies? Or did Detective Millette mean casualties? Like someone finding the officer's card on her dead body.

The rest of the day passed as slowly as a snail meandering across a tar pit. Hallie kept revisiting the panicked moment when she recognized what the mystery envelope contained and Brody's dark look as he left the station for his meeting with the legal beagle and Mr. Murderous Lange. Hard to say if the interviews she conducted with models on the job today would even turn out usable. And none of her fellow models had a clue where Alicia got her bracelet.

Hallie arrived home late in the afternoon. Sighing, she let her purse slip off her shoulder onto the couch, while she continued toward the bedroom, squeezing the thick carpet with her toes as she walked. Her pumps dangled from her right hand, and she carried her personal mail in the other. There was a package, but this had a return address she recognized.

She sat down on the end of the bed, laid the box beside her, and sorted through the envelopes. Junk, a bill and several cards in colorful envelopes from Berglund relatives. She smiled as she read the cards. Then she unwrapped the small container from the couple who had raised her when her parents couldn't. Uncle Reese and Auntie Michelle were right on time for her birthday as always. She'd forgotten about the occasion for most of this horrible day.

Lifting the cover revealed a gorgeous silk scarf in jewel-bright tones of gold and red and blue set off by rich cream. She squealed and ran the soft fabric between her fingers. This would be the perfect touch with several of her work outfits. The gift made another reason to call her aunt and uncle tonight.

Slipping the scarf around her neck, she went to the jewelry box on her chest of drawers and took out the bracelet her mother had given her when she was a child. Then she opened a compartment and removed a gold filigree locket.

In one palm, she cupped the bracelet; in the other, the locket. One gift from her mother, the other from her father. Gently, she opened the locket and a pair of smiling faces stared back at her, the woman's smooth and ebony, the man's rugged and pale. She used to wear those pieces constantly on those few occasions when Mom and Dad both had to be away. If she hadn't had them on when the orphanage workers spirited her from the stricken compound, she would have nothing from either of her parents. Everything Iver and Yewande Berglund had worked for went up in flames that day. And Hallie lost everything dear and familiar in one fell swoop.

The strong, practical faith of her father's brother and his wife here in the States had been her healing balm and a new start. Because of their rock-steady guidance, the "blessed hope" that she would one day be reunited with her parents for eternity was as real to her as her next breath. But for now, she held these momentos dear. Her hands closed around the pieces of jewelry.

With her treasures, Hallie went into the living room and settled on the easy chair. She punched in her aunt and uncle's number on the cordless phone.

"Christ Fellowship parsonage. Pastor Berglund speaking."

Hallie chuckled. "I'm looking for good counsel, Uncle R. Do you have any for me?"

"Hallie, how great to hear your voice. Happy birthday! Hang on a sec, and let me get your aunt on the phone, too."

The line went quiet, and then a click sounded. "Happy birthday to our favorite newscaster."

"Oh, get outta here, Auntie M. You don't even receive Channel Six in Eau Claire."

Her aunt snickered. "That doesn't mean you can't be our favorite reporter."

"Okay, I'll stop arguing. I never did win with you anyway."

"And don't you forget it, young lady."

Hallie joined her aunt and uncle in laughter. "Thank you so much for the beautiful scarf. It's draped around my neck right now."

"You're welcome, sweetheart," Uncle Reese said. "Did you have a good day?"

"Kind of dismal. Yesterday, too. I do have need of counsel, or rather information. To your knowledge, did my parents know anyone named Drayton?"

"Doesn't ring a bell," her uncle answered. "Mean anything to you, hon?"

Her aunt hummed. "I'm coming up blank. Why do you need to know? Did you meet someone who claims to have known them?"

Hallie fingered the bracelet and locket in her lap. "I saw someone who was wearing one of my mom's etched armbands…only the woman isn't able to tell me how she came by it."

"How can anybody not know where they got something they wear?"

Uncle R snorted. "I never know where anything I'm wearing came from. You do all the shopping. Remember?"

"Well, at least—"

"That's not what I mean," Hallie interrupted. "The person is dead."

Her aunt gasped.

A huff came from her uncle. "What?"

Hallie gave them the condensed version of everything,

except her demented foray into that bad neighborhood last night. She would never have done that if she'd trusted Brody a little better. She was coming to see that he was a man of his word.

"You found a dead body, were chased by a killer and got a death threat in the mail, and you're just now calling us?" The scold was plain in Aunt Michelle's tone.

"It got too late to try last night. Besides, there was nothing you could do. And today I've been beating the pavement nonstop. I've interviewed numerous people who knew Alicia, but no one could tell me where she got the bracelet that was clearly special to her. Why would a bracelet made by my mother be so important to someone else?"

"We're mystified," her uncle said. "We'll pray that you get the Lord's direction on this. There must be some purpose that you were the one to find poor Alicia."

"We'll be praying for the young woman's family, too," Aunt Michelle inserted. "Where are they from?"

"Some little town way up north, but that's about all I know. I need to talk to them." Hallie's fingertips tapped a tattoo on the chair's armrest. "Surely, they'll be coming to Minneapolis to claim the body, but in a case like this, I have no idea when it will be released for burial. I'll call the morgue and see if release has been scheduled. Thanks, you two."

"We didn't do anything," her uncle said. "Just let you think out loud."

"Um…there's something else I've been thinking. I'm not sure how to ask this."

"Don't hold back on our account." Aunt Michelle's tone was warm but firm.

Hallie smiled. These good people never hid from the truth. "So why do we hardly ever talk about my mom and dad?" There, she'd said it out loud.

Seconds of silence answered from the other end.

"I wasn't aware that we avoided the topic." Her uncle's words were measured and cautious. "Haven't I always told you stories about when your dad and I were kids?"

"Sure, but that's not the same thing as talking about him as a grown-up. About the mission work. About them as a couple in Africa."

"Ahh." The knowing sound came from her aunt. "You're finally ready for *that* pilgrimage. Honey, we've spoken little about those things because we weren't there. I'm sorry to say we hardly knew your mother, though we plan to rectify that loss in eternity."

"When you came to us," her uncle said, "you were so traumatized we thought it best not to pick at you with questions. We figured you'd open up and talk about those years when you were ready. Instead, you threw yourself into becoming an American girl and really never did revisit that time in your life."

Hallie's heart squeezed. Uncle Reese spoke the truth. The avoidance lay with her. Some part of her psyche feared that talking about her early years would conjure up the horror contained in that single last day. Maybe now she was ready to explore her Nigerian heritage.

"Possibly the 'pilgrimage,' as you put it, Auntie M, is bigger than merely finding out how Alicia came to have a bracelet made by my mother."

"I wouldn't be surprised," she answered.

"You know." Uncle R's tone was thoughtful. "Stuck away in my church office, I believe I have a small box of old newsletters from my brother's orphanage. If I can find it, would you like me to send the material to you?"

Hallie's breath caught. "Oh, would you? That would be wonderful!"

They made small talk for a few minutes, and her aunt and uncle urged her to use caution in her investigations, but they didn't panic as those with lesser faith might. Hallie ended the call and yawned, but it was too early for bed. Time to go out and pick up a few groceries for her bare cupboards. A few tummy rumbles signaled her body's complaint about lack of sustenance since breakfast this morning. She left her work suit on but changed into flat shoes and kept her aunt and uncle's gift around her neck. The soft feel of the scarf and the love that went with it comforted her.

Her thoughts galloped during the drive to the store. No doubt Brody had made sure Damon got a good lawyer—not some underpaid public defender. Alicia's death-dealing boyfriend could hit the streets on bail tomorrow. If she was right, and the taunting package she'd received came from Damon, how could she see the act as anything less than a threat that he might carry out after his release?

And what about Brody himself? Except for his constant harping on Damon's innocence, he actually seemed pretty sensible. He just needed to decide whose side he was on. The victim's or the killer's? Or how about hers for a change? His solid bulk standing next to her this afternoon had felt awfully good. Not that she'd ever let him know that.

Forty-five minutes later, she left the store with two bags of groceries dangling from one hand and her purse and car keys from the other. Dusk was closing in, and muggy heat from impending summer had lightened its grip on the atmosphere. She headed for her car a couple of aisles over. The place was busy tonight with families and business people shopping after work. Her gaze swept the area as she walked. No one seemed to be paying her any attention. With Damon still behind bars, why was she even nervous? Still, that business with the curtain cord had spooked her. All afternoon, she'd felt like hostile eyes were watching her every move. A fertile imagination could be a terrible thing.

Her car lay dead ahead, three slots down. She pressed the button on her key chain to unlock the doors. A noise came almost on her heels, and she whirled. A large, black and brown body hurtled into her, knocking her off her feet and onto her back. Everything in her hands flew in different directions. Her head bounced against the asphalt, and blackness swirled through her vision. Hot, stinky breath invaded her nostrils, and weight pressed against her chest. Her vision cleared to find a long dog snout in her face below a pair of canine eyes almost the same color as hers. Slobber dribbled onto her face.

"Get off me!"

The dog growled, grabbed her scarf in its teeth, and took off like its tail was on fire.

Hallie lunged to her feet, heedless of her bruised shoulder blades and tailbone. She raced after the canine thief, dodging between cars and around people who stared like she'd gone nuts. Her scarf waved from the animal's jaws like a mocking banner as he charged to the edge of the parking lot and darted around a hedge. Hallie rounded the line of bushes and stopped, panting.

She spotted a tufted tail disappearing into a narrow alley between two businesses. Hallie took a step forward then froze. Her purse! Her car keys! She'd left them behind to chase the dog. Gasping, she whirled and tore back to her car.

Groceries were scattered on the pavement, and her car keys lay where she'd fallen, but where was her purse? Her life was in there! Pulse hammering in her throat, she got down on her hands and knees and looked under the line of vehicles. A gust of breath left her lungs, and her joints went weak. There it lay under the bumper of the nearest car. She crawled over, snatched it up and hugged it to her chest. Then she sat right there on the ground, trembling. Tears trailed down her cheeks, washing against the stickiness of dog saliva.

Her gaze darted around to see if anyone was watching. No one lurked in the vicinity except a lone man in baggy jeans, walking away with his hands in his pockets, head down beneath a red ball cap.

Sniffling, Hallie rose and gathered up her things. The place around her neck where the scarf had rested felt empty and cold, and now she could go home to an equally empty apartment. *Happy birthday to me.* Why had she never seen before how great it would be to have someone to share her life with at the end of the day?

EIGHT

The next morning, Hallie trod through the front door of the station and headed for Daria's desk, legs encased in lead. What was the matter with her? She loved her job.

The crow's feet at the edges of the receptionist's eyes scrunched tight as she assessed Hallie up and down. "You tie one on for your birthday last night? You look like something the cat dragged in."

"The dog, actually." She smiled, but the effort turned out more like a grimace. "And, no, I spent the evening at home... alone."

Daria's lips pursed in a sympathetic moue. "Kind of a letdown after the great bash the night before. You've got some pretty special friends there."

Hallie's smile succeeded this time. "I sure do." Better let go of her pity party and appreciate the relationships God had given her. She leaned an elbow on the counter. "Vince in yet?"

The receptionist checked her computer screen. "Sorry, hon. He'll be out all day on assignment."

Hallie puffed out a breath that fluttered her bangs. "I'll have to hit him up tomorrow for a favor then and hope it's not too late."

She headed for her cubicle. She'd try calling the morgue herself and see when Alicia's body would be released, but they could be secretive about those things unless you had an "in" with someone. As a veteran of the crime beat, Vince would have known who to contact.

The morning flew by as she dove into her notes for the Minnesota model story and screened some film with the producer. He seemed very pleased with what she and Stan had accomplished so far, even made noises about a possible series for the morning show. If that much coverage for a single story didn't get a reporter's juices flowing, nothing could. Yet a dullness seemed to have taken hold of Hallie's heart.

A call to the county morgue did nothing to shake the feeling off. She got the runaround from two people. One of them said they were ready to release, but the parents hadn't made an appointment to claim the body yet. How weird was that? The other person denied that tale but refused to say when the body would be made available to family. Didn't anybody know what was going on in their own department? Or were they deliberately giving her the brush-off? *Vince, what a bad day for you to take off on another story.*

At noon, she did a segment for the news on a topic unrelated to the Minnesota model feature, and then continued to work on notes and video clips. Midafternoon, she met up with Stan to take off on another interview with a model wrapping up a shoot. This one could get interesting. The models she talked to yesterday said that Alicia and Jessica Parsons were bitter rivals.

On the way out the rear exit, she passed Brody's office, locked up tight, lights out. Her heart gave a little pang. It might have been nice to bounce her dog saga off Brody, and her frustrations with the morgue personnel, but he was busy championing the cause of the unrighteous. She firmed her lips and followed Stan out the door.

Outside the courtroom, Brody ended a call on his cell phone with a smile. He'd hit a homer. Now if this next call scored, he'd be batting a thousand. Brody punched in a number and leaned his shoulder against the wall, tapping his loafer against the floor. She'd be out doing interviews, so chances were she wouldn't answer. He'd just leave a voi—

"Hallie speaking."

The throaty female tone knocked the next thought straight out of Brody's brain.

"Hello?"

He snapped his jaw shut. "Hi, Hallie. Brody here."

"Really?" Her question reflected genuine surprise. "Is this a courtesy call to give me the results on the arraignment?"

"No, we haven't gone in yet. But I did succeed in getting us an appointment that should nicely repay that favor I owe you."

Silence fell for two heartbeats. "Which are you trying to do—exasperate or intrigue me?"

"The latter, for sure. Exasperating you seems to come naturally to me."

"You noticed. I'm impressed." Her dry tone held a touch of humor.

A grin took over Brody's face. The woman was a fun sparring partner. "When do you think you'll be back to the station? I've made…um—certain arrangements, and I'd like to include you."

"I thought you weren't coming in today."

"Turns out I'll be doing the evening broadcast after all. My sub had an emergency come up, and I couldn't leave Wayne in the lurch. As soon as this court thing is over, I'll be there."

"Good of you."

Was she mocking him or complimenting him? Brody shook his head. Inscrutability was an art form with Hallie.

"Yank the rabbit out of your sleeve already," she said. "Stan is pulling into a parking space, so I've got to go."

"Just show up at my office as soon as the evening news is over. You won't be sorry."

"If I am, you will be, too."

"I'll take that as a solemn promise."

"Count on it."

The connection went empty. Brody cradled the phone, chuckling.

What was Brody Jordan up to now? Hallie frowned as she climbed out of the van in front of the Sheraton Bloomington Hotel where Jessica Parsons, a Monique Agency model, was doing an advertising shoot for the hotel chain. The man surprised, annoyed, enticed and amused her in a one-minute conversation. He possessed multifaceted skills, all right.

Coming up beside her, Stan laughed. "Jordan gets under your skin quicker than anybody I've ever seen. There's always big-time sparks in the air when you two collide." He fluttered his fingers around her head.

Hallie lifted a brow at her cameraman. "You should see a doctor for those hallucinations. How did you know that was Brody, anyway?"

"Like I said. Sparks." He grinned and sauntered toward the glass front doors of the soaring structure.

Swallowing further retort—like she'd give him the satisfaction—she hustled after her cameraman, passed him and entered the hotel first. Personnel at the front desk gave them directions to find the indoor pool. They entered the chlorine-scented area in time to see a sweating man in a suit and tie wave his clipboard toward a corner of the pool hidden by a half wall topped by artificial green plants.

"That's a wrap." The man turned on the heel of his Gucci loafers and pranced toward the elevator from which Hallie and Stan had just come. Sounds of equipment being packed up came from over the wall.

A moment later, the svelte model sashayed into view, white towel draped over one shoulder. Her rich brunette hair was slicked back from a classic-featured face, and she wore a one-piece green and cream suit with a cleavage dip nearly to her navel.

Hallie stepped forward, hand extended, as Stan got Norman busy. "You must be Jessica Parsons. I'm Hallie Berglund from Channel Six news."

The model barely brushed Hallie's hand with hers. "Yes, Ms. Monique said you might be stopping by. Too bad you missed the shoot. We did some fabulous things today."

Hallie barely subdued an eye roll. "Sorry about that, but we're not allowed to film during a paid gig. That's copyrighted material."

"Oh, sure. Well, you're here now, so what can I tell you about myself?"

"Jessica." A man toting a tall piece of lighting equipment strode up with a white garment in his hand. "You forgot your robe."

The model giggled and flicked a heavy-lidded look at the technician. "Thanks, I'd forget my head if it wasn't fastened on." She returned her gaze to Hallie as she slipped into the skimpy beach cover-up that concealed the cleavage but accented the long legs. "My mother always said I should have been a blond."

"Why don't we go to a table over by those plants?" Hallie nodded toward some potted greenery. "And you can tell me how you got into this business."

For fifteen minutes, Jessica talked about entering modeling school as a child, spending the majority of her free hours either taking classes or working shoots, and the narrow, age-bracketed window of opportunity—determined somewhat by talent and ambition but mostly by hard work—to break into the top model category. "Modeling is a way of life for me. It's where I get my biggest highs and my lowest lows. I tell you, it's shark-eat-shark."

"I can believe that," Hallie said. "The models I interviewed yesterday told me you and Alicia Drayton took a few nips at each other from time to time."

Jessica flipped her mostly dry hair over her shoulder. "She was a stuck-up icicle. How dare she step into the career ten years later than I did, play around with the business on a part-time basis, and expect to get the same major gigs?"

"Like the Fashion for Fibromyalgia benefit coming up in a couple of weeks?"

"Exactly. The witch had to have performed some kind of magic to get Ms. Monique to put her on the roster for that one."

"It couldn't have been because she was that 'rare natural,' as one of your coworkers called her?"

A distinct snarl left Jessica's throat. "Everybody has to pay their dues. You don't get the world on a platter for nothing. Daddy paying her tuition through school, a hot boyfriend, pick and choose her modeling gigs. I knew karma would get her sooner or later."

"Karma?"

"She was asking for something bad to happen. Nothing was ever enough to make her happy. And, apparently, no one deserved her trust. You can't get close to someone who treats you like you're a criminal suspect. I'm not surprised Damon Lange eventually got a belly full of being used by her. She sucked up his love into the black hole of her heart and gave nothing in return." The model stopped and blinked. "That was kind of poetic. I'll have to remember that line if I'm wanted as a character witness on the stand or something."

Hallie looked away. Stan was still filming, eyes big, mouth agape. Evidently, she wasn't the only one boggled by little Miss Jessica's outburst. She turned her gaze back toward the model. "Can I ask you one final question?

"Do you know where Alicia got the elephant bracelet she wore when she wasn't working?"

"The el—? Oh, the African armband. No, I don't know where she got it. She treated it like a talisman though. Freaked if she couldn't find it right away after a show. I know, because I moved it to a different spot in the dressing room one day just to see what she would do." Jessica's cobalt eyes glittered.

This one was a shark for sure. The other models had been friendly and open. But they'd also been realistic in their acknowledgment that the big time wasn't within their reach. This was a bread and butter job with an ordinary private life to enjoy away from the haute couture.

Hallie rose, not offering her hand for a shake. "Thank you for your time, Jessica. You've been most interesting."

The model bounced up. "Let me know when this is going to air, will you?"

Hallie waved. "I'll communicate through Ms. Monique." She walked away briskly.

Stan tagged behind her into the lobby then scooted ahead

and poked a finger at her as he walked backward. "Now there's a murder suspect that I like—er, don't like." He turned around and fell into step.

Hallie buzzed him like a game show loser. "Sorry to bust your bubble, but if Alicia died in a fatal catfight, both parties would be covered in scratches, not to mention bald spots."

Stan shot her a fake pout.

She laughed. "I'll give you this, though. The deceased was no fairy tale princess loved by all. She had enemies."

On the ride back to the station, Hallie closed her eyes and leaned her head back. They were building a treasure-trove of film about the modeling industry in Minnesota. More work lay ahead, interviewing fashion designers, event planners, photographers, hair dressers, makeup artists and the list went on.

She wasn't getting quite the picture of Alicia she had expected—not the needy, insecure type who clung to any affection she found, no matter how dysfunctional. Still, the woman had possessed an unnatural fixation on Damon that would have made it easy for her to stay with him despite abuse. Maybe in her case the abuse wasn't entirely unprovoked, but nothing justified what she'd seen in the living room of that coed house.

What had Alicia's housemates seen in her relationship with Damon? She needed to put them on her list to interview.

And the part about Daddy paying the college tuition meant that Alicia worked for spending money, not to put herself through college. No wonder part-time was plenty.

What would Alicia's parents say about the daughter who'd been wrenched from them so horribly? If nothing else, they'd be Hallie's best bet to find out about the bracelet. Surely, they knew where it came from. She'd found out a whole lot of nothing today.

She *had* to track down Alicia's parents.

But first, corner Brody. What was on that guy's agenda? She'd go back to the station to watch the evening news broadcast for the outcome of Damon's arraignment, and then maybe she'd hang around and see Brody afterward. Or maybe she wouldn't.

"We're off the air."

The director's voice through the intercom of the control room released Brody from his chair behind the long desk on the news set. His stride ate up the distance to the door and up the hallway. Would she be there? He reached his office, and his stomach clenched. The door was slightly ajar, just like he'd left it, and no Hallie loitered in the hallway. It had probably been expecting too much for her to be interested in anything he had going, but he thought he'd baited the hook fairly well.

He opened the door, stepped inside and halted. "Well, ah…hello." Did that inane greeting escape his mouth? He cleared his throat. There she sat, dressed in a navy blue jacket and skirt, long legs crossed at the knee. She turned her head, and a pair of ear bangles swayed against her elegant neck.

She frowned at him from his guest chair. "You sound surprised to see me. Should I have waited outside the door?"

"No, of course not." Brody hustled past her and plopped his news script from the evening broadcast onto his desktop. "I'm glad you decided to hang around." He settled a hip on the edge of his desk.

She shrugged. "I'm surprised you've got something scheduled tonight that involves me. I thought you'd be off celebrating Damon's release on bail. Dramatic footage there on the courthouse steps when Damon walked out with his lawyer on one side of him and you on the other. You whisked him away pretty quickly. Where have you stashed him?"

"Far away. You don't need to worry about him."

She snorted. "Says the man who saw what the guy sent me yesterday."

"Let's not go there. Okay?" He raised his hands, palms out. "We've got better things to think about. I've offered to treat

Alicia's roommates to ice cream in about an hour, downtown Minneapolis. Can I buy you a treat, too?"

Her full mouth widened into a smile that lit her deep brown gaze. If Brody didn't know better, from the fizz going off on the inside, he'd think he just gulped a swig of seltzer water.

"For once you're ahead of me, Jordan." She rose. "The roommates were on my must-see list. I suppose if I have to eat ice cream to make it happen, I could force a little down."

A few minutes later they settled into Brody's Impala, and he headed the vehicle toward I-94. "We've got a little drive time. Ask what you want to know about me and Damon."

"I intended to." She darted him a shuttered look. "And I suppose you'd like a little quid pro quo on what my modeling interviews yielded so far."

"The thought crossed my mind." Brody held his gaze on the road. They'd missed rush hour, so traffic wasn't too heavy, but he couldn't let her see how eager he was to trade information. "I've been thinking deeper than that."

"Should I be afraid?" A grin sneaked onto her face.

Brody chuckled. "Very afraid."

She laughed.

"No, seriously," he said. "We both want the same thing, so why shouldn't we work together?"

"The same thing? That's a pretty big stretch."

"Not really. Maybe we have opposing opinions on Damon's role in Alicia's death, but we both want to see that the guilty party pays for her murder."

She turned away and looked out the passenger side window. Finally, she angled her head toward him. "I think you're reaching with that assessment of the situation. Your primary concern is getting Damon off, and the best way to do that is to prove someone else did it, or at least provide enough evidence that someone else could have done it in order to remove him as the main suspect. I don't know if I want to be a party to that effort."

Brody resisted the urge to take the next exit, head back for St. Paul, and dump her cute highness off at the station. Why had he wanted to bring her along in the first place? And why was he so irritated with her? Maybe because there was a nugget of truth mixed in with her contrariness. But truth could work both ways. "You could be right…to a degree. But are you sure your insistence that Damon is a murderer isn't a little bit influenced by your prejudice against athletes? My guess is you got burned by some fool who thought being good at a ball game gave him free license with women."

Red crept up her neck. "You're surmising and missing the mark. Yes, I think professional athletes are mostly an arrogant lot. But if I'm prejudiced, it's against abusers of any stripe."

"There, again, we agree. About the abusive people, I mean. Controllers, manipulators, batterers. I'd like to bundle them all off to Antarctica where they can enjoy each other's company, and the rest of us can live in peace."

"Poor penguins." Hallie clucked her tongue. "But I like your style."

They grinned at each other.

"Jocks aren't such a bad lot, you know," Brody said. "Many of them are Christians."

Hallie lost her grin. "So was Teresa's boyfriend, Mason… or so he claimed. Didn't stop him from inflicting diabolical torment on her heart, mind and body."

"Sounds heavy. Who are Teresa and Mason?"

His passenger stared straight ahead toward the freeway, but the distant look in her gaze said she probably wasn't seeing much of the road. "You've met my BFFs Jenna and Sam. I had to leave them behind when I graduated first and went to college. I thought I'd be miserable without them, but wonderful Teresa turned out to be my roommate. Funny. Kind. Smart. We hit it off straight away…and then Mason happened." Breath hissed between her teeth with a sound like a punctured tire.

"Touchy subject?" Something bad enough to leach the color from her face.

"Let's get back to business." She smacked her palms against the seat. "Cough up what's so special about your relationship to Damon that you'd risk your life for him in that neighborhood…and that he'd let you bring him in."

"Fair question. I'm his Big Brother."

Her jaw went slack. "His b-brother? That woman you said was his mother, she—"

"Nope, she's not my mommy-dearest. For that, I genuinely thank the Lord. My parents are happily retired in a senior village in Florida. Sorry, I didn't make myself clear about relationships. Damon grew up in Elk River, a town a little north and west of the Twin Cities. That's where I graduated from, so I took on a kid from there in the Big Brother mentorship program."

Her brow smoothed. "Not like George Orwell's *1984* Big Brother, then."

He laughed. "Well, we do keep a close eye on our protégés. In this program a guy volunteers to provide a male role model for a less fortunate kid. He was a handful. Still is, obviously. I've been on his case—literally—since he was in fifth grade. We've been through a pile of trouble together—near-brushes with the law from foolish decisions, his mom in and out of treatment, the constant mental and emotional affects of being born a crack baby. After he graduated high school and headed for college, his mom moved to the Cities right behind him. Not sure that was a good thing for Damon, but I'm proud of the young man he's become and his prospects for a great future."

Hallie huffed. "Prospects that would be seriously dimmed by a murder conviction." She pursed her lips. "I can see why you'd be willing to fight for his innocence." Her gaze zeroed in on him. "But what if he's guilty?"

A slow smile spread across Brody's face. "He can't be. I may know him better than his own mother. He's not physically capable of committing what was done to Alicia."

"Now that's a problematic statement to make about an acclaimed athlete."

"Damon becomes ill in the presence of violence toward women. He developed that phobia from exposure to all the abuse he witnessed from his mom's poor choices in—er, companions. If he'd even thought about hitting Alicia, he would have been hugging a toilet."

"And this is provable how? Any prosecutor would claim he's putting on an act."

Brody frowned. "That's what Damon's defense attorney said, too. I just happen to know it's the truth."

"If Damon doesn't hurt women, then how come he chased me at the coed house?"

"There's where you're again misinterpreting what you experienced. He wasn't chasing you. He was trying to escape the house and had to get past you to do it."

"I suppose he told you that."

"He did, and you have to admit it's a reasonable explanation." He tucked the Impala into a parking spot outside the ice cream parlor.

"Hmm. I don't know about that, but we're here now, so we can tackle the issue again later. I hope Alicia's roommates show up." Hallie turned her head this way and that, eyeing pedestrians on the sidewalks.

Brody checked his watch. She was right about interview subjects sometimes chickening out. "We're a little early. Let's go inside and wait for them."

She gathered her purse, and they entered the cool interior of the shop. From behind the serving counter, several youthful faces of wait staff focused on them. Most of the small, round tables were occupied by customers, but Brody snagged a pair in the corner and pulled them together, along with five chairs.

"Nice and cozy." Hallie nodded. "Uh-oh!" She pointed out the window that took up most of the front facade of the building. "Somebody's leaving a flyer on your windshield."

"I hate that." Brody scowled and hustled out the door. Didn't people have anything better to do than annoy their fellow man and waste good paper?

The broad-shouldered guy by the car must have heard him coming, because he took off at a lope and disappeared into the evening masses, baseball cap bobbing. Brody didn't even get a glimpse of his face. He snatched a folded white sheet from beneath his wiper blade, balled it in his fist, and went back inside. Hallie was standing where he'd left her, mouth agape.

"What's the big deal? It's probably just some advertisement." He headed for the waste can against the wall, but Hallie caught up to him and grabbed his arm.

"If I were you, I'd read that." Her grip tightened. "His cap resembles one on a guy I saw last night after a dog stole my birthday present."

"A dog stole your birthday present!" Was this woman losing it from all the stress lately?

"Later. Just find out what the note says."

Slowly, Brody unfolded the paper. Words stared back at him in bold, block letters.

ALICIA HAD MORE THAN ONE VISITOR THE DAY SHE DIED

NINE

Hallie shivered, though she hadn't so much as ordered her ice cream yet. If the guy who left this note on Brody's car had been lurking around in the store parking lot last night, then the scarf-snatching wasn't necessarily a fluke incident topping off a very bad day. Her breath snagged in her throat. Someone must be following her wherever she went. She opened her mouth to blurt out her alarms when three college-age women in shorts outfits and sandals entered the store.

Brody gave her a stare that promised further discussion, tucked the paper in the back pocket of his khaki slacks and waved at the newcomers. They smiled back. He shepherded them all into line for treats. While they waited, they exchanged introductions. Erin Weeding was from Spicer, Cassidy Beyer hailed from Duluth, and Jackie Kim came from Rochester. She was premed and swamped in summer school, while the other two were working and saving for the fall semester. Every one of them was a cheerleader for some type of college sport. They all vied with wisecracks, hair flips and long-lashed glances to tempt the famous Brody Jordan dimple out of hiding. None of them mentioned Alicia.

Hallie folded her arms and hung back. If these ladies were bent on falling all over a television personality, how were they going to get the conversation around to something serious? Didn't they give a flying pom-pom that their roommate was dead?

Soon they settled at the tables with various frozen concoctions. Hallie glanced at Brody, surrounded by coed attention. He spooned a bite into his mouth and gave her the barest nod. She wrinkled her nose at him. Fat chance she'd be able to arrest the women's attention long enough to get a question answered, but she might as well try.

"So where are you all staying now that your house is—um, off-limits?" She strained a smile from one to the next.

Jackie's face hardened. The others looked away. Erin's lower lip quivered.

"We're still processing. Y'know?" The premed student shrugged an eloquent shoulder. "This whole thing has shaken us up. It'd be worse if one of us had found her."

Three pairs of wide eyes focused on Hallie, while Brody kept his gaze on his ice cream. Heat rippled through her, leaving a damp chill on her skin. "It was…pretty bad."

Cassidy showed her palm. "Spare us the details."

"Gladly."

Jackie nodded. "So we figure you're not just some disinterested reporter nosing around, and we should be candid with you. We discussed it on the way over here."

Sure, when you weren't giggling about the hot WDJN sportscaster. Hallie stuck her spoon into her strawberry cheesecake ice cream. "We'd like to understand more about Damon and Alicia."

Jackie tilted her head, straight black hair falling over one eye. "So ask what you really want to know. Where we're living now isn't important, and griping about temporary accommodations sure isn't why we're here practicing our flirting skills on a TV mug old enough to be a lead professor."

Brody went bug-eyed with a spoonful of chocolate chip cookie dough in his mouth.

Hallie choked back a laugh then gave up the fight and hooted, while the others laughed too, including Brody. She had to admit the man was a good sport. "My humble apologies, ladies. I had about written you off as puff-cakes. My mistake. Now suppose you fill us in on how Alicia was as a roommate and what you observed about Alicia and Damon's relationship." She tucked a bite of ice cream into her mouth. The rich flavor flowed over her tongue, almost as delicious as the conversation that suddenly sounded promising.

"She was mean." Erin twirled a honey-brown strand of hair around her pointer finger.

"As a roommate or with Damon?" Brody inserted the question.

"Both. Wouldn't you think that was rude when you talk to a person, and they just brush right past you? And the things she said to Damon. I don't see why he put up with it for so long."

Cassidy waved her spoon. "Oh, Erin, you took her too personally. She said what was on her mind, and didn't care who heard it. And at times, well, she was like in her own little world. I don't think she ignored you on purpose. Too much going on inside to pay attention to small talk…and you do tend to jabber on quite a bit. But that's just your way, and we love you whatever."

Erin's cheeks bloomed a becoming pink. "Thanks…I think."

"You're both missing the subtleties of Alicia," Jackie said. "She played head games. A pro at it. Because Damon was whipped in love with her, he got the full load. Her favorite one with him was 'come hither, the better to mark you with my claws.'"

"Explain." Brody set his spoon down on his napkin. "I've seen glimpses of this behavior myself, but I'd like to get a clearer picture."

"Well, like it was pretty common for her to be all warm and excited on the phone about some dating plans, then when he shows up she turns all diva on him, and nothing's good enough. When they'd get home from an evening out, either they were going at it hammer and nails or hanging all over each other. Never any middle ground."

"She'd stir the pot with us quite a bit, too." Cassidy nodded.

Erin leaned forward. "You mean the way she had of turning

the corners of her lips down and twitching an eyebrow, while she comes with 'you're wearing that today?' Like you were about to step out the door in your pajamas or something."

Jackie chuckled. "Trademark Alicia. I finally figured out she was just messing with my head and paid no attention. She wasn't all that bad when you got used to her ways."

"No, I guess not." Erin sounded skeptical.

"Jackie's right." Cassidy gave her spoon a lick. "Erin's the newcomer in our house, so she hasn't had a chance to get oriented to personalities. There were plenty of times Alicia was pretty cool. She helped me with my calculus homework. Yuck!" She made a face.

Hallie let the last bite of ice cream slip down her throat. "What about Damon? Did he get angry over her treatment of him?"

"Not as often as I thought he should," Erin said.

Jackie nodded. "He was pretty patient with her."

"Damon had his own issues," Cassidy added. The three women exchanged glances.

Hallie pushed her empty bowl away. "How so?"

"He was an absolute freak about being on time," Jackie said. "When Alicia wanted to rile him, she'd dilly-dally and make them late for something."

"Yeah." Cassidy nodded. "You could set your watch by him showing up on our doorstep every afternoon at four o'clock all sweaty from his run between his apartment and our house. He'd come even if he knew Alicia wasn't going to be there, trot up onto the porch, and turn around and head back, because that was his route."

Brody smiled. "Damon finds comfort in routine, and being punctual shows a person is reliable. He sets a lot of store by that trait from too many let-downs in his life."

"So what have we got here? A Head Game Diva matched with a hot-tempered OCD jock? Sounds like a recipe for disaster to me." Hallie shot Brody a pointed stare. Let him wiggle out of this one.

"But not necessarily murder." Brody wagged a finger at her.

Jackie nodded. "So you two are on opposite sides of this issue. Makes for an interesting dynamic between coworkers. Or are you two more than that?"

"Hardly," Hallie blurted, torches igniting her cheekbones.

"I don't think so." Brody's answer trampled over the top of hers, and his face lost color.

The trio of coeds started laughing. "Gotcha!" Erin chortled. "We know way too much about the body language of love to be fooled by mere words."

"Don't make us dig up the old Shakespeare quote about protesting too much." Cassidy's dancing azure gaze moved from Hallie to Brody and back again.

Brody shifted in his chair. "How about answering another question. It's self-evident that Damon showed up on time at your house from his run yesterday, since he was found there at that time. But did Alicia have any other visitors yesterday afternoon? A source says she did."

A source? Hallie glared at him. How could a reporter qualify a note tucked onto a windshield as a legitimate source? Still, it was a good question and a neat dodge away from that romance nonsense.

The women gave each other blank looks. "We have no idea," Jackie finally said. "None of us was home."

Brody frowned. "Did she ever get other visitors than Damon?"

Cassidy tapped her lower lip. "Come to think of it, no. I don't think she had other friends. Her cell phone contact list could fit on one screen. She was a nut about her privacy, refused to open a Facebook or MySpace account. Said such things weren't secure. Of course, guys were always interested but she froze them out."

Hallie wadded her napkin in her fist. "So there were no other men in the picture?"

"Damon went ballistic if another guy looked at her sideways," Erin said.

Hallie shot Brody a gloating glance. He shrugged.

"The only regular contacts we know about were over the

telephone," Jackie said, face sober. "Mostly about work, but at least once a week she talked to her parents. They never came for a visit, though, and she never went there."

"We always dreaded those conversations," Erin inserted.

"Why was that?" Brody leaned toward the green-eyed coed.

Hallie reined in her impatience. Why pursue that line of questioning? If the family never showed up in person, they were irrelevant as suspects in the murder. However, they might have information about the bracelet.

Jackie snorted. "Well, something made Alicia the way she was. We never could tell if it was her mom or her dad that tweaked her the most, but we could count on her being a candidate for a ride on a broomstick when she got off the phone with them. Usually, we made ourselves scarce until she got over it by the next morning."

"You three apparently deserve medals for living with Alicia." Hallie shook her head. "I know what it's like, though, needing to keep the peace so you don't lose a rent-sharing roommate. I'd like to ask an off-topic question now. Do any of you know how Alicia came by the African bracelet she wore?"

Cassidy blinked at her. "She said she got it from her mother. Why?"

"It was made by *my* mother."

"How weird is that!" Erin laughed.

"Really weird," Hallie agreed. "So Alicia was fond of the bracelet because her mother gave it to her? She must have gotten along with her mom then."

"Not necessarily." Jackie shrugged. "I think in her mind she connected the bracelet with Damon somehow."

"That makes no sense."

"I know, but a lot of things about Alicia didn't exactly gel."

"Or Damon, either," Cassidy added.

Brody stacked the empty throwaway bowls together. "A pair of wounded souls finding what comfort they could in each other. But often inflicting more hurt in their fumbling around for wholeness."

"Deep!" Jackie narrowed brown eyes. "Are you sure you're *not* one of our profs?"

The Brody dimple peeked out, his gaze fixed on Hallie. "To my fellow reporter I'm just a humble sportscaster covering dumb jocks playing stupid games." He winked.

Hallie bit her lip. The floor might as well open up and swallow her. The trio of cheerleaders burst out laughing. Hallie released a chuckle. If Brody could laugh at himself, she could do the same.

"Good one," Erin said as the threesome rose and headed for the door.

"Thanks for the treat." Cassidy bobbed her blond ponytail.

Jackie waved and smirked with one side of her mouth as she followed the others outside.

Hallie stared after them. "Those women are full of surprises."

Brody pinned her with a scowl. "So are you. How come you didn't mention a stolen birthday present on the drive over here?"

"You need a bodyguard!"

Had Brody just shouted at her? Hallie stared at him from the passenger side of the vehicle. She'd barely finished explaining about her early morning incident. If he fumed any harder, steam would erupt out his ears. "You're mad at me because I was standing there minding my own business and some wild German shepherd jumps on me and grabs my scarf?"

"The same creep who probably sent you that curtain tie and has information about Alicia's death." He shot her a tight-lipped glance. "Maybe *he's* the killer, and you're on his radar. Have you thought about that?"

Hallie gulped. "Who's to say Detective Millette's not right. Maybe he's just a nut-job playing games with the news reporter?"

"A kook who's stalking you is a less threatening possibility?"

She gazed out the window at passing hotel towers, chain restaurants and glass-faced corporate headquarters buildings. "I guess not."

Brody sighed. "Sorry for yelling at you. I was scared."

"For me?" Warmth spread around her insides.

He shot her a long-suffering look. "No, the Easter Bunny. You do that to me a lot."

"Scare you? How?"

"You have a short memory about the neighborhood you visited last night."

"Oh, that." She spread her hands toward him. "I had to do it for Teresa. I couldn't let another killer escape justice if I could turn him in to the police."

"So this Mason killed Teresa and was never convicted?"

She let her arms drop to her sides. He'd never get it even if she told him about what happened. "Not exactly." The words escaped in a mumble between clenched teeth.

Brody pulled into a restaurant parking lot. "Then your reasoning eludes me, but let's put something more substantial than ice cream in our bellies, while you give me the scoop."

"And I suppose you want that report on my model interviews."

"Glad you remembered." His face softened into a teasing grin, and a knot unwound inside Hallie.

It might not be so bad to let someone else in on her private nightmare. If he passed this test, she might be ready to finish her about-face on this particular jock and admit him to her human being hall of fame. Where else did a guy belong who recently put himself between her and suspicious characters in a bad neighborhood, insured that a murderer he personally cared about turned himself in, and included her in his private investigation, knowing full well she didn't agree with him about Damon?

She followed Brody into the restaurant, smiling. A few minutes later, they placed their orders, and he gazed at her expectantly.

"Nothing about Teresa and Mason until after the meal, or I won't be able to eat."

"Fair enough."

Brody listened with furrowed brow while Hallie recounted her conversations with the modeling agent and her clients.

"My original assumption about Damon as the manipulative abuser has been reversed," she admitted when she finished. "Apparently, Alicia filled that role."

Brody nodded as he sipped at a cup of post-dinner coffee.

"But that doesn't change what I saw or my belief that Damon killed her." She twirled the straw in her glass of Dr. Pepper. "Abused people can snap and retaliate drastically against the abuser."

He set his cup down and draped his arm over the back of the empty chair beside him at their four-person table. What would it feel like if she occupied that chair instead of the one across from him? Hallie shook herself mentally. Where had that thought come from?

"True enough," he said. "But you know my reasons for thinking that didn't happen."

"Brody, you've got to face facts. There's no one else with a motive."

"There has to be. We haven't found that person yet, but we'll keep digging."

She rubbed a hand across her forehead. "At least you're including me in this quest. You're more stubborn than the ox that used to pull our neighbor's cart."

"You had a neighbor in Wisconsin with an ox?" Brody's mouth puckered.

Hallie laughed. "No, the ox is one of the few vivid memories I still have of the Nigerian village where I was born." Her grin faded. "I suppose I'd better quit putting off the moment of truth. But you're going to get the abbreviated version about Teresa and Mason."

"Whatever you want to tell me." He leaned forward and planted his elbows on the table.

She closed her eyes, then popped them open. No, that was inviting bad visions into her head. "As I told you, Teresa got to be my best college friend. For most of a year, we hung out together like a pair of twins. She'd had a tough time in life, a lot of insecurities, but she was really coming out of her shell in college.

"Then just before summer break, she met this guy who was a local football god. Grew up in the town—big, fanatical following—and went on to college at home where he could keep on being the big fish in the little pond. I never liked him from the first. He'd bought into his fame and become a legend in his own mind. She knew I couldn't stand him, but Teresa was so flattered he asked her out, she was like a kitten with a new toy. I didn't have the heart to—" She bit her lip and then expelled a long breath. "I never told her he hit on me first, and I turned him down cold. I thought she'd figure him out on the first date. I should have seen the danger. Maybe she'd still be alive."

She stared at her empty plate and fought the lump in her throat. A big hand covered hers. She gazed up into Brody's gray eyes.

He met her look, steady and gentle. "Whatever happened was not your fault."

"Maybe." She heaved a sigh. "But I'm still haunted by what might have been. Let me finish my story." Tucking a rebellious strand of hair behind her ear, she straightened her spine. "I went home for the summer, but Teresa didn't have the best environment to go back to, so she signed up for summer school. When I returned to school in the fall, she was still my roommate physically, but Mason had taken over her mind and will. She didn't make a move without his say-so.

"As if that wasn't bad enough, I started noticing bruises on her. She'd just laugh about being clumsy, but pretty soon I came to suspect the truth. Mason wasn't content with abusing her mentally and emotionally, he controlled her with his fists, too. I confronted her, but speaking the truth nearly ended our friendship. I went to the school authorities, but they treated me like a liar. Their favorite son involved in anything unsavory? Never!"

Something like a growl came from the man across the table.

Hallie's lips twisted. "My feelings exactly. Then the worst happened."

"He killed her?"

She met his bleak stare. "He might as well have." She gurgled a sound between a bitter laugh and a sob. "He broke up with her."

"What?" Brody stared.

"I came back from a weekend at home, walked into my dorm room, and found her in bed…with an empty pill bottle on the floor beside her. Her face was so white and cold." She choked and planted her forehead on one palm. "To this day, that moment haunts me in my dreams."

A low whistle emanated from across the table. "So when you saw Alicia, you thought you'd found another dead victim of abuse, and you were willing to charge the gates of hell to see that justice was served."

Hallie raised her head. "You do get it. I didn't think you would."

"I understand. That doesn't mean I approve. I'd just as soon have your skin stay whole and healthy, thanks very much."

A bemused smile quivered on Hallie's lips. "Not to mention yours."

He tilted his head back and laughed. "A secondary consideration, I assure you."

Brody took Hallie's arm as they left the restaurant, and she didn't pull away. In fact, she leaned toward him, gaze scanning the parking area. "I'm looking, too," he told her. "No lurking stalkers so far."

She smiled up at him and let him escort her to the car. As she settled into her seat, she grimaced. "I suppose we'd better make a stop at the police station with that note."

"I'm sure they'll want to know what's up." He started the car. "I hope you're right, and we're dealing with a harmless crackpot, but whoever this joker is, he's bold."

"And he may know something about Alicia's death that would tend to cast doubt on Damon's guilt."

His pulse sped up. "You admit he might not have done it?"

"That's not what I said, Mr. Jordan, but I'm willing to hear all the facts. Actually, I'd like to talk to Damon myself."

She *would* ask that. He clicked his tongue. "I suspect the authorities would have a fit if their chief witness interviewed the accused."

"It took a lot for me to even suggest the meeting, considering how I feel about Damon, but I suppose you're right. If he's so innocent, maybe you can tell me why he says he ran when I walked in."

"You scared him."

"*I* scared *him?*"

"You're more intimidating than you know, Hallie Berglund."

She snorted. Brody forced himself to grin. No need to let her guess how much he'd wanted to hold more than her arm on the way to the car. Intimidating to this once burned, twice shy guy? In spades!

At the police station, they waited on a hard bench for a good half an hour before a detective saw them. Not Millette. She was off duty. He took the note into evidence custody and got their statements about the incidents of yesterday and today, then promised Millette would get back to them if she needed anything else from them.

An hour and a half later they finally pulled up outside Hallie's apartment building. She looked over at him. "Thank you for an—ah—interesting evening."

"I guess that's a good way to describe it."

Hallie shook her head, and the small bangles on her earrings gave a sassy sway. "I thought the police would be more excited by that note."

"Why should they be when they're convinced they've got their man?"

"I'm on their side, Brody." The words were said with a concerned light in her eyes. "I wish you'd face facts. I *saw* him with the murder weapon in his hand."

"Which he removed from around Alicia's neck in hopes that she would breath again."

"So he says." The elegant planes of her face set in stony lines. "For your sake, I wish I could believe that. But I'm with the police—all the evidence points one way."

"Then let's find the truth, and the evidence will take on new meaning."

"Ox!"

"At your service."

Her scowl transformed into a half-grin. She waved and stepped out onto the curb. Brody waited until she disappeared into the vestibule of her building. At least she was safely home for tonight.

Tapping his fingers on the steering wheel, he gnawed his lower lip. How much did bodyguards cost these days?

TEN

Vince Graham leaned back in his desk chair and twiddled a pen between his fingers. "You want me to call in a favor with my contact at the morgue and find out when Alicia's parents are coming to claim her body?"

What was up with the smirk on the guy's face? Hallie shifted her weight from one leg to the other. "Isn't that something you'd like to know yourself?"

"You got me there." Vince nodded. "It's just that Brody told me if I ever gave you dangerous information again, he'd personally clean my clock."

"He threatened you?" She planted her hands on her hips. "Unbelievable! And what's dangerous about calling the morgue? Unless they're doing Frankenstein experiments down there."

Vince laughed. "Just thought you should know you've got a protector."

"Oh, puh-leeease." She needed to have a talk with Brody about this nonsense. People might begin to think the two of them had something going on when they'd barely started having conversations deeper than "hello" when passing in the hallway.

"Okay. I've already checked in with the morgue once or twice on this subject and got vague replies. I'll call again, as much for myself as you."

"Thanks!" Hallie tossed him a smile and returned to her desk.

Her phone was ringing when she got there. She answered it and heard the voice of Detective Millette. Hallie eased into her chair. "What can I do for you today, Detective?"

"Those clothes you were wearing when the dog bowled you over, what did you do with them?"

"You don't waste time on pleasantries do you?" She laughed.

"Not in the job description." But a small chuckle accompanied the deadpan words. "We hope you've done nothing with them except maybe put them with your dirty laundry."

"I'm sorry. It was a work outfit. I sent it off to the cleaners the very next morning."

Millette expelled a swear word. "Sorry about that, Ms. Berglund."

"Hallie, please. At that point, I had no idea the scarf-snatching was anything more than a freak incident. I didn't realize the man I saw near the scene was anyone suspicious until the same guy left the note on Brody's windshield that night."

"I understand, Hallie. We were just hoping…well, never mind."

"Did the note offer any useful leads?"

"Other than to confirm that there's an individual out there with an unhealthy interest in Alicia Drayton's murder case, no."

"This person also seems to have an unhealthy interest in me, as well. Do you think it's the person who sent the curtain tie? I'm still leaning toward Damon, but—"

"Unless there really was someone else at the murder scene, which this unsubstantiated note claims, we have to lean in that direction as well."

"Ahh. Then the tie was a match to the one that killed Alicia."

"Yes. Letting you know this much and urging you to extreme caution until we catch this man was the other reason I called. I can't answer any more questions."

"I respect that."

"Thank you, Ms.—Hallie."

They ended the call, and Hallie bowed her head, a dark

feeling chilling her heart. *Lord, I haven't felt this scared since…You know when. Help me to discern the truth, and the police, and Brody, too. Truth may be the only thing that will keep any of us safe.*

Right now, she'd love to run to Brody for his input, but he wouldn't be in until later this morning. She went in search of Stan to go over film in the editing room and then immersed herself in the work. A rap sounded on the doorjamb, and she jumped. Stan snickered. She scowled at him then swiveled her chair to find Vince entering the room.

"Walk right into the morgue like you own the place, but no cameras inside." He poked a finger at Stan, who sniffed. "Ask for Steve Ellis." He nodded toward Hallie.

"Aren't you going to be there?"

"That's iffy. James Drayton told the folks at the morgue that he and his wife Cheryl would be there early this afternoon to view the body, but their hometown mortuary isn't coming for it until Saturday. I guess Mr. Drayton has business in the city for another couple of days." Vince wrinkled his nose. "I need to be at the courthouse this afternoon for a different story. I'll hustle over to the morgue when that's done, but I might miss the action."

Hallie pursed her lips. "I've got a live segment at noon about the new baby animal exhibit at the Como Zoo, but I'll do my best to get to the morgue around one."

"Good enough for me." The crime reporter flashed a thumb's up and strode out.

Hallie frowned at Stan. "That is so strange."

The cameraman puckered his brow. "I thought it worked out good for both you and Vince."

"No, I mean about Alicia's parents. She's been dead for three days, and they're only arriving now?"

He shrugged. "Yeah, well, I think we already guessed she had some messed up stuff in her background."

"I wish I knew more about that background. I've accessed several sources and find out almost nothing. And, no, they're not in the Witness Protection Program or anything juicy like that. They live in Thief River Falls where James has been a Pennington County probation officer for nineteen years. Before that, he worked for a big oil company in communications. Cheryl does in-home day care. They have no other children besides Alicia, and their telephone is an unlisted number. Oh, and they've both got alibis for the time of the murder. Cheryl was looking after half a dozen children, and James's attendance is verified at a meeting in Moorhead. That's about it. I'm not seeing anything more coming from other news services either."

Stan waggled bushy eyebrows. "I heard through the cameraman grapevine that the dad is a piece of work. He gave the Pioneer Press photographer the bum's rush right off his porch and into a hedge. The bushes were hurt more than the newspaper guy, but I guess James Drayton is ferocious about his privacy. Must come from all those years of working with cons."

"Figures." Hallie snorted. "Brody and I found out yesterday that Alicia was paranoid about her privacy, too. She must have come by that characteristic honestly. I don't know if I'm eager or afraid to meet these parents of hers."

Two and a half hours later, Hallie pulled her car up to the Hennepin County Medical Examiner's Office, a nondescript building hunkered in the shadow of the Metrodome. A taxi idled in a parking spot nearby. She checked her watch and frowned. It was almost one-thirty. Were the Draytons already inside? Getting out of the zoo had been a trick with all of the elementary schools in the area participating in baby animal day. She'd raced off and left Stan to pack up his gear and follow in the station van.

Hallie locked her car and hurried into the building. She sniffed the air. No stench of dead bodies, just a whiff of some kind of men's aftershave. Must be wafting from Mr. Slick behind the counter. She approached the front desk, and the bald man lifted his gaze from a stack of paperwork. She looked into a pair of long-lashed eyes almost as brown as hers. His blue silk shirt, unbuttoned around the man's bull neck, stretched across linebacker shoulders. The man stood, his gaze alight with a kind of interest that left her cold.

"And what can I do for you today?" His smile flashed.

"Vince Graham sent me to see Steve Ellis."

The grin widened. "Then you've found the right man, beautiful." He leaned toward her with his knuckles resting on the high counter. "Hallie Berglund, WDJN news reporter, has never darkened the doorway of this establishment. I'll have to thank old Vince for finally sending you my way."

Hallie stretched her lips into a polite smile. "Can you tell me if the Draytons have arrived to see their daughter?"

"Just went back there." He jerked a thumb toward a door to the side. "Ugly deal, what happened. Too bad your beautiful eyes had to see something like that." He clucked then went back to grinning. "You have a seat, and we'll visit until they're done back there."

Hallie turned away, crossed her eyes and stuck out her tongue, then took a stuffed, vinyl-covered chair against the wall. When her face showed toward her host, it was once more composed. "How did they seem when they arrived?"

He shook his head. "Like a pair of coiled springs. Best not be too close when they go off. But don't worry, I'll run interference for you." He licked his lips. "Riding this desk is my day job. Pays the bills, you know. My passion is weight-lifting. This is going to be my year to win the regional title. Let me tell you…"

The next ten minutes passed in a litany of outrageous physical feats, punctuated by the occasional phone call he needed to answer. Did the guy really think this level of narcissism impressed any woman with more brains than a slug? At least he didn't actually require Hallie to respond to his monologue. Her background information on Brody showed that he'd once been a real athlete compared to this bozo's wannabe. Whether or not he'd been the cocky type back then, she couldn't say, but now Brody possessed true class…and smarts.

"Hey ya, Stevie!" The call announced a short, pudgy man

in a sports shirt and khaki pants barging through the front door. Hallie recognized a freelance news stringer. "The Draytons make an appearance yet?"

"Outside." Ellis pointed toward the door. "I can't have a bunch of reporters clogging up the reception area."

The stringer jerked his chin at Hallie. "You let someone from Channel Six in here."

Muscles in the morgue-worker's neck tightened visibly. "She's here on personal business."

"Yeah, right, and I'm a hyena."

"You said it first."

The stringer spat a foul word and charged out. Ellis winked at Hallie. She responded with a minimal flutter of the fingers. This guy had done her a huge favor. How soon could she expect him to offer her the grand opportunity of a date with him?

A shush of air announced the inner door opening, and two people emerged from the viewing room. A medium-sized man had his arm around the shoulder of a slender woman who sobbed into a palm pressed against her eyes. The man's pale face and cold expression surrounded a burning gaze that dared anyone to intrude on their grief.

Hallie rose. Maybe she should have waited until another time, but when would that be? She stepped forward and intercepted them at the exit. "I'm Hallie Berglund. I wanted to introduce myself and tell you how sorry I am for your loss."

The woman lifted her head away from her hand, and Hallie looked into the reddened, puffy eyes of Alicia's mother. Cheryl Drayton was lovely, even with tragedy emphasizing fine lines around her delicately sculptured mouth and eyes. Here was the source of Alicia's looks. A whiff of something on her breath said that the woman had needed to imbibe a little fortification to face the viewing of her daughter's body. "B-Berglund? You're the one who found my daughter."

The hoarse rasp tugged at Hallie's heartstrings. If she could get some kind of commitment that this pair would talk to her later, she could save her questions for another day. "That's right. It's only fair to warn you that there are reporters outside waiting to talk to you."

James drew himself up stiff. "You're a reporter, too. Nice try at an exclusive interview, but we won't be manipulated for public titillation." He put himself between his wife and Hallie, opened the door, and shepherded Alicia's mother through.

Shouted questions and camera-flashes greeted their appearance. Hallie slipped out behind the couple who now faced video cameras and extended microphones from a half dozen news personnel, including Stan, who was busy filming.

Cheryl turned and hid her face in her husband's shoulder. James pressed forward, half dragging her and shouting "no comment," among some colorful descriptions of what the reporters could do with themselves. They reached the curb amidst continued staccato-fire questions.

"What happened to our cab?" James's question came out a growl.

Hallie took note of the smirk on the freelancer's face. Dirty trick, sending it away. She scowled at him and touched James's arm. He glared down at her. "My car is right there." She pointed up the block. "No interview required."

Cheryl sent a beseeching gaze toward her husband. "Let's take the ride."

Hallie led the way with Cheryl close behind and James following, still snarling angry words at the pursuing horde. Alicia's parents both climbed into the backseat of the Honda Civic and shut their doors on questions. A few moments later, Hallie steered her car into traffic.

She vented a small laugh. "I do love tweaking the noses of my fellow reporters."

"No interview. Remember?" The man's harsh voice cracked enough to remind her that she was dealing with a grief-stricken parent.

"No worries. I'm not here on behalf of WDJN." Even though Vince no doubt thought she was, or he would never have made the arrangements with Steve "Muscleman" Ellis.

Later, she'd have to apologize profusely to Vince for lack of scoop. But what would she say? "Sorry, Vince, I was too busy finding out who I am to bother about my job?" Sure, that would go over like a lead balloon.

James gave a skeptical grunt. "Then why did you go to the trouble to accost us almost the instant we hit town?"

Cheryl made a shushing sound. "She came to give her condolences."

"You're too trusting, darling."

How did her husband make the endearment sound like an insult? Hallie glanced into the rearview mirror and caught Cheryl biting her lower lip.

"You're both right," Hallie said. "I do have questions to ask, but not for any newscast, and I did come to tell you I can relate to your pain."

"Unless you've lost a child, you couldn't possibly," James fired back.

"Try both parents in one day when I was still a child myself. Surely, there is some loss equivalent in that."

Quiet blanketed the car, and Hallie let it last for long seconds. "Where are we going, by the way, so I don't keep zigzagging aimlessly?"

"We're at the Days Inn across from the Mall of America." Cheryl's answer came in soft, breathy tones, like she continued to battle tears.

Hallie turned the car south toward I-494.

"All right." James grunted. "You've piqued my curiosity. What questions are you burning to ask?"

"If you'd rather set up an appointment for another time, I'd—"

"I don't believe in putting things off."

"Very well." She took the exit onto the freeway and merged with 75-mile-an-hour traffic. "Were you by any chance supporters of Iver and Yewande Berglund's orphanage in Nigeria about twenty-odd years ago?"

A hissed breath came from Cheryl. "Wh-why do you ask such a thing?"

"Never heard of them." James's flat statement trampled Cheryl's stutter.

Hallie darted a glance at the rearview mirror. Alicia's mother looked like someone had white-washed her face. Hallie swallowed. What kind of minefield was she charging into? "I'm trying to make sense of a mystery. When I came upon your daughter, she was wearing a two-inch wide, brass and copper bracelet etched with marching elephants. Yewande, my mother, made that bracelet."

Stone silence met the pronouncement.

"Cheryl, someone told me you gave the armband to her. Is that true?" If Hallie hadn't been checking in her rearview mirror, she would have missed the woman's wordless nod. "I'd like to know where you got it. My mother never sold her work commercially. She gave it away to people she cared about. The armband had to originally belong to someone she knew and held dear. I'm trying to reconnect with my Nigerian half, and finding that person would help."

"I really don't think I—"

"My wife picks up baubles at estate sales all the time. Who knows where she got this African armband you're talking about."

Hallie's insides did a slow burn. The man had all the sensitivity of a billy goat. He'd equated her mother's loving handiwork with a garage sale trinket. "Mr. Drayton, your wife is a grown woman. I'd appreciate it if you'd respect her enough to let her answer for herself."

"Oh, now, let's not blow this out of proportion." Cheryl's words gushed forth like she was trying to dowse a flash-fire. "I must have gotten the bracelet at an estate sale. In that case, the original owner is dead. I'm sorry, dear."

"May I speak now?" The temperature of James's words could freeze an Eskimo.

"Of course," Cheryl tittered.

Hallie let him make what he would out of her lack of response.

"I appreciate your search for roots, young lady. Youth

today lack anything like appreciation for their ancestry, but we can't help you in this matter. We have a funeral to plan."

"The bracelet meant a lot to your daughter, sir. She wore it all the time, venerated it. That doesn't happen with an item that has no roots, as you put it, in a person's heart."

"If that's what you're basing this interrogation on, then you're sniffing up a false trail. Alicia's flights of fancy and attachments to odd things and people have always been beyond me to figure out. She's had professional help for this sort of thing, medication, et cetera. She was doing well here in Minneapolis…until she decided to flaunt herself in front of cameras and take up with that white trash basketball player." He let out a guttural sound.

"You didn't approve of Alicia's part-time job or her boyfriend?" Hallie glanced over her shoulder.

James was as red as the crimson on her stolen scarf. *Whoa!* He'd better not have a heart attack in her car.

The man leaned toward her. "One degraded her, and the other one killed her."

Hallie focused on her driving just in time to take the exit toward the hotel. No one spoke another word as they drove past the Mall of America then turned on Killebrew Drive. She pulled up outside the hotel main entrance, fished around in her purse and turned toward the couple. "Let me give you my card. If you think of anything, please give me a call."

James snatched the rectangle of cardstock. "I'll give you this—you're tenacious." He poked his wife, who was blinking at Hallie like a rabbit in a yard light. The woman jerked and escaped out her side of the car. He scooted across the seat and followed his wife onto the pavement. Then he turned and stuck his head inside the vehicle.

"You're going to be testifying against the man who killed our daughter. Correct?"

"I believe so."

"I'd advise you to concentrate on doing your duty. We'll be watching."

Was that a warning of retribution in those slate-gray eyes?

He slammed the door and strode away, herding his wife ahead of him.

Hallie shivered. Alicia's father was a very creepy man.

ELEVEN

Brody approached Hallie's work cubicle late in the afternoon. Her day must have been tough, judging by the way she sat slumped over some doodles on a note pad. "Looks like you could use a listening ear."

She straightened, and warmth flashed in those brown eyes then dimmed. "You volunteering to get dumped on?"

"Try me."

She shrugged and looked down at her doodles. "I had a call from Detective Millette this morning."

A fist squeezed Brody's insides as she shared what the detective had to say. "I told you that you need a bodyguard. Maybe the station will spring for one."

"Not on your wireless microphone. I've got no desire to be followed around by a bodyguard. That would really set my interview subjects at ease. I'll be careful wherever I go. I promise."

"And I promise to be more ornery than an ox if you don't."

A smile played with the corners of her mouth. "I wouldn't expect anything less." The amusement dimmed and she sighed. "I met with Alicia's parents today, but got a whole lot of frustration. The only newsworthy bit was James Drayton's rabid dislike of Alicia's career and her boyfriend."

"Doesn't sound like a complete bust."

She curled her upper lip. "Yeah, well, I got nothing but

lies about my mother's bracelet. I keep hitting a brick wall on that one."

"Sorry to hear it. Let's go grab a snack at the food court and chow down in the park. A little fresh air would do us both good."

"Sounds lovely." She let out a weary sigh. "I was ready to ditch this joint for today anyway."

A short time later they settled with cookies and bottles of water onto a bench in the block-wide park across the street from the station.

Hallie turned toward him. "I hear you pledged bodily harm to Vince on my account."

"Blabbermouth," he muttered. "Feel free to dump the details on me about today's adventures with the Draytons."

She laughed and little tingles spiraled down Brody's spine. He stiffened. He had to stop reacting that way to this woman. The description of her fruitless encounter with James and Cheryl Drayton halted his eating half way through his peanut butter cookie. "Are you saying the guy threatened you?"

She wrinkled her nose. "More like he intimidated me. Well, not even quite that. I got the impression I was supposed to be cowed by his anger and manipulated by his grief."

"An abuser?"

"The signs were all over Cheryl in the way she interacted with him. It wouldn't surprise me to find out the woman has a drinking problem. I smelled alcohol on her breath. I suppose Alicia got her Dr. Jeckyl/Mr. Hyde personality from James's treatment as well."

"Did you see bruises on his wife?"

"No. James may be the psychological and emotional type of abuser. In some ways, those are the worst kind. The wounds they leave are invisible and only God Himself can bring true healing."

"Amen to that!" Brody chomped another bite.

Hallie studied him, head tilted to the side. "You're a unique sort of guy in this day and age—a gentleman and a believer. Have you always had it together, or were you arrogant and heedless in your glamorous youth?"

Brody polished off his cookie and wiped his hands on a

paper napkin. "I assume you refer to my brief flirtation in college with the possibility that I might be drafted into the NFL. In that case, then *ignorant* and heedless would be an apt description. My parents would never tolerate me being stuck on myself, but I had no clue life might not turn out exactly as I'd envisioned." He placed his hand over his right knee. "A blown kneecap and a bad divorce sobered me up in a hurry. Er—rather, it sent me down a rocky path of alcoholism, so I'm familiar with Mrs. Drayton's particular bondage. I even had a DUI once. Near tragedy made me bosom-buddies with God real quick, and He sobered me up."

"Hmm." She dipped her chin. "I think there's a lot of story in between those lines."

"Maybe I'll tell you sometime. What brought on the question anyway?"

She huffed through her nose. "I've had to ask Daria not to put calls through to me from Steve Ellis, the man at the morgue. I did nothing to remotely hint that I was interested in him. But since I returned to the station, he's called twice suggesting dating plans. Like I should be overawed by the size of his biceps or something. Where do these guys get this attitude?"

"From a deep well of insecurity." Brody sipped at his water. "Physical prowess of any kind—whether it be beauty or brawn—is fleeting at best. If that's all a person has going for them, they scramble to capitalize on every moment and deceive themselves that everyone else thinks the same way."

"Are you sure you didn't major in psychology in college?"

"Just communications. I swear." He lifted a hand in pledge.

Hallie crumpled her wrapper and napkin in a pair of fists. "Jessica, one of the models I met yesterday—she's living in that illusion. As much as I disliked her, I can almost feel sorry for her when I look at her life with your insight."

Brody took her crumpled paper and strolled over to the garbage can. "Ready for me to walk you home before I head back to the station to get ready for the evening news?"

"Walk me home? Are you serious?" She stood and hitched

her purse up on her shoulder. "You can see my apartment building front door from here."

"Humor the stubborn ox, would you?"

She grimaced then led the way toward the intersection.

Brody fell into step with her. "If you try to talk to the Draytons again, would you mind taking me with you?"

"How did you know I planned to make another run at them?"

"C'mon! We're both reporters."

She grinned. "I'd like to get Cheryl alone for a little while. I had the feeling she wanted to say more, but her husband's presence held her back. Maybe you can help by distracting James."

"Oh, goody. Feed me to the lion." He chuckled.

"You can handle it, big ox like yourself."

They both laughed as they crossed the street. Near the metal sculpture outside her apartment, Hallie turned and gazed into his eyes. "So where have you got Damon stashed? I know good and well you wouldn't let him go back to his mother's, and his place and yours will be under surveillance by a flock of media hawks."

"Off the record?" Giving this particular woman that information could pay off big-time in establishing mutual trust, or it could backfire into major problems for him and Damon.

Hallie twitched as if startled. "You know, when I asked the question I wasn't thinking as a reporter at all. But I can see how you might have the idea I'd run to Vince with the answer, since we've been tossing favors back and forth. No one will hear the location from me. I just want an idea where he's at for my own peace of mind."

Brody searched her face for the least hint of calculation. Her gaze remained open and clear. Of course, Deborah had been pretty good with the innocent stare when she wanted something, too. *Get off it, Jordan.* Hallie wasn't Deborah, though it had taken him this long to start figuring that out.

"All right. I called in a favor. Damon's house-sitting for a friend in a quiet little neighborhood in Anoka. The guy got a temporary job transfer that might turn permanent so the house is sitting unoccupied. Damon's got no vehicle of his own, so he's pretty much stuck there."

"Anoka." She sighed. "Well, thirty minutes by car is better than walking distance. And your answer was just right. Enough information to soothe my soul, but not so much that I have specifics."

Brody spread his hands. "Do you want the address?"

"You'd give it to me?" She leaned toward him.

"In a heartbeat." Wasn't that his heart trying to knock a hole in his chest at her closeness?

"You'd really trust this 'cheerleader type'?" Her gaze went earnest, and she drew away.

He sucked in oxygen he hadn't even realized he'd stopped inhaling. "A what type?"

"You heard me. You called me that straight to our boss Wayne Billings's face the day I started at WDJN."

"I said you were a cheerleader type?"

"Loud and clear."

He tugged his left earlobe. "Well, if I did, I don't remember it, but I do know one thing. I meant the term as a compliment."

A chuckle spurted between her lips. "From your perspective I guess you did. For me, the term is synonymous with giggly jock groupies. What does it mean to you?"

"I suppose your interpretation is the negative side of that coin. There are some who behave that way. I see cheerleading as a sport in itself. They've got competitions every bit as grueling as any other athletic contest. But if I applied the description to you, I suspect I was thinking in terms of grace, tenacity and teamwork."

"You meant it that way? I thought—" She stopped and bit her lip.

"You thought what?"

"I figured you were telling Wayne I'd be no good for anything but fluff assignments. I've been trying to prove you wrong ever since."

Brody slapped his forehead. "So some of the crazy risks

you've taken for a story, like sneaking into that illegal union/management meeting, were all about what I said?"

She scowled. "Don't take too much credit, Jordan. Giving you the raspberry was only a secondary motivation. I probably would have leaped in with both feet anyway. Those jerks didn't need to get away with cheating people."

Brody sighed. "I agree. It was a great story, but I wish you had let someone know what you were up to in case you ran into trouble."

"Someone like you?"

"Exactly."

She grinned at him. "Teamwork, eh? The quarterback and the cheerleader?"

He cleared his throat. "I was a running back."

Chuckling, she dug her key card out of her purse. "I think I might just learn to like you, Jordan." Her voice ran warm and smooth. She slipped into the building and the door closed behind her while he stood and stared. Turning, she waggled her fingers at him then walked through the inner vestibule door into her lobby.

What do you know? She'd decided he wasn't on a level with pond scum after all. Shouldn't this former running back be racing away pell-mell? Probably, but he couldn't, not with so much at stake for Damon. He'd just have to endure the thrill and the risk of hanging around Hallie Berglund.

By 6:30 p.m., Hallie had worked out in the apartment complex gym, taken a refreshing dip in the pool, showered and dressed in a soft blouse and denim shorts. Now, she finished buckling her wedge-heeled sandals and headed out the door toward the elevator. If Brody could see her leaving the building alone, he'd pitch a fit, but she wasn't about to start living like a rabbit in a hole because of some oddball fixated on her connection to Alicia's murder. Not even her own fears were going to do that to her.

She took the elevator to the private underground parking garage. Stepping off, she paused and scanned the area. The place looked deserted, but the ticking of an engine signaled someone had recently returned home and parked. The sound seemed loud in the silence. Gripping her purse strap, Hallie headed for her car, gaze darting around. Why had she never noticed how footfalls echoed in this enclosed space or how many shadows there were? Her skin prickled. She swallowed and increased her pace. At her car, she scanned the front and back seats. Empty. Then she unlocked the vehicle quickly and hopped in, slamming and locking the door in near simultaneous motions.

Her breath sawed in and out of her lungs. *Quit being an infant!* There was no threat here but her own heebie-jeebies. She pressed her hands together between her knees and commanded them to steady.

A few deep breaths later, she stuffed her key into the Honda's ignition. The engine purred smooth as a kitten, a soothing sound, as she left the garage. Setting her chin, she headed toward the bridal shop for a final fitting on one of those gorgeous emerald green bridesmaid's gowns Sam had picked out. Her gaze kept flitting to her rearview mirror in case she could pick up on anyone tailing her, but saw nothing suspicious. Still, her stomach stayed wrapped in knots. Okay, so maybe it would be comforting to have that big ox riding shotgun.

He'd done a number on her whole perspective on life at WDJN with that revelation about "grace, tenacity and teamwork." Who would've thought Brody respected her as a reporter when he had always avoided her presence like a case of chicken pox?

A few minutes after seven, Hallie parked her car in the lot between the arms of a U-shaped strip mall populated by boutiques and specialty shops. She walked through the door of the bridal shop to find her friends already there, and Jenna in the throes of gown-modeling in front of a three-way mirror. The frown and puckered brow said that Jenna was having her usual body-image struggles. Some women would kill for such a generous figure. So what if a little extra fluffiness went with the package? She might as well enjoy who she was.

"You look fabulous!" Hallie said as Jenna and Sam spotted her and waved her over.

Jenna sighed. "I was hoping to lose ten pounds by now instead of only five. There's no way I can shave off the rest by tomorrow night."

"Tomorrow?" Hallie shot a mystified look at Sam. "The wedding is over a month away."

Sam smirked. "Jen's got a hot Friday night date with you-know-who."

"No, I don't know who." Hallie shook her head.

"Really? He hasn't mentioned their plans?" Sam chuckled. "Maybe he doesn't want you razzing him since you work with him every day."

Hallie searched her memory banks and came up with a picture of her cameraman and Jenna with their heads together, yakking a mile a minute at her surprise party. "Stan Fisher? You're kidding!"

Jenna's pale complexion turned fire-red from the scoop neck up to her hairline. In the green gown, she now resembled a shimmery Christmas ornament.

"That's terrific!" Hallie wrapped Jenna in a bear hug. "That guy had better count himself the most fortunate man on the planet to have scored a night on the town with my beautiful BFF. And," she drew back and touched the tip of her friend's pert nose, "he'd better treat you like royalty, or he'll answer to me."

"That's probably what he's afraid of." Jenna's face finally found its smile. "We're going to one of those places where we get to try our hand at new recipes and eat our own concoctions."

"But you cook at work all the time."

Jenna shrugged. "I don't experiment on the restaurant customers. This will be a chance to try out some wild and crazy cuisine. Maybe I'll find something new to put on the menu. Besides, it's common ground. I like to cook, he likes to cook, and we both like to eat, only he doesn't show it like I do." She looked down at herself and one side of her mouth drifted south.

"Honey, let me tell you some model-mania horror stories."

"Later," Sam inserted. "Here comes the seamstress with your gown, Hallie."

In the next moment, she was whisked away into a changing room, then turned this way and that, and prodded and pinned. Finally, she was released from her duties and got to watch Sam try on her elegantly simple wedding gown. In between oohs and aahs, Hallie filled her friends in on Jessica and her skinny little world of desperate competition.

"Okay, so I get the picture," Jenna said when Sam left to remove her gown. "Don't get caught up in svelte syndrome. It's a false standard anyway."

"See? I knew you were a wise woman." Hallie offered her palm to receive a high five.

When the bride-to-be returned in street clothes, Hallie strolled with her friends toward the exit.

Sam sent her a sober look. "You're carrying on with the Minnesota model story in typical Hallie-the-trooper fashion. But how are you really holding up since the murder?"

"Yeah," Jenna said, "even for you that was gutsy to go through your entire surprise birthday party without saying a word to anyone about a dead body."

"You're not mad at me for keeping mum, are you? I couldn't talk about it right then without falling apart, and everybody was having such a good time. I didn't want to ruin the party."

"Angry? Are you kidding?" Sam laughed.

"You're the one that went through a nightmare," Jenna added.

Hallie threw an arm around the shoulder of each friend. "What did I ever do to deserve such great buds?"

Laughing, they all stepped out into waning sunlight and balmy evening air. A breeze wafted the scent of cooling tarmac their way.

Hallie pointed toward the coffee shop next door. "Let's grab a snack. I have a bunch to tell you about the bracelet on Alicia's wrist. If anybody's going to understand how I feel, you two will."

Half an hour passed with soothing Chai tea and conversation that meandered back and forth between the upcoming marriage and the recent murder.

"I'm afraid the more roadblocks I run into, the more I'm obsessed with finding out about that armband." Hallie drained the last of her tea.

"I don't think it's unreasonable at all for you to want to know how your mother's craftsmanship ended up with Alicia." Sam polished off her scone and dabbed at her mouth with a napkin. "So what's the next step?"

"A couple of things. I'm working on Brody to let me talk to Damon Lange. As much as I dread the prospect, he may be my best source of information if the Draytons won't talk. Of course, I plan to try again with them—with Cheryl anyway. Brody's going to help me, and—"

"You keep mentioning Brody," Jenna interrupted. "Are you talking about Brody Jordan, that hot sportscaster? I thought you couldn't stand him."

Hallie dipped her head. "We're learning to get along."

"Ahhhh!"

"Mmm!"

Jenna and Sam's knowing noises overlapped.

Hallie glared from one to other. "It's strictly a professional arrangement. We're also doing a little investigating into the murder, but from opposite convictions about Damon Lange's guilt. It's a pretty interesting relationship—competitive cooperation." She laughed.

"I don't see how you can resist that dimple." Jenna's elbow found Hallie's ribs.

"Says the woman intrigued by my cameraman's food fixation."

They all snickered, then Sam stuffed her napkin into her foam cup and sat back. "The media is crucifying Damon since the murder was so gruesome. Even WDJN is in the act."

"Vince Graham, our crime reporter, is as positive as I am about Damon's guilt."

"What about objectivity in the media?" Jenna tapped the tabletop with a pointed finger.

Hallie curled her lip. "That's the ideal, but seldom the reality. But the hype has probably had an unintended negative affect on my personal life. I seem to have attracted unwanted attention as the sole witness to the crime."

Jenna's eyes widened. "How ironic! The media's hounding *you*."

"Not that so much." Hallie told them about the curtain tie, the scarf-snatching and the note on Brody's windshield. Her friends were glowering at her by the time she finished her account.

"Woman," Sam said, "you'd better start checking in with us several times a day, or we're going to go bonkers worrying about you."

"That goes double for me." Jenna jerked a nod.

Hallie rolled her eyes. "You and Brody are trying to gang up on me. The police are aware of events. If someone even sneezes funny in my vicinity, I'll report it. I promise." She got up and tossed her empty cup and paper plate into the trash then turned and yawned and stretched. "I'm beat. If you're determined to look after me, why don't you walk me to my car?"

They left the coffee shop, and Hallie's friends took up positions on either side of her. She laughed and hooked her elbows around their arms as they strolled toward her vehicle in the nearly deserted parking lot. "I feel like I should start singing, 'We're Off to See the Wizard.'"

"Why don't we?" Sam started the tune in her sweet soprano.

Between sputtered chuckles, Hallie added her alto, and Jenna chimed in off-key but enthusiastically. They reached the Honda parked by itself under the pale glow of a light.

Hallie suddenly stopped mid-word and let out a yelp. Her feet rooted to the pavement and a chill coursed through her veins. Her friends' voices trailed off beside her.

She stabbed a finger toward wicked gashes in the side of her car. "Somebody keyed my paint!"

"That's not all they did." Sam's voice came out a high squeak.

Hallie followed the direction of her pointing finger. At the sight of the bloody body on her windshield, a scream ripped through her throat, echoed by her friends.

TWELVE

The sound of his cell phone dragged Brody out of a doze on the couch. He sat up with a groan, and ran his fingers through his hair. What did a guy have to do to get a little shut-eye? He'd just lain down. The phone went on with its ringtone, and he picked up the offending instrument. The number on the caller ID looked only vaguely familiar.

"'Lo." The abbreviated greeting came out thick and grouchy.

"Brody Jordan, you had better get a rein on your protégé quick, fast, and in a hurry!"

The feminine snarl on the other end of the connection brought him fully awake. "Hallie?"

A muffled noise like a suppressed sob answered him. He heard the sound of excited voices talking in the background and then came the squawk of a two-way radio like in a police car. His pulse spiked, and he scooted to the edge of the couch. "What's going on? Are you okay?"

"I'm all right. My car's not."

"You had an accident." He shot to his feet. "Where are you? I'm on my way."

"This was no accident. Somebody gashed the driver's side of my car with a sharp object, probably a key, while I was at my bridesmaid's gown fitting with Jenna and Sam. They also left a gruesome gift plastered across my windshield—a dead squirrel. Flat as a pancake. Probably roadkill, but whoever did this thing smeared the guts all over the glass." Her voice broke at the end of the sentence. "It was… horrible!"

"What?" The word came out a muted bellow. "That stalker found you at a bridal shop? And now he's raised the ante by taunting you with dead animals. This is getting way serious, Hallie." He started pacing the carpet.

"What makes you think the stalker did it? There's no note this time, just malice pure and simple. That spells Damon to me."

"You think Damon did it? That's impossible." He stopped pacing. "I'm not at home. I've been with him all evening, and he never left the house."

The man in question wandered into the room from the kitchen with a bowl of popcorn in his hand. "Who's on the phone?"

Brody held up a forestalling hand and turned away. "Give me the address, and I'll be there as quick as I can."

A deep sigh met his ears. "There's no point in you making the trip. The police are about done here. My friends will help me clean up the car, and then I'll drive straight home. We'll be gone before you could make it."

"Not without me on your tail, you won't. So wait right there with your friends."

"Why don't I just see if one of these nice officers will follow me home?"

Brody grunted. Why did he feel disappointed that she'd turned down his help? "Let me talk to the officer in charge, then."

"Why? So you can assure her that your pet boy was a homebody tonight?"

He did a mental ten-count. Hallie might not be the prima donna he'd assumed, but she could still be aggravating as all get-out. "Your leap to conclusion wasn't my first concern, but if she wants to ask me about him, I'll tell her. So humor me, and let me speak to the officer."

"Oh, o-okay." The broken, deflated answer sucked the wind out of his annoyance. She tried to put on a good front, but she must be scared stiff after something like this. No wonder she was slinging accusations.

"Hey, hang in there, Hallie. We're going to catch whoever's doing these things."

"I'm counting on it, Jordan."

He smiled. That sounded more like his Hallie.

The jumble of voices and radio static grew louder. Faintly, he heard Hallie informing someone that Damon Lange had been snug at home with another person all evening.

"Detective Millette. You wished to speak to me?"

"Brody Jordan. Remember me?"

"I certainly do, sir."

"I hope you people are going to take this matter seriously. Chances are excellent that this was not a random occurrence."

"Mr. Jordan, we always regard stalking as a serious issue, but we can only go where the evidence leads. We cannot enforce a restraining order on a phantom or arrest thin air."

Brody suppressed a growl. "I understand your point, but she needs protection. Aren't the police supposed to protect and defend?"

A few heartbeats of silence passed then Millette released an audible breath. "Ideally, I agree with you, but unfortunately, we don't have the manpower to assign an officer to everyone who may potentially be the target of a criminal. That's the reality."

"So you have to wait until *after* someone is assaulted in order to assign personnel?" His tone raised several decibels.

"Settle down now, sir. We have investigators on the criminal activities of theft and property damage. However, leaving a leaflet on your window isn't a crime. But, hopefully, we'll catch this guy before he escalates to harming Ms. Berglund."

Brody's heart tripped over itself. Sure, he'd known the risk was there, but hearing it spoken so matter-of-factly by this officer of the law shot ice into his core. If anything happened to Hallie, he'd—what? So, he'd watched her from afar for three years, but they'd only spent significant time together in the last couple of days. Was he that easily snared by a pair of big brown eyes? "Excuse me. What did you say?" He'd missed a comment by the detective.

"I assured you we'd make sure Ms. Berglund got home safely tonight."

Brody cleared his throat. "I'll count on that then. Thank you. Could I speak to her again?"

Dead air lasted a second or two. "Hi." Hallie's voice sounded gentle and a little shy. "I heard most of that. You have quite the lung power when you're riled."

"Yeah, well, I shouldn't have been such a hard case with the detective. She's doing her job the best she can."

"Speaking of jobs, I still have mine to do. Now, before you launch into the lecture," Hallie let out a small laugh, "I promise to take the skyway to work and walk over in a group of people I know from my building. I can't just hunker down in my apartment. This guy is not going to run my life. I should be perfectly safe at the station, and when I'm out, I'm generally with Stan."

Brody snorted. "Like he'd pose a threat to a gnat."

She giggled—a lovely sound to Brody's ears. "He could always slug someone with Norman."

A reluctant smile spread his lips. "There's always that. Do you still want to take another run at the Draytons tomorrow?"

"You know it…and, Brody?"

"What?"

"Thanks for caring." She broke the connection.

Brody pulled the phone away from his ear and stared at the screen like he could reach out and touch Hallie through it. If only.

"Was that the Berglund woman?" The question was accompanied by the crunch of kernels. Damon had taken a perch on the arm of an easy chair where he held a fistful of popcorn close to his mouth. His long legs had no trouble reaching the floor from that height.

Brody flopped back against the couch. "Hallie Berglund, yes."

Damon's eyes narrowed. "So what's she trying to pin on me now?"

"Considering her opinion of you and the threat she poses to your freedom, she decided you must be the culprit who keyed the side of her Honda and left a roadkill present on her windshield."

"You make her accusation sound almost logical." Sparks lit Damon's pale blue eyes. "You've got a thing for her, haven't you? Should I wonder whose side you're on?"

Brody fixed the young man with a stern gaze. "Give the paranoia a rest, will you? When have I not been on your side?"

"Do you blame me for the thought? I'm looking at a murder trial." He rose and plunked the half-full bowl of popcorn onto the glass-topped coffee table. "My Alicia's dead, and rather than look for the real killer, they want to convict the only man who truly loved her." Muscles in Damon's jaw knotted.

"Relax. Finish your popcorn. Going ballistic tonight will *not* help." Brody sat up and took a handful of kernels. "I know the situation bites, but believe it or not, Hallie's helping me investigate behind the scenes. She's an honest reporter. If she finds something that exonerates you, she'll say so."

Damon wilted into the easy chair and propped his forehead on his hands, fingers buried in his thick blond hair. "I hope you're right." He lifted his head, gaze weary. "You've got it tough, too, man. Googly-eyed over the woman whose testimony could blow up years of your effort and sweat—me." He jerked a thumb at his chest.

Brody stopped chewing. "I'm not gaga over Hallie Berglund. She's a fascinating woman, that's all."

"Suuure." Snickering, Damon reclaimed his bowl of popcorn.

Brody stood and stalked toward the door. "Since you're all settled in here, I'm going home to get some rest." He turned with his hand on the knob. "I'll pick you up in the morning for our strategy meeting with your lawyer."

"I'll be here." A sly grin drove the shadows from his young face. "Give my regards to Hallie…er, on second thought, maybe you'd better not mention me. Spoil the romance, you know."

Damon's smug cackles chased Brody out the door.

* * *

The next day passed in a blur for Hallie, as in-house tasks claimed her time. Hopefully, no one noticed she was only half tuned in to her work. Images of her damaged car, the tiny battered body on her windshield, Damon Lange's furious face as he raised the murder weapon in her direction, and the cold glitter of James Drayton's eyes kept jumbling up in her mind and drove concentration out the window. Maybe she should have stayed home after all.

She called Brody at three o'clock and found him in his office. "Can you get away now? You'll have to drive. My car's in the shop."

"I'll meet you at the back door."

In the car, his gaze searched her face. "You okay?"

"I'm fine. Really. Just a little distracted today. The Draytons are at the Days Inn in Bloomington."

"What if they're out browsing?"

Hallie shrugged. "They have to come back to their room sometime. But I figure since Mr. Drayton said he had business in town, maybe Cheryl's there alone. I didn't call ahead though, because I want to take her by surprise if I can."

"I hope you're right." Brody frowned. "I don't want to leave you cooling your heels in the lobby when I have to get back to the station for the evening newscast."

She chuckled. "You think someone's going to try to mug me in the hotel lobby?"

"Let's just say there's too many scary things happening that seem targeted at you. And from my perspective, an un-identified murderer is on the loose."

She bit her lower lip and gazed out the window at the crawling traffic around them. "I picked a rotten time of day to start this expedition."

"We'll survive the home-going masses. We might as well pass the time getting to know one another. You have a fasci-nating background. So tell me about your parents and your childhood in Nigeria."

Hallie's stomach clenched. "I'd like to. I really would. In

fact, I've recently been thinking about those years more than I have since I left, but…" Her voice trailed away.

"There's trauma associated with the sudden loss of your parents getting in the way."

The man totally got it. How about that? Hallie laughed. "You know, for a dumb jock, you sure are smart."

Brody guffawed. The laugh lines sprayed around his eyes were at least as appealing as that much-lauded indentation on his cheek.

"I'm going to give it a try. Where shall I start?" She clasped her hands together in her lap.

"What's your earliest memory?"

"That's easy. My mother singing a folk song in Yoruba tongue while she boiled rice at the stove."

"Do you sing?"

"In the church choir. I'm an alto, like she was."

"Do you look like her, too?"

Hallie pulled her purse up from the floor and dug inside. She found the locket she'd tucked in there this morning, along with her childhood bracelet. "I brought a couple of things to show the Draytons, including this." She opened the locket and held it toward him. "Here. What do you think?"

He hazarded several glances at the photos. "You've got your mom's regal bone structure, and her mouth and eyes, but the long, straight nose and thick, arching eyebrows are definitely from your dad."

She snapped the locket shut. "That's what I think. My parents always did give me the best of themselves."

"What's your happiest memory of them?"

Hallie pursed her lips and closed her eyes. "Ummm, oh, yes. My parents screaming and hugging each other when I made a goal during a soccer game with the orphanage kids." She scrunched up her face. "Then there's my mother teaching Sunday school in one room of the cement block church. She had such a gentle presence, so full of the love of God. I feel her now. I see her smiling." Hot tears welled up and traced warm paths down her cheeks.

She scrambled for a tissue in her purse. "I had no idea I'd turn into a gusher this easily."

"Lots of buried things bubbling to the surface, and you've been under extra stress these past few days. You loved your parents, they loved you. That's precious. Do you want to talk about how you lost them?"

"N-not now." Hallie sniffed and finished wiping her cheeks. "I'll look like a puffy-lidded raccoon if I approach the Draytons after that discussion."

"Maybe a teary-eyed plea would loosen up some information."

She scowled and wadded up her tissue. "I'm not going to manipulate them."

Brody shook his head. "I don't think that'd be manipulation, just honest emotion."

Hallie took in a quivering breath. "I'm not ready to talk about my last day in Nigeria yet."

"Okay. So, how about those Minnesota Twins?"

"Now you want to discuss sports?" She gave a watery giggle. "What about the weather instead?"

"Hey, I'm not the station meteorologist, but I think rain is on the way."

Hallie studied the low, dark clouds drifting in from the west. "It was pouring the afternoon before I left Nigeria, like it does every day in the rainy season."

"I thought you didn't want to talk about that."

"Maybe just nibble around at the edges. I need to start getting this out." Her heart rate climbed like she was about to leap off a cliff. "They died in a plane crash—a small, private plane. We lived in a village near Lagos, but they were headed over to the delta area of the Niger River to pick up a pair of orphans. Twin sisters. My mom didn't usually go on these trips. But when I whined about her leaving, she told me the little girls were afraid of men, and she needed to be there to calm them. At that time, I didn't know what she meant by that like I do now."

Brody sent her a grim glance and headed the car off the freeway onto the Highway 77 exit.

"They never reached their destination," Hallie continued.

"Plane trouble? Weather issues?"

"Neither, but I didn't find out any details until later." Hallie fell silent, watching the Mall of America drift past beyond Brody's profile. How could she put in a nutshell such a complicated issue when she understood so little about it herself?

She rubbed her palm along the seat upholstery between them and frowned. "The delta region has been a hotbed of strife and violence for a long time in Nigeria, fueled by greed over oil fields in the area. My parents' plane was shot down by a guerrilla group who thought they were taking out executives of a hated oil company. Somebody's communications got messed up that day, and my parents and their pilot died for the mistake."

"That's terrible."

"Yeah. But I didn't yet know my parents were dead when the orphanage was raided in the night."

Brody exhaled a low whistle as they turned off the highway onto Killebrew Drive. The first raindrops spattered the windshield. "Raided? You're kidding! These same guys who shot down the plane?"

"No, locals. But that part of the story can wait. The horrors that taint my memories of Nigeria are mostly tied up in those terrible minutes at the orphanage. I only heard secondhand about my parents' deaths, but *this* I experienced. Here we are anyway." Hallie pointed toward the yellow-and-blue sunburst sign outside the hotel ahead and to their right. "Time to see if we can get past Dragon Drayton and talk to his captive maiden. I need her to be honest about where she got the bracelet. Maybe whoever had it before Alicia's mother can tell me more about what happened and why. I was pretty little and scared and very confused at the time."

They parked and went into the hotel. At the front desk, Brody introduced himself and Hallie, and offered to show ID, but the clerk grinned and said he watched WDJN news all the time. Hallie smiled and asked for the Drayton's room.

The man's grin fell away, and he shook his head. "I'd call their room for you, sure thing, but it wouldn't do any good."

Hallie stepped closer to the desk. "I understand they've

probably been pestered by the media, but I'm hoping they'll
spare me a few minutes since I did them a favor yesterday."

"Media? Sure." The clerk scratched his head. "But that's
not why I can't contact them. They packed up and moved out
about a half hour ago. Paid for the room but the guy said they
weren't staying in it."

"What?" Hallie said.

"Why would they do that?" Brody chimed in at the same
time.

The man shrugged. "Weird dude. Claimed someone was
watching them."

Heart sinking, Hallie exchanged glances with Brody then
returned her attention to the clerk. "Do you have any idea
where they went?"

"Not a clue."

Why did every move she made toward finding out about
the bracelet end in disappointment? Her shoulders slumped,
and she looked up at Brody. "I'm so sorry to bring you on this
wild goose chase."

"No problem." He pulled a card from his wallet, along with
a green bill, and handed them both to the clerk. "If you hear
from them or get an inkling where they're at, give us a call,
and I'll match the donation."

The man behind the counter slid the offering into his palm.
"You got it."

They went out the door and stopped on the sidewalk underneath the entrance canopy. Rain pounded the pavement and
brought welcome freshness to the muggy air.

Hallie turned to Brody and put a hand on his arm. He
gazed down at her, brows knotted. She drew herself up to her
full height, only a few inches shy of Brody's. "I only have one
source left to explore, and you're the only available liaison.
I need to talk to Damon."

THIRTEEN

That soft, elegant hand on the crook of his elbow could turn him any direction she wanted him to go. And those big, brown eyes… But he couldn't give in. The police and the lawyers on both sides of the case would have conniption fits. Not only that, but Damon would be sure to take exception to her opinion of him and come off belligerent when he needed to be cool and sincere. Tact was not that young man's middle name.

Brody backed away from the tempting touch. "Tell me what you want to ask him, and I'll get the information."

"No good." She shook her head hard enough to disturb a tendril of dark hair from its restraint. The hair bounced against her cheek, and Brody curled his fingers into fists to keep from smoothing it behind her ear just so he could feel the texture.

"I don't merely want to ask him about the bracelet," she went on. "As a return favor to you, I'm going to give him the chance to tell me what happened in that rental house, and I want to be looking him in the eye when he does. You claim he's innocent." She poked his chest. "I'd think you'd want him to convince the main witness against him."

Brody sucked in a breath and closed his eyes. "You could talk an umpire out of his call." He looked her in the face. Raw hope stared back at him. "I promise only one thing. Damon and I will discuss the possibility. I'll let you know."

She smiled, and the sun came out, though the rain still poured. Brody sprinted into the torrent and brought the car up under the canopy.

Hallie piled in, still smiling. "Thanks."

Brody shook his head. "For keeping you out of the rain or actually considering your cockamamy request?"

"Both. And for helping me look for answers to my personal riddle when you don't have to. Lots of men would take pleasure in my frustrations if I was set on making trouble for someone they consider like a brother."

"I haven't forgotten about receiving my share out of this odd partnership. I want every scrap of information you get from your interviews with people in the modeling world."

"Then I guess you'll have to be my escort to the Fashion for Fibromyalgia benefit the Friday after next. Stan hates wearing tuxes, so he was just going to meet me backstage before and after the show. But now I won't have to be a fifth wheel at some table."

"It's a date."

"So it is." She sat primly on the passenger seat, chatting about nothing in particular, all the way back to her apartment.

Brody dropped her off and got to the station in plenty of time for his broadcast. Afterward, he headed straight toward the house where Damon was staying. As he turned the last corner onto the proper block, he groaned long and loud. A couple of news vans skulked in front of the house. The media had found their quarry.

Brody and the lawyer had decided the young basketball player's emotional condition was too volatile for more than a brief, official statement on the courthouse steps before they whisked Damon away. Evidently the hidey-hole hadn't been secret enough, and he meant to find out who had ratted them out. But first things first.

Brody pulled into the driveway past a For Sale sign on the lawn. When did that go up? It explained a lot. His friend Trent must have decided to sell, and Damon probably had a visit from a Realtor today, and the Realtor had hot cell phone fingers to the nearest news outlet.

Grumbling under his breath, Brody pressed the button on the door opener his friend had lent him, along with the house—*thanks for nothing, pal*—and pulled into the attached garage. Snug inside, the steady rain ceased pattering against his vehicle. Brody got out and went in through the kitchen door, calling for Damon. No answer. His chest tightened. Had the kid been spooked and ran off when he'd seen the reporters outside? Brody charged through the silent house. He opened the door to the bedroom Damon was using and spotted a large body sprawled on the bed. Brody exhaled a long breath and leaned a shoulder against the doorjamb.

"Damon?"

The body didn't move.

"Damon!" Brody rapped sharply on the door casement.

"Huh?" The young man stirred. "Wuzzup?"

"What are you doing in bed already?"

Damon sat up, rubbing his face. "Already? What time is it?"

Brody checked the luminous face of his watch. "Not quite seven p.m."

"Oh, man!" He got off the bed and stretched. "I've been sacked out since midafternoon when that Realtor dude left. I'm beat all the time. Must be boredom. There's nothing to do stuck inside these walls."

"You'd better be up for an interview pretty quick. The media's going to be hounding you until you give one. Even now there are a couple of news vans sitting outside in the rain."

Damon grunted. "No wonder the door bell rang a few times while I was sleeping. I did what you said and ignored it." He scowled. "Who do I gotta talk to? Not that Berglund woman."

"Any on-the-record interviews will be with Vince Graham. We were going to schedule one with him anyway. Promising WDJN the first exclusive was the only way I wasn't going to get in major trouble at the job for hiding you."

"Can't you do the interview?" His tone edged toward a whine.

"We've been over this already. The public would scream foul. Vince will be tough but fair, and you're going to have to be tough back, but calm and controlled." He jabbed a finger at his protégé.

"Hey, I'm the king of cool." Damon sauntered past Brody into the hallway and headed for the bathroom, clothes and hair rumpled.

Brody snorted. "And I'm Samson smiting the Philistines single-handedly."

Damon turned at the door to the bathroom, gaze sober. "To me you are." He disappeared inside.

Brody returned to the living room, shaking his head. That kid always did know how to turn him to mush. He sat down on the couch and planted his forehead on his palms. He'd have a bone to pick with Trent later, but he'd do it gently. The guy was a brilliant computer technician but didn't have a clue about people. Probably swore the Realtor to secrecy and thought that'd be good enough.

In a few minutes, Damon emerged with his hair combed and a fresh shirt on. Then they put ham sandwiches together in the kitchen. Brody bit into his just as his phone jangled.

He took it from the pocket of his sports shirt. *Hallie,* he mouthed to Damon and flipped the phone open. "Hi, sunshine." His jaw froze in mid-chew. Did he just call Hallie Berglund *sunshine?* The smirk on Damon's face said he had. Maybe she didn't notice the unconscious endearment. He forced the bite of sandwich down his throat.

She laughed. "You sound like you've got a mouthful."

"Just a couple of guys scarfing down sandwiches."

"So you're with Damon right now." Her voice took on a note of uncertainty. "Um, have you talked to him about my proposition? He tells me what he knows about that bracelet, and I give him a chance to explain himself about Alicia's death."

"Not yet, but I'm working up to it. Had a crisis to deal with when I got here."

She gasped. "Oh, no! Did he make an attempt on his own life?"

"Nothing like that." He scowled at Damon, who was bobbling his eyebrows up and down. "The media found him. I need to find another place to stash him."

Damon stopped the eyebrow dance. "You make me sound like a piece of luggage."

"Can it!"

"What?" Hallie's tone darkened.

"Not you. This annoying kid brother of mine is giving me a hard time." He waved Damon out.

The young man exited the kitchen, chuckling.

Brody returned to his conversation. "He's in a good mood right now because he yanked my chain, so I'll sound him out after we hang up. I might need to give him a little time to get used to the idea though."

"Hmm. You know, I'm going out on a limb here, giving you my opinion, but the last place anyone would look for him now is the most obvious."

"My place."

"Bingo!" She laughed.

"Ms. Berglund, you're a genius."

"Well, at least the arrangement will be a lot more convenient for you. But I'm not sure I've done myself any favors, since the guy will now be closer to me."

"You sure you want an eyeball-to-eyeball talk with him?"

"Only if you're there, Jordan."

"It won't happen otherwise."

Two hours passed in fruitless phone calls to mid-range hotels and motels from every area of the Twin Cities and suburbs as she tried to locate James and Cheryl Drayton. Hallie keyed off her latest attempt with an audible growl. She uncurled from her easy chair, stretched and padded toward the kitchen in her pajamas and bare feet. Another cup of tea sounded divine. This one with a little honey in it to soothe her overused voice.

She returned to the living room as her phone rang. The caller ID said unknown caller. That usually meant a tele-marketer. But after nine o'clock at night? That was an unusual time for them to be operating. She keyed the button. "Hello?"'

"Graves Hotel," a male voice grated in a gravelly base.

"Who is this? What do you want?"

The line went dead. Hallie stared at the phone with her mouth open. She set her tea on the side table with a quiver-ing hand. The sensation of being observed, even in her private apartment, crept in upon her. Every inch of her skin crawled. There was no way anyone was watching her here, but someone knew she was looking for the Draytons, and that someone meant her to find them.

What about the Days Inn clerk? He knew she and Brody were looking. No, it couldn't have been him. He would have identified himself and asked for more money. Besides, that guy had Brody's business card for contact information, not hers.

Hallie eased into her chair, swallowing against a dry throat. She picked up her tea mug and took a gulp. Heat scalded the roof of her mouth. She choked and wiped her lips with the back of her hand.

The call could be a prank to get her hopes up. The Graves Hotel had five stars—way above the price range of Days Inn. An unlikely roost for a probation officer and a day care provider. Of course, if Alicia's parents had been paying her college tuition, they must have money tucked away some-where. Or maybe James had gotten wind she hadn't given up on talking to them and made the phone call himself to play with her head. Only one way to find out.

She found the listing in the phone book and punched in the number.

"Graves Hotel, Minneapolis. How may I help you?"

The mellifluous female voice soothed Hallie's frazzled nerves. "Give me James and Cheryl Drayton's room, please."

"One moment. I'll ring you through to their suite."

Hallie's heart leaped. They were there! Then the phone was

ringing again…once…twice…"Hello?" Cheryl's tone was tentative.

"Mrs. Drayton, this is Hallie Berglund. I only want a few minutes of your time, and then I'll let you alone."

"You shouldn't have called, Ms. Berglund. I can't…well… I've said all I can say."

"Is your husband there, Mrs. Drayton?"

"James has gone to the fitness center." The woman's voice fell to a whisper.

"If he's not there, then what are you afraid of?"

"I'm not afraid." The tone turned flat. Cold.

Hallie strangled the phone in her grip. She was so close to answers. She could feel it. "Yesterday, I had the impression you wanted to tell me more about the bracelet than your husband would allow. Here's your opportunity to do the right thing."

"Young lady, you have no idea what you're asking. I got the armband from a man I loved a long time ago. Before James. Things didn't turn out well with him. He made a terrible mistake and—" A sniffle came over the line, then a gurgle like she was swallowing a drink. "I know nothing about the person who made it. I passed it on to my daughter without James's knowledge, and now I wish I'd tossed it in a lake. Please stop pestering us, or we'll file suit for harassment."

"Those words sound like your husband's, Mrs. Drayton. Not yours. Besides, it's difficult to get an injunction against a reporter for asking questions."

"Your questions are personal. Not news."

Hallie's eyebrows climbed. Cheryl Drayton was smarter than she acted. "One last thing then. What was this man's name? If I have that much, maybe I can find out how he came upon the bracelet."

"I've told you more than enough already. I mustn't talk about him."

"Did James threaten you not to?"

A whimper met the question. "What does a piece of jewelry matter? You can have the thing, for all I care. Please, pleeease…" A man's voice called in the background, far enough away to be in another room of the suite. "Leave us alone." The woman's voice dropped to a feather of sound, and the line went blank.

Hallie let out a strangled cry and resisted the urge to fling the phone across the room. What was the big secret? Hallie went still. Didn't Mrs. Drayton realize that teasing a reporter was tantamount to laying scent for a bloodhound? Who was this man who had given her the bracelet? Digging into Cheryl Drayton's distant past just jumped to top priority.

Well, not quite. First she needed to fill Brody in on the fruits of her evening. She was bursting to tell somebody, and he was the closest to the situation. Her finger paused over the phone. No, maybe calling him was a bad idea. That would make twice in one evening and might give him the wrong idea. What idea was that? That he anchored her in the midst of this confusing, dangerous investigation? The harsh, grating voice of the man who'd told her the Draytons' location played again in her head. She shivered.

Okay, maybe calling Brody was her best option. She picked up the phone just as it rang. The caller ID showed a familiar number. She grinned and answered.

"Hi, Brody. Did you manage to whisk Damon out from under the reporters' noses?"

"Hello at last. You *have* been diligent on the phone. I've been trying to reach you for an hour. To answer your question, yes, Damon curled up in my trunk—quite a feat for a guy his size—and I drove off with him nice as you please. We're at my place now, and our fellow nosey newsies," he laughed, "are still camped outside an empty house. How about you? Any success?"

"Yes and no." She told him about her inroads into the yellow page hotel listings without results and then the anonymous phone call that had supplied the answer.

"You need to report that call to the police, Hallie." Brody's tone was urgent.

"What are they going to do about it?"

"It's not so much what they can do. It's making sure these contacts are documented."

"Makes sense."

"You agree?"

Hallie snickered. "Did you think I was going to argue with you?"

"Well…uh, yeah."

"Brody Jordan, I promise after we hang up, I will call the police and report the incident. Satisfied?"

"Quite. And I think you'll be pleased to know that Damon has agreed to meet with you sometime after we get him through a recorded interview with Vince, which should be early next week."

"That's terrific…I think." She pulled her bare feet up into the overstuffed chair. "I'm nervous about talking to him."

"Not half as nervous as he is to face *you*. Now, give up the info. You haven't said yet whether your mystery caller's hotel tip panned out."

Hallie gave him the lowdown on the conversation with Mrs. Drayton. "I'm starting to think that woman has a past she'd rather remain undisturbed."

"Like mother, like daughter, I think Alicia had things to hide, too. I'm going to dig around in her background, and then we can compare notes."

"Don't we already have a pretty good idea what her life must have been like, growing up under James's thumb? I'll bet coming here to college made her feel as if she'd sprouted wings and flown to freedom."

"That's the thing. Damon tells me Alicia was only going to be a sophomore this fall. We knew she was twenty-one years old, and we assumed she was going to be a senior. There's considerable time unaccounted for between high school graduation and coming to the University of Minnesota."

Hallie sat forward. "Maybe she stayed home for a couple of years."

"According to Damon, Alicia let it drop that she escaped the happy family home for a year or so before being dragged back. Starting school at the U of M was a new release for her. Damon's not sure what she was doing that year out of the nest, but I intend to find out."

"Go for it!"

"There's my cheerleader." He chuckled.

"Smart aleck." She blew him a raspberry then laughed with him.

Later that evening, Hallie snuggled down into her pillow in bed. The police had been interested but frustrated by her report about the anonymous caller. She could relate. Discouragement had dogged her heels all day, but right now her heart was lightened by an inkling of hope that she still might find answers. What was it about Brody that buoyed her spirit?

"Thank you, Lord, for sending me an unexpected friend," she whispered into the darkness. She might even entertain notions of something more if they kept getting along like this. Wouldn't that blow the minds of everyone at the station? She drifted to sleep, smiling.

A distant sound of drums invaded her dreams. The pounding drew closer…closer…a familiar rhythm. She'd heard those drums long ago in a faraway place. Her heart battered her ribs in time with the drumming.

Fire bloomed. A bonfire, bright and sizzling, and around it whirled a dancer with brilliant colored robes in red and purple and white flapping around a scarecrow body. The man wore a plumed headdress that flowed nearly to his knees. Matted tendrils of hair, braided like ropes, covered his face.

Hallie struggled against the pull of the drums, and the fire, and the dance, but her feet remained rooted. Nearer, nearer, the dancer whirled, until…suddenly, he leaped toward her.

The hair flew back from his face, and she stared into Damon's furious blue eyes, but the dancer's face was not Damon's. Pock-marked skin couldn't mask the features of James Drayton. Yet the voice that spoke held the gravelly tones of the man on the telephone tonight.

"The past holds the future."

She woke with a cry and lunged upright in bed.

FOURTEEN

Since her car was still in the shop, Jenna and Sam picked Hallie up on Saturday morning for a day at the lake. Sam was full of final wedding plans, and Jenna reported that she and Stan were still casually dating, emphasis on *casual*. Hallie returned to her apartment in the evening, sunbaked and pleasantly weary. Her wild dream and the question marks surrounding the bracelet and murder lurked in the back of her mind, but the time away had refreshed her.

On Sunday, she caught a ride to church and sang in the choir. She invited her friends over for an afternoon of vegging out in front of a rented movie, then spent the evening doing research for her modeling story and on Cheryl Drayton. A public record search engine yielded a tidbit that would interest Brody as much as it did her.

Monday found her at her desk bright and early confirming interviews with modeling event promoters, advertising executives and makeup artists. She only had two weeks to wrap up the modeling story because the special segment was scheduled to air in ten-minute bites on the morning show throughout the final week in June.

The rest of the morning was consumed by an interview, and then picking up her car at the body shop. When she returned to the station shortly before noon, a note from Brody lay on her desk. *Can we grab lunch together?* Humming under her breath, Hallie punched in his internal extension number.

"I'm starved," she announced when he answered. "Can we do better than the food court? If we go over there, people are going to start gossiping about us being together so often."

"Wise woman. But as far as I'm concerned, they should get used to the sight."

Warmth spread like butter under sunlight inside Hallie. "Sweet-talker." She laughed.

"Let's grab something at Cossetta's then and make it a nice, long walk."

Frowning, she looked down at her feet. "We-e-ell, I did wear my low heels today, but that's still quite a trek."

"It'll give us time to talk privately, not to mention a little exercise."

"You've persuaded me."

They left the building through the reception area under Daria's wide-eyed stare. "Hey there, you two," she called as they went out the door. Hallie turned and waved at the receptionist, who answered with a grin and a nod.

"Daria approves." Hallie chuckled as they headed up the sidewalk under a blue sky feathered with pale clouds. "But there won't be anybody at the station who doesn't know that Hallie Berglund and Brody Jordan went to lunch together."

"I can handle that." Brody strolled beside her, one hand in the pocket of his tan slacks. "But I wish I had more of a handle on Alicia Drayton. I'm a little annoyed by my inability to locate a birth certificate for her. Do you think James and Cheryl adopted her? Those records are sealed in a lot of states."

"Negative. Alicia looked too much like her mother. But I can probably tell you why you're not finding the birth record." She chortled and did a little skip.

He stopped and stared down at her. "Go for it before you pop like a balloon."

"James and Cheryl were hitched in a Vegas chapel a little over nineteen years ago."

"But Alicia was twenty-one."

"Exactly. Alicia may have been born out of wedlock. I

suggest you search for Alicia's birth certificate under Cheryl's maiden name of Gerris."

Brody whistled under his breath. "That does explain a few things."

"Like why no birth record for Alicia *Drayton,* and why Cheryl is touchy about her past. Maybe the man who gave her the bracelet was Alicia's birth father, though how he got his hands on one of *my* mom's bracelets I have no clue."

"It also means that James adopted Alicia at some point in order for her to bear his name. Though that record would probably not be public."

"Yes, but the juicy part is if we find a birth certificate for Alicia *Gerris,* the birth father's name might be listed." She rubbed her hands together.

"And maybe not."

"Don't be a killjoy. I'm thinking positive."

They batted around theories for the rest of the journey to the Italian eatery. As they stepped inside Cossetta's, Hallie inhaled the delicious mix of spicy odors. She got into the queue for the salads and pastas, but Brody darted into line for a whopping slice of pizza. They met with their selections upstairs at a tiny table in the crowded dining area. The noise level kept conversation at a minimum while they ate.

Back outside with full stomachs, they retraced their steps toward the station at a slow pace. Brody's head swiveled this way and that as they walked.

"You act like you've never seen this neighborhood before. Or are you looking for something in particular?" Brody shrugged and continued his odd vigilance. Hallie smiled. "Ah, you're watching for my stalker. Y'know, this whole time we've been walking together, I haven't thought about him once. I must feel really safe with a big ox for a protector."

"I was actually hoping to draw the guy out if we made enough bait of ourselves."

"So that's the ulterior motive for this long-distance walk, and you didn't say anything. I'm not sure whether I should be mad at you or not."

"'Not' would be nice."

"I'll cut you some slack this time, but next time you take me along fishing for bad guys, you need to let me know."

"Deal."

A comfortable silence settled between them, punctuated by the sound of their footfalls. The rhythm brought to mind the drumbeats from Hallie's dreams, only that pace had been wild and strange. What if she stopped keeping these dreams to herself? Brody had surprised her more than once with his understanding.

They reached Sibley Street and stepped out with the green light. A Papa Morelli's Pizza car shot past them illegally, narrowly missing their feet, and they jumped back.

"Crazy driver!" Brody scowled at the vehicle.

Hallie shrugged. "There are more than a few around this city." She touched his arm, and he turned his head toward her. "Can we take a few minutes' breather in the park before we go back to the grindstone? I'd like a bench over by the bridge and little waterfall."

"Any particular reason for that spot?"

"It's a peaceful place to discuss a disturbing dream I had." Should she really tell him? He'd think she was nuts. And what if talking about her Friday night apparition invited the other, darker dreams? The ones with the children screaming. But the impulse to speak had ambushed her, she'd followed it, and now it was too late to put that cat back in its sack.

"You look scared."

She glanced up at him as they crossed the street in a group of other people. "I am."

He made a movement with his arm, as if he would put it around her, then pulled back. She hugged herself as they entered the park. They took the diagonal walk until they reached a vacant bench near the gentle rush of the waterfall. When they settled in, he did put his arm across the bench behind her with his hand lightly resting against her shoulder. Amazing what comfort a small human touch could bring. She sent him a tight smile then stared down at her hands clasped together in her lap.

"Any time you're ready," he said. "But no sooner."

A pent-up breath left Hallie's lungs. This guy understood things in ways she'd thought only her dearest girlfriends could, and she hadn't even told *them* about the dream. Haltingly at first, then with increasing flow, she described everything she heard and saw. The moments played out in her mind's eye as vividly as if she was still in the nightmare.

Brody shook his head when she finished, and the hand on her shoulder clamped tight and squeezed. "What do you think all that means?"

Hallie lifted her gaze to his. "You don't think I'm crazy?"

"Why should I? We all dream strange stuff at times. My nightmares usually come from eating too much spicy pizza." He issued a brief chuckle, and Hallie smiled. "But never mind my indigestion. It sounds like your dream has significance for you—the robes, the drums, the dancing."

"Those things are related to the native Yoruba religion of orisha worship."

"Who's orisha?"

"The question would be correctly phrased, 'Who are the orishas?'"

"Ah, a religion of many deities."

"Oh, yes, hundreds! Maybe you'll understand better if I tell you that in the States and the Caribbean, the religion brought in by Nigerian slaves has morphed into what we call voodoo. Really dark stuff. The particular orisha in my dream specializes in disease, a nasty fellow, and worshippers go out of their way to appease him. My parents protected me from most exposure to the pagan ways, but I picked things up here and there. Mostly from other school children. Nigeria is around forty percent Christian, actually, a number exceeded only by the Muslim population. But the small percentage who cling to the ancient idol-worship can be rabid about it. I know this firsthand." She suppressed a shudder.

Brody rubbed his chin. "So your subconscious has thrown together the evil you've experienced in this last week with an evil from your childhood."

"Exactly! And it's like solving the mysteries of the present will require uncovering the truth about the past."

He took his arm from around Hallie's shoulder and twined his hand with hers. "Whatever that involves, I'm with you."

She studied their fingers locked together. "At this time last week, I would've laughed in the face of anyone who told me I'd say this to Brody Jordan, but honestly, there's no one— other than God—I'd rather have on my side right now."

Brody's chest expanded, like he'd sucked in a gallon of air. His gaze trapped hers. Was he going to kiss her? What if someone from the station was watching? Did she care?

His shoulders slowly relaxed, and he touched her lips with a fingertip. "We need to get back to the office, but hold that thought. I'm sure going to." His gaze held a solemn promise that sent pleasant tingles through Hallie.

He tugged her to her feet, and they walked back toward the station side by side, hands almost touching but not quite.

Brody hung up the phone after talking with the Dean of Admissions at the University of Minnesota. He dropped his pen onto the blotter. Twenty-four hours had passed since Hallie had bolstered his hope with her mellowing toward Damon, but the possible lead on Alicia's birth certificate had fizzled. He had found no record of an Alicia Gerris being born to Cheryl Gerris. And now nothing from the university either.

A knock sounded on his door. "Come!" Brody barked.

Hallie stuck her head through. "Am I in danger of having something thrown at me, or dare I step inside?"

He waved her in. "Sorry about that. I just checked with the U of M, and Alicia didn't transfer any credits from another university when she enrolled here. What was she doing that year away from home?"

Hallie settled into his guest chair, hugging a short stack of dog-eared and yellowed papers. "My guess is she took up with a man. In her situation, she'd grasp at anything to get out of that house, and chances are she'd pick a loser. Young people from abusive homes have no clue how to find a healthy relationship."

"You're probably right. Looks like we'll have to go to the memorial service and ask some questions around Alicia's hometown. Interested?"

"You found out when the service is?" She leaned toward him, face expectant.

"The Johnson Funeral Home in Thief River Falls was only too happy to tell me that, although Alicia's body was cremated, there will be a memorial service in their chapel at two o'clock tomorrow afternoon."

"When do we le—oh, can you get away after you took two days off last week?" She let loose of the papers in her arms, and they flopped onto her lap. The sheets looked like old newsletters.

"I twisted Wayne's arm a bit until he saw this as an opportunity to gain leads that could mean new scoops for WDJN. He can't spare a cameraman, though, so it'll be just you and me. Besides, he's in a *very* good mood today."

Hallie gathered up her fliers and crossed legs. "I don't doubt it with Vince scheduled to interview Damon for the evening news. Are you worried?"

"Petrified, but praying."

"Oddly enough, I'm praying for things to go well, too. For your sake."

"Thanks. I appreciate that. Have you got something you wanted to show me?" He pointed toward the papers in her arms.

She hopped up and laid the short stack on his desk. Excitement radiated from her. "My uncle sent a packet of old newsletters my parents issued from Africa. They were waiting for me yesterday when I got off work. I spent the whole evening poring over these. It's like the pictures from the place I lived, the people I knew, and the words written by my dad have unlocked the floodgates of *happy* memories of Nigeria. I wanted to share a couple of things with you."

"I'm honored." Was he ever! Of all the people she could include in her personal journey of rediscovery, she'd made him one of them. Who would have believed it?

She opened a ripply-edged copy of the *Living Hope Home Newsletter*. "Look here." She pointed to a photograph on the bottom left page.

About a dozen children gazed at him from a backdrop of trees and landscape not found in America. Most of the kids were grinning, but the littlest—about toddler age—had his thumb in his mouth. Brody pointed toward the head of a girl toward the middle of the group. "That's you."

Hallie laughed. "How did you guess? Just kidding. It's obvious. My Caucasian blood betrays me. Now wait." She laid a regular photograph beside the newsletter picture. Three children mugged for the camera in front of a very American Dairy Queen.

He pointed to the middle one. "That's you."

"Right again, you clever man. The other two are my cousins I grew up with, Uncle Reese and Auntie Michelle's boy and girl. It felt so strange last night to look at that photo of me among the orphanage kids and be the lightest-skinned, when I've gotten used to being the darkest one in the family pictures. But that's not all. Here." She produced another news-letter.

In the top right photo a man and woman stood hand-in-hand in front of a small airplane. Their closed-mouthed smiles were understated but warm. Brody recognized the regal carriage of the woman's head and the strong slash of the man's eyebrows. The characteristics were reflected in the elegant lady who shared these personal treasures with him.

"Your parents," he said.

"Brody Jordan, I'd like to introduce you to my father, Iver, and my mother, Yewande."

"Pleased to meet them." He gazed up into Hallie's glowing face. "Their daughter does them proud."

"Oh, you." She colored. "Check out the man in the background. He was the pilot who died in the crash with them."

Brody studied the picture. An indistinct figure, a tall, lanky man stood with one hand on his hip, the other on the nose of the plane, and one ankle crossed over the other with the toe of his shoe planted against the ground. Though the picture was grainy, a miniscule strip of white betrayed the man was grinning.

"I remember him now." Hallie tapped the picture. "Mr. O'Halloran. He was a three-month intern, checking out the mission field to see if it was the Lord's will that he come permanently. Full of the 'old Irish mischief,' he was. At least that's the way he put it." She chuckled. "But as I recall, he wasn't always happy-go-lucky. Sometimes he was serious and thoughtful. Mom said he missed people back in the States. I'm going to see if I can find any immediate relatives. Maybe one of them has an inkling why Cheryl Drayton would have one of my mother's bracelets."

"Excellent thinking."

She gathered up the newsletters. "There's lots more memorabilia here, but it'll have to wait. I have a ton of work to do in order to free up my schedule to head for Alicia's service tomorrow. I have a good feeling we'll discover something important." Cradling the fliers, she charged out of the office.

Brody leaned back in his chair. Which investigation did she mean? The bracelet or the murder? The way things were going, Damon wasn't any closer to being off the hook, and the leads were dwindling to nothing. Unless something truly startling came to light, Damon's lawyer would have a tough row to hoe in order to create reasonable doubt in the minds of jurors. He didn't blame Hallie for thinking Damon was guilty. If he didn't know the kid, he'd think so, too.

FIFTEEN

Hallie sneaked a peek at Brody's somber profile in the driver's seat as they headed up I-94 on the first leg of their five-and-a-half-hour journey to Thief River Falls. Dawn had brushed the car's interior a ruddy gold.

"Damon did all right in the interview," she said.

Brody's upper lip curled. "Damon's something like Dennis Rodman, a stellar player but prone to controversial antics on and off the court. He didn't do himself any favors with that crack about the brain-dead public."

"To tell you the truth, I about choked on my Dr. Pepper over that one. Otherwise, he was fairly well-mannered, even when Vince needled him about his fights with Alicia."

"Good thing old Vinnie didn't say anything inflammatory about Alicia's character, or the kid would've blown a gasket."

"He really loved her, didn't he." Hallie shook her head. "But that doesn't mean he didn't kill her."

"I know. I loved my wife, even long after the divorce, but there were lots of times I could have cheerfully throttled her."

Hallie wrinkled her nose. "People say that kind of thing, but there's very few who actually followed through. From the comments you've let drop, I take it she's the one who left."

Brody hummed an affirmative. "It took me a while to figure out that she hadn't married *me*. She married my potential for fame and fortune. Growing up in an affluent home, she'd never lacked anything as far as material possessions, and she wanted it to stay that way. Plus, I was her ticket to what she saw as the fast life of glamour as a pro ball player's wife. I wrecked my knee, and her dreams with it, in my senior year."

"Pretty shallow dreams, if you ask me." Hallie laid a hand on his arm. The muscles beneath her fingers were relaxed. Evidently, he wasn't still bothered about his losses. That spoke of maturity and healing. He must not have nightmares about his past. Lucky him. "Did you get together in college, or were you high school sweethearts?"

"I met her my first day on the practice field at Penn State. She was, get this, a cheerleader." They both laughed. "Two years ahead of me in school, she was sophisticated, cool, beautiful. Her hooks were into me before I even knew what happened, and I sure was a sucker for those enormous hazel eyes. I'd daydream about the beautiful babies we'd have together, only she wasn't eager to start a family. And she was right about that, as long as we were in school. Now, I think she never would have wanted kids to play havoc with her figure."

Hallie snorted. "A few stretch marks are nothing compared to the joy of a new life."

"My philosophy exactly." His dimple appeared.

She socked him in the shoulder. "Says you. You wouldn't have to live with them."

"I'd adore each one as a badge of honor on my wife and the mother of my children."

Blinking her eyes, Hallie looked away. Whoever got this guy would nab herself a gem. "Funny he isn't taken already."

"What did you say?"

Hallie sucked in a breath. Had she spoken that last thought out loud? Evidently so. Heat crept up her neck. "I was just wondering why you haven't remarried. I mean, since you want a family and all."

The dimple disappeared. "Believe me, for several years after the divorce I wouldn't have wished myself on anybody. Sure, I managed to graduate with a degree, but I'd lost what I thought really mattered—my game and my wife—and the bottle was my big solution to the pain. I barely hung on to a gig as a radio announcer. The station owner was a Christian, and he relentlessly invited me to church. I know he was praying for me, too."

He stared ahead in silence, a muscle in his neck twitching, as if reliving an emotional time. Then his shoulders eased back, and he shook his head. "Remember how I told you I'd had a DUI. That was my lowest point. I narrowly avoided killing myself and a carload of teenagers. If by sheer fluke I hadn't hit the ditch on the wrong side of the road at the last instant, it would have been a head-on collision. And next time I wouldn't be so lucky. I knew it like I knew my name. But there was no way I could beat the bottle on my own. When my boss visited me in the hospital and asked if he could pray with me, I threw myself at the foot of the cross, and I haven't left since. Jesus delivered me from the bottle, not some program, though I have nothing against those if they point people to the ultimate solution. Now I'm waiting on God for the *right* Mrs. Jordan."

He shot her a pointed stare. "So what about you?"

Huh? She blinked at him. Was that some sort of offhand marriage proposal? He was teasing her. A laugh stuttered between her lips.

His color deepened. "That didn't come out right. What I meant was, why aren't you all wrapped up in marital bliss with a couple of children to liven up your life?"

"Good question. I used to scold myself for being too picky, but now I think I've held off because I haven't felt whole enough in myself for that level of union with another person."

"Good answer. Are you getting closer to readiness?"

Was she? "I hope so, but I'm not sure. There are still some things…"

Hallie watched cropland interrupted by groves of trees and farm sites slide past her window. Not entirely. What held her back? Questions about a bracelet that she hadn't known existed eight days ago? No, her search for answers about Alicia's armband was only a catalyst for an inner exploration that had needed to happen for a long time.

The memories of her early years were emerging from the fog, but one big, dark splotch still kept her from making peace with the way the most innocent era of her life had come to an abrupt end. Maybe it was time to put the horror in perspective. If she talked about what happened, could that be a positive first step? A man who'd conquered his own personal tragedy might have a good pair of ears, but did she have the courage to speak?

Her fingers tightened around the armrest on the passenger door. "They found out my parents were dead. No one had told me yet, but they knew, and they came."

"Who came?"

"The orishas." Her words came out a strained whisper. She cleared her throat. "Just people dressed up like them. I know that now, but I was too young and terrified to realize that at the time. A mob struck our compound in the night and set fire to the buildings. I remember…" She reached for her bottle of water in the cup holder and took several sips.

"We don't have to go there if you don't want." Brody's tone was gentle.

"I do want." She spoke fiercely. "It's just that I *don't* want to stir up the nightmares."

"So talking about it brings on bad dreams?"

"Yes…no! I don't know." She went stiff with realization. "I haven't asked myself that question, because I *never* talk about it. Sometimes I start thinking about that night, and then I stop myself. When I don't turn off the memories quickly enough, I have the nightmares. But you know," she smacked her knees with her palms, "I'm tired of being afraid of something that happened over twenty years ago. I'm going to talk about it, and if I dream, I dream."

"Go for it!" Brody sent her an approving grin.

"That's my cheerleader!" A gust of cleansing laughter left Hallie's chest. She was going to do this. She set the water bottle into the holder and allowed her thoughts to drift back in time.

"African nights can be so black, and clear, and peaceful. I had a window in my second floor bedroom that I liked to keep uncovered so I could look out until I fell asleep. This night was an ebony blanket of stars when I went to bed believing all was well in my world. I woke up from a sound sleep with the smell of smoke in my nostrils and the sound of my playmates' screams in my ears. One of the workers raced into my room and grabbed me out of my bed. He wasn't gentle, but I don't suppose he had time to be. I had bruises the next day.

"My memories from that moment on are fragments of sensory impressions. The darting of flames. Heat on my skin. The stink of burning wood and scorched brick. And the screams!" A shudder rolled through Hallie. "The children that I'd grown up with—my friends—were crying for help. I begged to go get them, but the worker rushed me outside to a waiting jeep. We raced off in a spray of gravel, and all I could think was that I'd failed my parents by not helping the others. With the screams growing fainter in my ears, I looked back, and that's when I saw the orishas whirling in their robes by the light of the blaze. The picture is seared into my brain."

Drained, Hallie slumped back against her seat. "It's irrational, I know, but I still battle the sense that I disappointed my mother and father by not stopping to save the other children. Later, after that horrible night, and all I wanted was my mommy and daddy, I was told my parents wouldn't be coming for me—ever." She lifted her head and glared toward Brody. "The whole village knew of my parents' deaths the afternoon before the raid, but the orphanage workers had opted not to tell me until after I'd had a good night's rest. Right!"

She settled against the seat and closed her eyes against the prickle of tears. A drop slid down one cheek, and she swiped it away. A big, warm hand closed around the fingers damp from the tear.

"You're no disappointment, Hallie Berglund. To anyone. I have no doubt that when your mom and dad hug you in heaven, you'll find out that they're so proud of you they could bust."

"I hope you're right, Brody Jordan." A great lethargy drew her toward sleep, and she didn't resist.

* * *

Brody glanced at Hallie sleeping on the passenger side. She hadn't even stirred when they went through the stop and go lights in St. Cloud. They'd traveled northwest on Highway 10 for two hours now, and she continued breathing deep and steady with her long lashes feathered against her high cheekbones. She needed the rest. She'd been under many days of strain, both personal and professional.

He had to give her, and that aunt and uncle of hers, a lot of credit that she turned out a Godly, stable woman after such a traumatic departure from Africa at a tender age. Lots of people grew up into unresolved messes with fewer losses in their lives than hers, though it sounded like repression had been one of her coping tools. Finding that bracelet had stirred her to face her fears. In that respect, Alicia's tragedy had worked for good in Hallie.

Now if they could find out the truth about the murder for both Alicia and Damon's sakes, resolution might be found for everyone. It would take a miracle, though. But if God could arrange that Hallie would choose him, of all the unlikely people, to honor with her private pain, Brody had to believe he would help the two of them find the answers they sought.

He touched a strand of the dark hair spread against the headrest of the passenger seat. She'd worn her hair loose today. He liked it a bit tousled and not so controlled. Maybe as she let loose some of the hidden things inside of her, he'd see a little more of the free spirit he sometimes glimpsed. Now *that* was something to look forward to.

A good-sized town loomed ahead. Brody slowed the car and then pulled over at a convenience store and gas station.

Hallie groaned and lifted her head, eyes blinking for focus. "Where are we?"

"Detroit Lakes. I'm making a pit stop to use the facilities and grab a sandwich."

"Sounds good."

They got out of the vehicle and stretched. Their gazes met,

and they laughed at their mirror actions. A few minutes later, they got back on the road, heading north on Highway 59.

"Feeling refreshed?" Brody said.

"Yeah, I am. Like some sort of long-term oppression has eased off. I didn't dream at all."

"You looked peaceful as a babe."

She smiled at him. "Since I'm all rested up, I'll take the wheel for the drive home."

"I'll take you up on that offer."

"And thanks for listening to my strange history."

"Unusual, for sure, but interesting. And I'm sorry those things happened."

"Me, too."

He glanced at her sideways. "Um, do you mind if I ask a few questions?"

"Shoot!"

"Why did the orisha-worshippers attack as soon as your parents were dead?"

Her gaze darkened. "They were scared spitless of my dad. With him out of the way, they didn't waste the chance to eliminate the Christian influence in an area they used to control. At least, that's how I've figured it out since then. As a kid, I was just confused by the whole deal."

Brody shook his head. "I hadn't pictured your father as an intimidating man."

She laughed. "He was a teddy bear. To me, especially. I worded that wrong. It wasn't really my dad they were scared of, but this Jesus he preached to anyone who would listen."

Hallie angled toward him and stretched her arm over the back of the seat. "You see, my parents didn't just look after orphaned children, they built a church that drew converts by the dozens. That's when the fanatical followers of the old ways started to hate us. Sometimes, they opposed us openly. I actually saw my father face down an irate priest who barged into one of our services shaking his rattles and yelling curses. My father calmly spoke the name of Jesus and quoted scripture from Revelation about the fate of the devil. Finally the priest clapped his hands over his ears and ran away shrieking. I was only five at the time, but that moment erased all question forever about which god is truly God."

"That's amazing," Brody said. "Even when your parents died, you didn't rethink that? Most people *blame* God when tragedy happens."

"That's just a misguided way of acknowledging him as the Supreme Being. Tragedy happens because people do terrible things to each other or just because this world is so messed up. God's the only hope for either of those things to change."

"No argument from me."

The remainder of the trip passed in discussing their game plan once they reached Thief River Falls. They needed to make the most of every minute during this one-day dash.

As soon as they drove into town, Brody guided the car toward the neighborhood where the Draytons lived, while Hallie navigated from an Internet-generated map. The well-kept rambler and split-level homes spoke of solid middle-class affluence—not doctor or lawyer scale, but not financial suffering, either. They cruised past the brown-and-white rambler with the Draytons' number on it. No cars sat in front of the double garage.

Brody consulted his watch. "Hard to say if James and Cheryl are home. They might be at the funeral parlor by now. We've only got about a half hour to do a whirlwind canvas of the neighbors, and then we need to head for the service ourselves." He turned a corner.

"Hey!" Hallie pointed toward the green-and-gold car that was pulling out of the Draytons' alley in front of them. "I saw a Papa Morelli's vehicle in front of Alicia's house the day she was killed."

Brody narrowed his gaze and fell in behind the car. "Change of plan. We're following this dude. If he leads us to a legitimate pizza parlor, we'll laugh at ourselves and go back to our original plan. We've seen this type of vehicle too often. Remember that close call when we were returning from our walk to Cossetta's?"

"It's not as if pizza delivery vehicles are uncommon." Her words were cautious, but the tone broadcast excitement. "I'm getting the license plate number." She dug in her purse and took out paper and pen as Brody stayed several car lengths behind.

The delivery car proceeded at a sedate pace through several turns and brought them into a busy commercial area. A good way ahead a light turned yellow. Brody tapped the gas to creep closer to the delivery car, and then the brakes to prepare to stop. But the driver in the pizza car gunned his vehicle and shot through the light as it flared red.

Brody smacked the steering wheel. "That's the second time someone's pulled that trick on me in recent history. You were the other one."

"I remember it well, but it seems like forever ago already. So much has changed."

Their gazes met, and Brody's heart did a little jig. Did he read personal interest in Hallie's eyes? He'd better, because he meant to pursue this woman with serious intentions as soon as they could get a breather from crises.

A car behind them honked. "Oops!" Brody headed the Impala through the intersection. "Did you get the license plate number?"

"Number, make, model, the ding in the left rear fender."

"At least one of us got something right."

"Don't beat yourself up, Jordan. We could be making a big deal out of nothing, but at least we can give the information to the police when we get home."

"Home nothing." He pulled into the parking lot of a grocery store and stopped the car. "I'm reporting it now. If this is your stalker who followed us all the way to Thief River Falls, I want him traced ASAP." He punched a number into his cell phone.

Hallie patted him on the knee. "Make yourself happy, ox. But it seems to me that *we* were following *him*."

Brody scowled at her as he was connected to the office of Detective Millette. His scowl deepened when voicemail picked up. He left a terse message and his contact information then snapped his phone shut.

"Back to plan A," Hallie said.

They retraced their path to the Draytons' neighborhood. Brody took one side of the street, and Hallie took the other. Twenty minutes later, they met at the car.

"I got zip," he told Hallie. "Nobody home."

"I found one very nice little old lady. She said the folks around here respect James and love Cheryl, and we should find most of them gathered at the funeral home. She'd be there herself if she wasn't feeling so poorly. Oh, and do you know what else she told me?" Her smug smile belonged on the Sphinx. "The Draytons moved here from 'up north.'"

"North! There's not much north of here but Canada."

"Oooh, give the man a prize."

"That's why we haven't found a U.S. birth certificate for Alicia," they said in unison.

Brody headed the car toward the funeral home. "There's one problem with the theory. My research has shown that James is a natural born American."

"Yes, but maybe Cheryl isn't. If Alicia is hers from a prior relationship, no records would show on this side of the border. Come to think of it, as long as we're digging on foreign soil, we might as well go whole hog and try to see if there's a record of a prior marriage for her in Canada. Checking out another angle can't hurt."

"I like the way you think, woman." Brody shot her a grin.

Shortly, they parked outside the funeral parlor. Hallie joined him on the sidewalk going into the building. He looked at his watch.

Her warm hand closed around his wrist. "Yes, I know we're late, but perhaps unwelcome guests are best served by slipping quietly into the back of the chapel."

"We won't go unnoticed forever. It'll be interesting to see what fireworks let loose then."

Wound tight and expectant, Brody followed Hallie into the building. If either of Alicia's parents knew anything about their daughter's murder, an emotional moment like this service might supply the crack in their armor that he needed to help Damon's case.

SIXTEEN

As the service concluded, Hallie touched the corners of her eyes with a tissue, careful not to smear her makeup. That Steven Curtis Chapman song about a life too soon over had nearly ripped her apart. She kept thinking about her friend Teresa, and how her young life was stolen by warped and manipulated thinking. Alicia, too, had been lost to something wicked in someone's heart.

She stood with the other guests and let people file past them to greet James and Cheryl, who waited near the front, flanked by live plants and sprays of flowers. The pastor had announced that the interment of the urn containing Alicia's ashes would be a private moment at a later time. Today, guests were invited to partake of a light lunch before heading home. The smell of coffee wafted from another room.

A touch on her arm drew Hallie's attention to Brody.

"How about we let the group around the Draytons thin out a bit," he said. "You visit with the women, and I'll mingle with the guys and ask a few questions. Believe it or not, guys are aching to talk when they think they have information someone else doesn't."

Hallie chuckled. "I can easily believe that. My uncle always said the men down at the coffee shop jawed more than any group of women he'd ever heard."

"Sounds about right." The Brody dimple twinkled at her. "Give it fifteen minutes and then I'll back you up while you approach the grieving parents."

Hallie glanced toward where the Draytons received condolences. Poor Cheryl. She stood like a wilted rose, and James
hovered as her protector—or was it her keeper—shaking
hands with those who came by.

A figure came between her and the Draytons. "Hello," said
a woman dressed in a navy blue pinstriped suit that identified
her as one of the funeral home workers. Her smile accented
sprays of delicate lines around her mouth and eyes that betrayed
her middle age, despite the solid blond hair. "You look familiar.
Where have I seen you before? Were you a friend of Alicia's?"

"I'm the television news reporter who discovered her body."

"Oh, my!" The woman's mouth pursed, then smoothed again
into the businesswoman smile. "From the Twin Cities then.
How nice of you to come all this way to pay your respects."

"I lost a friend some years back to a violent death. This hit
me hard and personally."

The woman shook her head. "The Draytons may have a
tough time going on after the loss. Alicia was their life."

"Do you know them well?"

"Not really, but Cheryl does day care for my granddaugh-
ter, Riley. I've had occasion to pick Riley up at their house
now and then. Cheryl sure did mope both times her daughter
left for college. And now this."

"Both times?" Hallie stiffened.

"That's right. But Alicia didn't finish her freshman year
when she went off right out of high school. Must not have
been quite ready for the change. Her parents definitely
weren't. She came home again for over a year and helped with
the day care before she tried leaving again."

Hallie's heart rate quickened. "Do you know where Alicia
went to college before?"

"Not specifically." The woman shrugged. "Just that it was
far away. Some place out of state, I think. Maybe the distance
was too much for all of them. Excuse me." She touched
Hallie's arm. "I need to check the refreshment table."

"Sure…ah, thanks for visiting with me." Hallie watched the
woman walk away. Such a tiny morsel of information, but at

least it provided a new direction for investigation. So Alicia had gone to college somewhere before the University of Minnesota. She must not have tried to transfer any credits from her failed attempt. Had she flunked out? That hardly sounded like the driven and composed straight A student from the U of M.

Hallie searched the crowd of strangers for Brody's familiar face. She needed to clue him in to ask people about Alicia's prior schooling. There he was. She took a step toward him.

"Ms. Berglund, we thought you might show up today." Cheryl Drayton's voice leaked sorrow.

Hallie turned and came face-to-face with both of Alicia's parents. James stood behind Cheryl, his nostrils and lips pinched. His gaze was fixed on his wife, but Hallie glimpsed the expression. Unfulfilled longing. She'd seen that look before in the eyes of men who gazed at something they craved—a boat, a car, a new gadget—that was beyond their means to have. James was anything but sure of his hold over his wife, and that made him all the more possessive.

"Here." Cheryl held a small box toward her. "You should have this."

Hallie accepted the box and lifted the lid. Her mother's handmade armband gleamed back at her. "How—"

"They returned all of Alicia's personal property not considered evidence."

Brody stepped up beside her, and the tightness in Hallie's chest eased.

"You both agree to give the bracelet to Hallie?" He stared from one Drayton to the other.

James stepped forward and put his arm around his wife's shoulder. "We both agree that this needs to be the final contact between us and her—and you, too, if you're with her."

"Brody Jordan, Channel Six sportscaster." He held out his hand toward Alicia's father.

The man ignored it and lifted his gaze toward something behind Hallie and Brody. She looked over her shoulder. A pair of stocky men dressed in suits, legs slightly apart, arms flexed at their sides, flanked her and Brody. Their gazes radiated menace. She'd seen their crew-cut heads in the honorary pall-bearer row during the service. Conversations began to go still around the little group as heads swiveled in their direction.

"Friends from the police department." James smirked while Cheryl dropped her gaze toward the floor. "They will escort you out of the building and follow you out of town."

Tension radiated from Brody's arm that brushed against Hallie's. No! He wouldn't start something here, would he? With his size and athletic training, he probably could hold his own, but— His hand closed around her elbow, and he guided her toward the door.

Hallie let out a pent-up breath as they stepped out the door into the afternoon sunlight. "Very dark in there."

"You said it," Brody muttered.

They got into the Impala and headed toward Highway 59. Hugging the box, Hallie looked back toward the unmarked police car on their tail. "I guess we're leaving town."

Brody rippled his shoulders. "Might as well. I think the wagons were starting to circle in there against us. I doubt anyone will say another word. I don't suppose you had any more luck finding out anything than I did in five minutes flat."

"Gotcha there, Jordan." She told him about Alicia's prior college attendance.

"Good job. You might get off the cheer squad and into the anchor chair yet." He held out a palm for a victor's slap.

Fat chance after that crack! She socked him in the shoulder.

He laughed. "Shall we go over our list of suspects and match them with what we know?"

"*Your* list of suspects. I already know who my suspect is."

"Humor me." He sent her a long-suffering look.

She opened the box Cheryl had given her and took out the bracelet. The cool metal rapidly warmed between her fingers.

"Your mom did pretty nice work there." His tone had changed from bantering to gentle. "Can I take a closer look when we stop for supper?"

"Certainly." She slipped the bracelet onto her wrist. It was bulky, but fit snugly enough around her wrist that there was little slippage, and yet it wasn't too tight—as if Yewande Berglund had made it for her adult daughter's arm, like she'd done the child's bracelet. Of course, the armband would fit any woman with slender wrists like Cheryl and Alicia's. Hallie traced the intricate elephant design with her thumb. Should she feel weird about wearing an article that had adorned a dead woman? If so, she didn't. The bracelet belonged where it was.

She put her hands in her lap, still fingering the design on the metal. "Stan had a couple of favorites for the job of killer."

"I remember Monique Rimes. Was that catty model Jessica the other one?"

"You got it."

"But?" Brody sent her an assessing glance.

"No motive for Ms. Monique. She had every reason to want Alicia alive. Jessica wouldn't have minded her rival dead, but she was doing a shoot at the time of the murder."

Brody grunted acknowledgment. "Well, here's my top contender—your stalker. And that worries me where you're concerned. A lot. No known motive, but that might become apparent when he's caught. Or maybe he's just a nut who targets beautiful women."

Hallie's heart did a little *ka-bump*. Brody thought she was beautiful. "Thank you."

"Huh?" He blinked at her.

She rolled her eyes at him. "Figures! You imply something really nice, and it's so off the cuff, you didn't even realize you said it." Hallie chuckled, shaking her head. "At least I know your words were sincere, since they came out minus any planning."

"Sounds like good feminine logic. I'm at least smart enough to go along with *that*." He sent her a bemused grin.

She answered with a mock scowl. "Okay, funny man, what about this stalker makes him your prime suspect?"

"His penchant for violence, for one thing. Grabbing your purse, keying your car."

Hallie frowned. How did she make sense of her confusion about the man? "Okay. The guy gives me the creeps, but maybe he's just choosing a really scary way to spur us on to keep investigating. The note on your windshield, the phone call when we were looking for the Draytons."

Brody's disgusted look said he considered her ready for the funny farm. "How can keying your car be called helpful?"

"Everyone's assuming he did that, but it still doesn't feel right to me. That was a malicious act—something done by someone with a score to settle or as the random act of an angry person. It's simply not consistent with the rest of this guy's actions."

"Oh, yeah, like stealing your scarf?"

"I haven't figured out what that was all about, but there's got to be an explanation."

"Exactly. He's crazy, and he might be a killer."

"Whoa, whoa, whoa!" Her thoughts backpedaled to that frightening night in the drug neighborhood. "He's the rock-thrower!"

"The what?" Brody stared at her.

"Eyes on the road, buddy."

He huffed and looked ahead.

"Try this on for size." She leaned toward him. "He threw the rock that broke the window at Damon's mother's house and maybe saved us all from being shot by a drug addict."

Brody's mouth made motions like a beached fish, and little splutters emerged. Finally, he burst out laughing.

Hallie crossed her arms. Let the man have his fun. She knew what she knew.

The guffaws ebbed to spurts, and he wiped his eyes. "I'm sorry. Truly." He waved a feeble hand in her direction. "If you knew that neighborhood, you'd realize that no one needs a reason to throw a rock through a window around there. Anyone could have done it."

"Exactly in the nick of time? I don't believe in so much coincidence."

Brody sobered. "You have a point there."

"At least you don't count me a total moron."

"Aw, honey, that's one thing I'll never think about you."

The sincerity in his gaze almost melted Hallie, but she gathered her arms closer against her chest. "Honey? Is that another slip of the tongue like 'beautiful' and 'sunshine'?"

Pink crept up from the collar of Brody's sport shirt right to his hairline. "You caught the 'sunshine' one, too?"

The poor man looked ready to sink through the seat. A snort of laughter escaped through Hallie's nose before she could stop it. He sent her a weak smile, and she gave up and laughed. "If you weren't so cute, you'd be in a lot more trouble, Jordan."

"Cute?"

"Easy to see you've never been in the electronics department of a store when the ladies are gathered around a demo TV set during the evening sportscast, going, 'Oooh, isn't he cuuuute?'" She put on a falsetto. "'I just loooove that dimple.'"

"You're kidding." His Adam's apple bobbed. "Aren't you?"

Her steady look answered him, and his eyes went wide. "You didn't know?"

"Why would I want to know something like that?"

"Another misconception about Brody Jordan busted. You were so stuck up about talking to me at the station, I figured you were mainly stuck on yourself."

"My avoidance of your candle-flame to this poor moth was pure self-preservation."

"I scared you?" Her own eyes grew wide.

"Still do, but I'm beyond worrying about getting burned."

Emotion clogged her throat and halted further words. This man stirred her on levels none other had touched before, but an overload of turmoil—inside and out—clouded her judgment. If she allowed their relationship to move beyond professional, it had to be when she could think clearly. She sneaked a look at his strong profile, and he met her gaze.

"So quit distracting me already." His tone was gruff, and

he glued his gaze back on the road. "Can we pull over in the next town and get a bite to eat? Then you can drive."

With his stomach pleasantly full, Brody settled into the passenger side of his Impala and reclined the seat so he could relax, maybe snooze a bit. He hadn't been sleeping the best at night, and today had been a tough one. Lack of rest must be why he blabbed to Hallie about his attraction to her. She probably thought he was rushing things, because she hadn't responded in kind, though she'd been bright and charming through the meal. He glanced over at her, and she smiled at him as she started the car.

"Next stop, home sweet home." She guided the car into traffic.

"What about James and Cheryl?"

"As what?"

"Suspects."

A light laugh answered him. "They both have alibis and anything but motive," Hallie said. "As much as I despise James and pity Cheryl, can you honestly see either of them beating and strangling their daughter?"

"Not Cheryl, for sure. James has the physical strength."

"Yes, but he's cool, calculating. Alicia's murder has all the earmarks of a crime of passion."

Brody hummed. "Passion may lurk beneath that icy exterior. And fear."

"You noticed the insecurity, too?"

"He turned a shade whiter when Cheryl handed you the box. That's why I asked them if they both agreed to give you the bracelet."

"Any passion in James belongs to Cheryl. I'm not sure an adopted daughter qualified for that much attention. He lives in constant dread of losing his wife. That's why he hangs on so tightly. And something about this bracelet," she lifted her arm, "stirs up those fears. Cheryl all but told me that Alicia's birth father gave it to her. I suspect James has always felt second fiddle to that man, which is why we need to find out who he was. But all this is a huge stretch with no support to create a motive for murder."

Brody sighed. "Unfortunately, I have to agree with you."

She angled an arch-browed look at him. "There's one suspect we haven't discussed."

"Damon?" A sour taste settled on Brody's tongue.

"He's the only one with all the factors in place—capability, motive, opportunity—not to mention the temperament for a crime of passion. I totally hate to see you hurt, but you need to face facts for the sake of your own sanity."

Brody studied Hallie's face. She sincerely cared about his feelings. At least that was a start in the right direction. "Thanks. I appreciate your concern, but there's only one problem with your evaluation. Damon didn't do it."

She frowned at him without a word.

He dug out his cell phone. "Which brings us back to the stalker. I'm going to call the detective on your case and see if she's traced that license plate number yet. I'll put the phone on speaker so we can both hear and talk."

The detective came on the line a minute later. "Millette here."

"This is Brody Jordan. I'm on the road toward home with Hallie Berglund. We're hoping you've been able to do something with the license information we phoned in earlier today."

"I'm glad you called…for a couple of reasons," the detective said. "First of all, yes, I did some digging. There is a Papa Morelli's in Thief River Falls, but none of their cars have a license plate number that matches the one you reported. I ran the plates, and come to find out, the number belongs to a car sold to a small-time dealer from a franchise here in the Twin Cities a few weeks ago. I'm following up with the dealer to see if he let it go to someone else without repainting it like he was supposed to do."

"Sounds like a plan," Brody said.

"Do you think this is a lead toward the stalker?" Hallie's words came out breathless.

The connection continued silent for several heartbeats. "You may well have caught a glimpse of him, yes. But unfortunately, since he apparently spotted you, he'll probably ditch the car somewhere. I've put out an APB, but that's about all I can do, except to let you know when and if the vehicle is found."

Brody bit back an angry comment. "What was the other thing you needed to talk to us about?"

"You're lucky there's not an APB out on *you.*"

"What?" Brody burst out in unison with Hallie.

"The precinct had a phone call from an irate pair of police officers in Thief River Falls."

"We've met them," Brody said, his gaze colliding with Hallie's.

"I told them about the stalker and the Papa Morelli's car, and they calmed down enough to hold off on issuing an immediate arrest warrant. But I'm asking you both to come in to the station and voluntarily give your fingerprints. It seems that James and Cheryl Drayton returned home from their daughter's memorial service to find their house ransacked, and they're screaming for your heads."

SEVENTEEN

On Friday, Hallie flopped backward onto her couch. What an eternal workweek! Fortunately, the latter half had returned to a normal level of hectic after that disturbing trip to Thief River Falls. Tomorrow's meeting with Damon should rev up the adrenaline quite a bit, and she wanted extra sleep—which was why she turned down Brody's suggestion that they take in a movie tonight.

Well, only part of the reason. She could fall for that big ox in a big way, but until they found some closure on Alicia's murder and the bracelet, personal involvement wasn't smart.

Was it?

Aack! She heaved to her feet and padded to her kitchen to rustle up a little supper. Sure, she was being wise to protect her heart. Unfortunately for that plan, she already liked Brody in the same measure she used to despise him, and that was quite a bit.

She found some leftover lasagna in the refrigerator, popped it into the microwave, and then poured a glass of milk. Her phone rang at the same time as the microwave beeped done. She picked up the phone. "Hello, Hallie here."

"This is Detective Millette. We've found the pizza delivery car, abandoned as we suspected, at a beach near Maple Lake, southwest of Thief River Falls. The vehicle is being examined as we speak, but I already know a couple of interesting things."

"And those are?"

"Dog hairs are on the seats."

"And?" An audible exhale met her question. "That doesn't sound like something you want to share with me."

"A female mannequin's torso was in the passenger seat with a scarf tied around its neck. The scarf matches the description of the one that was stolen from you."

Hallie's knees went weak. She backpedaled to a chair and sank into it. "A direct threat?"

"I'm afraid so." The detective cleared her throat. "There's more. The perp wrote a message in black marker on the torso."

"Do I want to know what it said?"

"Want to? Probably not. Need to? I think so. It said, 'Find the real killer before I find you.'"

Hallie closed her eyes and rubbed her forehead with her fingertips. "Thanks for the information. I'm not sure what to make of it, but you're right. I needed to know." She got up and took her steaming lasagna out of the microwave. "So on the break-in at the Draytons, are Brody and I headed for the hoosegow soon?"

"Negative. Neither of your prints was found in the Draytons' home. The PD up that way isn't happy about it, but they have nothing to hold you on."

She set her plate of supper on a cloth place mat at her table. "To them, I suppose we looked as guilty as a pair of hoods with our hands in the till."

"Frankly, they're now as eager for positive results on the pizza car as you are."

"In other words, they got skunked at the scene and need you to catch the stalker, and maybe he'll confess to the break-in, because that's the only way they'll solve the crime."

"Very sharp, Hallie." Amusement leaked across the connection. "But you didn't hear that much from me. Have you had any other incidents in the past few days?"

"Believe me, you would've heard from me if there'd been so much as a leaf rustle." She sat down at the table with her milk glass.

"Good. I suspect this stalker will lay low for a while after his close call. Besides he's got transportation issues now. Keep in touch."

They ended the call, and Hallie nibbled a bite of pasta. Too hot. She took a gulp of milk then picked up the phone and punched in Brody's number.

"Hello?" A man answered that wasn't Brody.

"Damon?"

"Uh…you must have the wrong number."

"Yeah, right. Brody'll probably scalp you for picking up his phone. I could've been one of those reporters trying to locate you. Put him on, would you?"

The young man grunted and muttered something ungracious about annoying women.

Moments later, Brody came on. "Sorry about that. He's going stir-crazy. I think that's one of the reasons he insisted on meeting with you outdoors tomorrow. But it's not a totally bad idea. The University of Minnesota Arboretum should offer quiet paths where we can talk. I'm making him wear the wig and sunglasses you got him, just to be on the safe side. That was a pretty clever touch, by the way." He chuckled.

"Glad you think so. Obviously, he doesn't have much appreciation for me."

"What do you expect? You're set on getting him sent away for murder."

"I'm set on doing what I believe to be right."

"I respect that, Hallie, and he'll figure it out, too…eventually."

"Excuse me if I don't hold my breath. But Damon's attitude is beside the point right now. I just got off the phone with Detective Millette."

She told him what the detective shared with her, and Brody went practically ballistic. He wanted to call off the meeting and lock Hallie away in protective custody, but she clung to the detective's logic that the stalker was without wheels for the moment, and they probably had a little reprieve. He reluctantly gave in. When she laid the phone down, her lasagna was lukewarm, but she ate it anyway.

Five minutes after eight o'clock the next morning found her at the Arborvitae collection in the Arboretum. In another hour, or maybe two, if the Twin Cities populace was especially lazy on a Saturday morning, the place would entertain many visitors. But for now, there were few people strolling among the cultivated displays of flowers, trees and shrubs. Lovely scents carried on the summer wind that bowed the brightly colored flowers and native grasses and set the trees waving at each other. Too bad this wasn't a day simply to absorb nature. She scratched under her ear where a trickle of sweat emerged from beneath the brown wig she wore, along with a pair of sunglasses.

So where were the two people she was supposed to meet? Had Damon backed out? Hands in her capri pants pockets, she watched the path. Brody came into view beside a tall, jeans-clad young man with endless, coltish legs and shaggy, dark hair topped by a cap that loyally proclaimed Minnesota Twins. Damon in disguise. Hallie knotted her fists and found her palms clammy.

Brody performed introductions, and Damon and Hallie nodded to one another, both sets of hands safely tucked in pockets. The ball player focused on her, but his eyes were hidden behind opaque glasses.

Hallie glanced toward Brody. "Could you ask him to take his glasses off while we visit? It's unnerving not to be able to read his expression."

Damon swiped the glasses from his face and scowled, his exposed gaze broadcasting scorn. "This was your idea, lady, and here I am. You don't need a referee to talk to me."

Gulping, Hallie took a step backward.

"Attitude, Damon, attitude," Brody growled.

Damon's shoulders slumped. "Yeah, I know I'm a pain to be around these days. I just wish—" He tilted his face toward the sky, eyelids blinking rapidly. "If only I would've gotten there early, she might be alive. You know? And we wouldn't even be having this conversation." He returned his gaze to Hallie, eyes glassy with unshed tears.

"So, tell me," she said, "what exactly happened in that house?"

"I trotted up the porch at 3:58 exactly—I looked at my watch—and went inside."

"Did you usually walk right into a house where four women lived?"

He shook his head. "No, I always had to knock, but she'd told me the door would be unlocked, and to just come in when I got there that day. She was going to have an interview, and she wanted me, and only me, there."

Hmm. Intriguing tidbit. "Go on."

"I walked into the living room and...found her on the floor." A choking sound escaped his throat, and his big hands formed fists.

Hallie edged closer to Brody. "I'm listening."

A shudder wracked the lanky frame, then Damon went still, his blue gaze steady on Hallie. "I got that cord off her and tried to revive her. That's why the police found my DNA all over everything. Then you showed up, and I got scared and ran. That's the whole ugly story. Believe it or not."

"Give me some space to think it over." Hallie took her hands from her pockets and wiped the palms against her pants. "Shall we walk up the path?"

"Okay. Sure." The ball player shrugged and cautiously fell into step a few feet from Hallie.

She checked over her shoulder and found Brody on their heels. He sent her an encouraging nod.

Damon kicked a rock off the path with cross-trainers the size of small boats. "Brody says you want to know about Alicia's elephant bracelet. I see you're wearing it." He gestured toward her arm.

"Does that bother you?"

He shook his head. "Can't say I really liked the thing anyway. Er, no offense. I understand your mom made it."

"What significance did it have for Alicia?"

"Well, for one thing, she got it from *her* mom, and it was

this big secret. I guess it was pretty rare for them to share anything private together. James didn't like it. Strange dude."

Hallie nodded. "On that we can agree."

"Her mom said the bracelet would bring her the love of her life. When we got together, Alicia claimed the thing was doing its job." He snorted a laugh.

"I don't buy into the talisman notion, either, and neither would my mom. She never fashioned a piece with anything in mind but the joy of her craft and sharing the love of God. But here's the million dollar question. Where did Cheryl Drayton get the bracelet?"

"Can't help you there."

"Can't? Won't? Which do you mean?" Hallie stopped and planted her hands on her hips.

Damon faced her. "Really, I have no idea. I don't think Alicia did, either."

She flopped her arms against her sides. "Do you have any idea how frustrating it is to keep getting a stone wall or a blank stare to a simple question?"

Damon scuffed his toe against the ground. "Then maybe the question isn't that simple."

She pursed her lips and looked away across the natural beauty of the groomed trees and flower beds and grasslands—all appearing so simple and natural, yet in reality complex and maintained by constant labor. "Maybe it's the answer that's hard."

Brody's chuckle drew their attention. He nodded toward Damon. "See? I told you she was smart."

The young man grinned. "Alicia was, too. Smarter than me. I loved that about her. Made her more interesting."

"That's a unique perspective." Hallie started up the path again. "Brody's probably told you that we think she attended college somewhere else before she came to the U of M."

"She never said anything about that."

"No clues, hints, casual references?" Hallie glanced up at his ball cap. "Team apparel?"

"Alicia wouldn't wear anything that ordinary. She liked

different clothes. Flowy things. I never even saw her in a T-sh—" He abruptly halted.

Hallie yelped as Brody sidestepped and nearly plowed into her. She backpedaled, tripped on a stick, and would have fallen except Brody's arms came around her at the last instant. His face filled her world. Those gray eyes smiled, and her limbs turned the consistency of oatmeal.

Damon slapped his thigh and hooted. "Sorry about that. It wasn't on purpose. But, say, those were pretty fast reflexes for an old guy."

"Old guy?" Brody turned Hallie loose and scowled at his protégé.

Hallie firmed her knees by an act of will, tugged her blouse straight, and settled her purse strap on her shoulder. How could that man not look half as flustered as she felt?

"You can beat me up later." Damon waved. "I just thought of something."

Hallie dragged her gaze off Brody and focused on the younger man.

"Alicia did have a Washington Huskies T-shirt under the seat of her car that she used as a grease rag."

"Good man!" Brody slapped Damon on the shoulder.

Voices coming from around a bend in the path halted conversation.

"You should probably go." Hallie looked from Brody to Damon and back again.

"What's the rush?" The tall young man strolled up the path. "Nobody's going to recognize me with this brown mop on my head. I got me some flowers to smell."

Brody shrugged and followed, muttering, "Stir-crazy."

Hallie brought up the rear, shaking her head. For most of an hour they explored carefully tended cultivations of trees, and shrubs, and flower beds along paths that skirted sparkling ponds. Damon actually did get right down on his knees and smell flowers.

"What do you think?" Brody came up alongside Hallie as she watched Damon bend and finger a gold leaf on a spirea.

"If I hadn't seen him at Alicia's house, I'd figure him for an overgrown kid on an outing."

"You'd figure right. There's nothing wrong with his intellect, or he wouldn't be able to hack it in college, but he'll probably always be a little childlike emotionally. Vulnerable. Volatile, but not mean. He had plenty of chances to go bad, and he passed them up."

Hallie refrained from answering. She wasn't ready to admit doubts were starting to peck away at her conviction concerning the young man's guilt.

A large tour group came toward them, and Damon straightened quickly. A nearby branch snagged his wig. Cap and all toppled off his head and crowned the shrub. His sweat-slicked golden hair glinted in the sunlight. The group separated and began to move around him, people shooting him sideways glances.

A man pointed toward Damon, and Brody's sharp intake of breath carried to Hallie. The man whispered to the woman next to him, and she gave a little cry, wide gaze fixed on Damon. Mutters of "murderer" flowed through the crowd.

Towering above the group, Damon's face flushed bright red. "That's a lie! I didn't kill anybody."

Brody bolted from Hallie's side. She stood rooted as he darted between milling people, grabbed Damon by the arm. He resisted for a moment, then turned and charged toward her up the path. His fisted arm struck her shoulder on the way past, and she flew backward, landing hard on her rear atop something that went *crunch.* Her purse!

On his way by, Brody yanked her to her feet. Like a galloping herd, they raced to the parking lot. Hallie spotted her car, veered off from the guys, and went for it. She stopped beside the driver's door, breathing hard, and groped inside her bag with a shaking hand for her keys. Where were they? She stamped her foot.

"Are you all right?"

She jumped and turned toward Brody's voice. "No thanks

to that *harmless* little child you insist on protecting from the consequences of his actions."

"I'm sorry that happened. I left Damon in the Impala to cool off. He wouldn't have hurt anybody, just engaged in a shouting match. He'll feel really bad about his reaction in a minute or so."

"Like how bad he felt after he killed Alicia? Sometimes it's too late for sorry, Brody." His sad gaze pierced her heart, but she turned away. "What is this?" Her fingers finally located her keys stabbed through a slit in the lining of her purse. She drew them out with a nest of little wires, bits of plastic, and electronic gadgetry dangling from the grooves.

Brody's eyes went big, the whites showing around the gray. "So that's how he did it."

"How who did what?"

"Your stalker. The guy planted that thing in your purse while you chased his pooch, and then he knew exactly where you were at all times. I had something like that on my old dog before he died. It's a personal tracking device."

EIGHTEEN

The Monday after the Arboretum disaster, Brody finally found Hallie at her workstation. She'd been out most of the day on assignments and interviews and hadn't returned his phone calls over the weekend. He approached her desk with caution. "Are we still on for Friday night?"

"Why wouldn't we be?" Her dark-eyed stare was cool. "The Fashion for Fibromyalgia benefit is the finale for my modeling story, and I need an escort."

All business then. His heart sank.

"You're not backing out on me, are you?" She leaned back in her chair.

"Nothing like that. I wasn't sure you still wanted me in that function."

Amusement sparked her gaze but didn't move her lips. "You're nothing if not exciting to be around, Brody Jordan. Why would a little ruckus discourage a reporter from working with a colleague?"

"Just checking." He forced his face to smile. "I'm following up on the Washington Huskies lead. If Alicia attended college in Seattle, I should know soon."

"Good. I'm still tracking down relatives of my parents' airplane pilot. My dad and uncle's central church headquarters might still have some records on Mr. O'Halloran."

"Okay. We'll touch base as new information surfaces."

"Check."

They waved at each other, and Brody went to his office. He closed the door, plunked into his chair and stared at his blank computer screen. He'd known that woman could turn him inside out if he gave her half a chance, but he'd plunged ahead in spending time with her anyway. Stupid! Because now all he wanted to do was get closer, and she was shoving him away.

On Wednesday, Hallie showed up at his office door, a pucker between her brows. Brody waved her in and motioned toward a seat.

She stood behind it, hands resting on the chair back. "I heard from Detective Millette. DNA results are a slow business, so nothing new on the trace found in the car, though they're still hoping for something conclusive. However, the lab techs were intrigued by the tracking device, since it showed signs of modification, and they got right on it. Evidently, my stalker must be an electronics whiz. He took a store model and installed a specialty lithium-iodide battery that would last almost indefinitely instead of the standard day or two, plus he lengthened the range on the thing. This guy was very serious about watching my movements. Plus," a little shudder rippled her shoulders, "he added a bugging device so he could overhear conversations."

Brody smacked his desktop. "No wonder he always knew what we were looking for!"

"He had his dog steal my scarf to give him a chance to tuck the device underneath the stiff bottom lining of my purse, so it would be nearly undetectable. He's clever, he's cool, he's determined, he's ruthless, and he's still out there." She pressed two fingers to the crease between her eyes.

Brody lunged from his chair and pulled her close. She didn't resist, but rested her forehead against his shoulder. Her breath warmed his collarbone, and reached deep inside him to wrap longing around his heart.

She released a hefty sigh then stepped away. "Thanks. I needed a hug, and your arms are strong enough to pack a little reassurance."

"I'm not going to let anything happen to you, Hallie."

She shook her head. "Nobody can guarantee anyone else's safety."

"We'll keep praying and trusting God."

"Right." A small smile bloomed. "I'm glad I can count on you for that, too."

Brody settled a hip on the edge of his desk. "You might be interested to know that Damon has consented to go on medication that will help calm his moods. He's always refused before—afraid the meds would slow his reflexes on the court. But after the incident at the Arboretum, he sees he has no future in basketball or anything else if he can't control himself."

Hallie responded with a frown and looked away.

"Yes, I'm aware the outlook on his continued freedom is grim," he said, "but we're going to keep thinking positive."

"Fair enough. I hope Mr. Stalker gets caught and confesses to the murder. If not, I'll have to take the stand at the trial next month and say what I saw. It won't sound good to a jury."

"I understand. You're doing your duty. Any word on that pilot?"

Hallie shook her head. "Twenty-year-old records for a guy who served on the mission field less than two months may be hard to dig up."

"I hear you. Chances of getting a birth certificate for Alicia are slim to none if we don't know what province she was born in. Ditto with a marriage certificate on Cheryl. But on a better note, I just got off the phone with the Dean of Admissions at the U of W. Alicia *did* attend there for about a semester and a half, but she dropped out abruptly."

She smacked her hands together. "Progress…finally."

"Hopefully, I'll have more to report soon. The dean's going to ask Alicia's supervisory professor to give me a call and answer questions about the circumstances surrounding her leaving school."

"More progress. Maybe." She walked to his door then

turned. "Pick me up at 5:00 p.m. sharp on Friday. Seating starts at six. It's a five hundred dollar a plate dinner, so have your taste buds revved up."

"No worries. I'll be there, tux and all. But the cost of the meal at these benefit things doesn't always guarantee the quality of the food." He made a face. "I've learned that over the years at sports functions."

"Yeah, well, maybe jocks have no taste." She winked and left chuckling.

Grinning, he settled into his chair. That woman was for him whether she realized it or not yet. Since when did Brody Jordan call it quits over a setback? Friday night was coming, and he still had good plays in his book.

Hallie stepped out of the elevator into her apartment building lobby. She stopped and looked around. There Brody stood, staring out the floor to ceiling windows onto the street outside. His tall, broad build filled out his tailored tux. A few minutes ago, he'd called, and she'd buzzed him into the building, but told him to wait downstairs rather than trekking all the way up to her apartment.

She glanced down at herself. Swarovski crystals sewn into the form-fitting bronze fabric of the spaghetti-strap gown twinkled back at her. The neckline plunged, yet covered completely, and a subtle jungle pattern in copper threads peeped from the under-dress beneath the split skirt that rippled aside when she walked. Her African bracelet gleamed from the polish she'd given it.

Would Brody like what he saw? Should she care? Her brain kept telling her to keep it professional between them, but her heart wanted to leap out of her chest into his hands.

Hallie's fingers tightened around the handbag she carried at her side. "Hello, there."

He turned and went still. A look washed over his face that compensated for every dime she'd spent on a new gown she really didn't *need*...except for Brody.

"Are you real?"

The husky words from his lips sent a tingle across her skin. She held out her hand. "Come here and find out."

Grinning, he stepped forward and curled his fingers around hers then brushed the back of her hand with his lips.

"Oh, my!" She barely suppressed a shiver. This man got to her way too easily.

He slipped her arm inside his and guided her out the door. "Our chariot awaits, but I see now I should have rented a limo. It's the least you deserve."

His warm gaze held good humor and open admiration. She smiled. This could turn into one of the best nights of her life.

Two hours later, Hallie hadn't changed her opinion. The ballroom of the Minneapolis Grand Hotel was the stuff of dreams with its marble foyer, warm color scheme, and host of sparkling windows along two sides of the room. Soft music, played by a small, string orchestra, wooed the guests into a happy mood. And Brody had been wrong in his warning about the meal. She'd savored every bite, laughing and chatting with the others at their table, one a noted stage and screen celebrity. Handsome as the actor was, her favorite moment was looking into her escort's storm-gray eyes as he dabbed a trace of house dressing from the side of her mouth with his linen napkin.

But now that dessert was about to be served, followed by a speaker for the cause of finding a cure for fibromyalgia, it was time for her to take temporary leave of pleasant company and cover the backstage bustle of a fashion show getting ready to start. She excused herself and slipped out into the hallway and meeting rooms teeming with models, hairdressers, makeup artists and assistants. Ms. Monique acknowledged Hallie's presence with a smile and a nod. Dressed in a long-sleeved, black dress belted at the waist, she directed the chaos with a master's touch. Aspiring supermodel Jessica waggled her fingers as a dresser did up the buttons on a knockout, lavender party dress. Wearing jeans and a sport shirt, Stan was busy moving from one group to another, filming the proceedings.

She joined him. "Looks like you're getting wonderful footage."

"Ex-cel-lent!" He enunciated every syllable. "Even a little cat-spat between a couple of models over a hair clip. Madame Monique straightened them out in a hurry."

Hallie noted a rotund, little man working with scissors on the bottom of a pair of treacherously high-heeled, slingback pumps. "Did you get a shot of that? Must be that trick Ms. Monique told us about. They scrape the soles so the model doesn't slip on the runway."

Stan obediently trained his camera in the direction she pointed. Then they moved away toward the next moment of interest, a model receiving a bouquet of mixed wild flowers from a smiling hotel bellboy.

"Do you have a fan on the hotel staff?" Hallie asked the stunning redhead.

The woman laughed. "No, this wasn't from him." She passed the bouquet off to an assistant. "Just one of the runway groupies paying his respects to his current favorite."

"Runway groupies? I've heard that term before. What does it mean?"

"Oh, that's what we call guys who are what you said... fans." Another assistant moved up behind the model and fastened a pendant around her neck. She paid no attention. "You know, like rock bands have groupies. Models attract them, too."

"So you don't know the person who sent you those flowers."

"No, and I don't want to, either. Given a little encouragement, a groupie can become a stalker real fast."

Hallie's heart stuttered, then kicked into overdrive. "Did Alicia Drayton have any runway groupies?"

"A woman who looked like that? Are you kidding? She was bound to, but I didn't know her well enough to say for sure." Color crept into the model's face. "I'm, uh, her replacement for this show." She gestured around the area. "Maybe someone else can tell you if any of the fans were giving her particular trouble."

Ms. Monique came up beside Hallie. "We're about to start the show. I have no problem with your cameraman continuing to film, as long as he stays out of the way, but I'll have to ask you to hold further questions until afterward."

Hallie squashed a spike of disappointment. She wanted answers now, not later, but she turned a smile on the model trainer and agent. "No problem. I'll have some specific questions for you then."

As she rustled toward her seat in the ballroom, Brody rose and pulled out her chair. She grabbed his arm as he took his place beside her. His eyes widened at her urgent whisper of information. Then the show started, and they politely ceased conversation, but Hallie couldn't say which of them fidgeted more as the models paraded fashions that only the people who actually paid for their high-priced seats at the tables could afford.

At last, the show concluded and someone got up to say a few parting words. Hallie grabbed Brody's hand, and they left the ballroom for the post-show meltdown in the modeling area. They found Ms. Monique accepting congratulations from a designer for a successful show. The man hurried away as they approached.

The agent turned toward them, glowing with a fresh triumph under her belt. "Ah, you've brought along the sportscaster as your escort. You two make a striking couple."

"Thank you," Brody said. "I need to tell you that Hallie's attracted the attention of a stalker, and we were wondering if it might be someone who was also stalking Alicia."

Ms. Monique grabbed one of Hallie's hands, and she braced herself for squeezing, but the touch remained gentle. "I am so sorry to hear that you're dealing with such a terrible thing, but I had no idea Alicia was being stalked."

"We don't know that either, for sure," Hallie said. "But—"

"She might have been having problems along that line."

Everyone turned toward Jessica's voice. The regal brunette stood with a pair of hot-pink pumps dangling from her fingers. "Alicia and I worked together a couple of days before she died. One evening a single white rose was brought in for her. No card. She jumped back and screamed when she saw the flower. Honestly, I'd never seen the ice queen so rattled. I rather enjoyed it."

"Jessica!"

Ms. Monique's rebuke drew color to the model's face, and her gaze dropped.

"What else can you tell us?" Brody prodded.

The young woman shrugged.

"Jessica Parsons, you will tell these people what you know," Ms. Monique said.

The model lifted her chin. "I don't *know* anything. I just saw Alicia grab the flower and ram it into the trash, and then mutter something like, 'That creep is *not* going to get back into my life.' That's it. Honest." She directed a pair of big eyes toward her agent.

"And you didn't think to tell any of this to the police?" Brody shouted.

Jessica paled before his red-faced fury. Hallie laid a hand on his arm. She'd touched softer cement blocks.

The model's lips trembled. "Why should I have said anything? I thought the killer was caught in the act."

Tension eased from the muscles under Hallie's fingers.

"I'm sorry, Ms. Parsons. My apologies to everybody." He nodded around the little circle. "I care about Damon Lange, and I don't want to see him shafted for something he didn't do."

Jessica brightened. "You think my statement might help? Just send the cops my way."

Hallie giggled. Must be nervous tension. She never made a sound that inane.

She thanked the model and the agent, and then she and Brody split up to interview anybody else who might know more about the white rose. A half hour later, Stan found her and said he was going home. Most everyone had already left the hotel. Brody came up beside her, hands in his pockets, shoulders slumped.

Hallie shook her head. "Looks like you had about as much luck as I did."

One side of his mouth lifted, and the Brody dimple appeared. "Well, hey, we have a new lead to sniff at. Let me take you home." He offered his arm.

Outside the hotel, Brody presented his ticket, and the valet brought the Impala to the curb. Hallie let Brody open her door and hand her into the passenger seat. His manner was deft and gentle, but she could swear the press of his fingers left a brand where they touched. A few moments later, he settled into the driver's seat, chuckling.

"What's so funny?"

"This brand-new car I'm so proud of. I'll bet the valet curled his lip all the way from the parking lot in this baby after having delivered dozens of BMWs, Mercedes and Lexuses."

Hallie laughed and patted the Impala's dash. "I have no problem with American-made."

"Then I'd better not tell you about the foreign-manufactured parts."

They both laughed. Conversation remained light all the way back to Hallie's apartment complex. Brody found a parking spot, and helped her out of the car.

"I'm walking you to your door." His tone left no room for argument.

As if she wanted to offer any! Of course, that was only because of the stalker out there and had nothing to do with the pleasure she got from walking beside him in the warm night, arm-in-arm. Her gown swished soft as water around her ankles. His leather shoes patted the sidewalk in steady rhythm. Too soon they stood inside the deserted lobby of her building.

Hallie turned to thank her escort and found his face inches from hers. The heels on her feet brought her nearly to his height. The corners of his mouth turned upward as his gray gaze lit. She licked her lips and sucked in a breath. His arms stole around her as easy as moonlight, and she let them. Her eyelids drifted shut, and she waited. A moment. Another.

Then his mouth brushed hers, feather-soft. Then firmer. Then his touch disappeared.

Hallie gasped and opened her eyes.

Brody stood a foot away, gaze sober and steady. "Thank you for an incredible evening." He turned and strode out the door.

Openmouthed Hallie watched him fade into the night. At last, she wandered to the elevator and got on board. Inside, she leaned against the wall, closed her eyes and relived the most marvelous kiss of her life.

When the door shushed open, she strolled up the hall toward her apartment, a silly smile on her face that she didn't care to wipe off. Music drifted from beneath her neighbor's door, but that didn't mean he was awake, much less home.

Hallie lifted her key to insert it into her lock and went still, rib cage squeezed tight. A pair of gouges on the jamb had never been there before. Slowly she straightened and backed away. Her door flung open, and a faceless apparition in black charged toward her.

Screaming, she whirled and ran, but iron arms captured her from behind. One clamped her arms to her sides, the other went around her throat, cutting off her air. She struggled, but to no use.

"Where is it?" A voice grated in her ear. "I know he gave it to you."

She gurgled, spots waltzing before her eyes. The man dragged her backward toward the privacy of her apartment, where he could do whatever he wanted with her. Weakness seeped into her limbs, but she sent one frantic command to her failing body. With every remnant of strength she rammed her spike heel onto her attacker's foot.

He howled, and his grip loosened. She whirled away, staggering. Her ankle turned, shooting fire up her leg, and she plunged headfirst toward the edge of her neighbor's doorframe. Pain split her skull. Then blackness and silence swallowed her whole.

NINETEEN

Quiet greeted Brody in his small two-bedroom rambler in South St. Paul. No television blaring. No music going. Only one light on in the living room. Carrying his tux jacket over one arm, he went up the hall toward the bedrooms. A quick check in Damon's revealed an empty bed. Where was he? Frowning, Brody left his jacket and shoes in his room and headed for his tiny office on the other side of the house, calling Damon's name. No answer. Maybe the kid was engrossed in a computer game.

A light glowed under the closed door, and Brody blew out a breath. "Hey, buddy." He opened the door to nobody home. A yellow sticky note was stuck to the PC screen. He snatched it and read, *Gotta get some air. Back soon. Probably before you get home, and then you'll never see this note. Ha! Ha! Oh, and some lady called from a university around 10:00 p.m. She said to call her back right away. Number's on the phone.*

Brody scowled. Fool kid! Well, at least he wasn't strolling the neighborhood in broad daylight. Brody turned and snatched another sticky note off the phone receiver. The number had a Seattle area code. Must be Alicia's former college supervisor. He settled into his desk chair and punched the numbers in.

"Ferndale residence," a mellow female voice answered.

"This is Brody Jordan, returning your call from Minnesota."

"Ah, Mr. Jordan." The tone sharpened. "I'm Professor

Gladys Ferndale. I was Alicia Drayton's supervisory professor when she attended here. Thank you for calling back yet this evening. I realize it's a couple of hours later there than here."

"I was told you had urgent information."

"Indeed, I do. In fact, I've already given it to the St. Paul police."

"The police!" Brody's breath caught.

"The Dean of Admissions filled me in on the reason for your inquiries. Alicia was violently murdered and a female colleague of yours has acquired a stalker? Is that correct?"

"It is."

"Then I'm afraid there is cause for alarm connected with Alicia's reason for withdrawing from college here at the U of W."

"Just a second. I want to write this down." Heart thudding against his ribs, Brody grabbed a pen and a notepad out of his top drawer. "Go ahead."

"This is so sad. I hate when things like this happen." Professor Ferndale heaved a breath. "When Alicia arrived at school, I noted immediately that she was like a confused creature escaped from captivity. She didn't say much about her background, except that she'd chosen a school about as far away from home as she could get.

"Soon, she took up with a senior student, a wild young man named Wyatt Rosenbaum. Red flags went up in my mind, but she did well in her first semester. However, into her second term, she gradually slacked off on attendance and her grades slipped. I attempted to counsel her on numerous occasions, but she brushed me off.

"Then I truly became alarmed when I began noticing bruises on her face and arms. That's when I took the liberty of calling her parents. They came and got her. The next day, Mr. Rosenbaum was in a two-car collision where several people were hurt, and he was found to be under the influence of drugs. His family's money had gotten him out of trouble in the past, but this time he ended up getting sent to prison for a five-year stretch."

Brody stopped writing. "So the man is in jail? How does this story relate to Alicia's murder and the stalking issue?"

"Let me finish."

"Go ahead." He poised his pen, a prickly sensation teasing the nape of his neck. This was the big break. He knew it.

"When the Dean told me about Alicia's death, at first I assumed the same as you did—that Mr. Rosenbaum couldn't possibly be a factor. But the matter bothered me, so I took the liberty of checking." A pregnant second of silence passed. "Three months ago, Wyatt Rosenbaum was released on parole. He failed to report to his parole officer eight weeks ago, and has been missing ever since."

The sheet of paper ripped beneath the pressure of Brody's pen. Expelling a pent-up breath, he threw the ballpoint down. "Is there any chance you have an old student photo of this Rosenbaum that you could fax me?"

"I've already sent one to your police station. I could do the same for you."

"Please." Brody gave the professor his fax number. "And thank you so much for coming forward with this information. You may have helped save another woman's life."

"Someone you care about personally?"

"More than I can say."

"Ahhh. I thought I heard that inflection in your voice."

"Very astute, Professor. Can you tell me one other thing about this Rosenbaum?"

"If I can, I will."

"I take it he might have had access to money through his family. Is he also the sort of man who would have particular electronics expertise?"

"Most certainly. He was studying to be an electrical engineer and was very savvy with computers, as well."

Gotcha! Not only would Rosenbaum have been able to modify the tracking device in Hallie's purse, he would have had the money for whatever equipment he needed in order to pick up the signal. "Thank you. That confirms an aspect of the stalking issue. I don't suppose you know if he had a dog."

"I'm afraid I can't help you there."

They ended the call, and Brody's fax machine chittered a minute later. The sheet that came out showed a head and shoulders shot of a young Caucasian man with a square chin and dark hair and eyes. Shade was indeterminate since the fax was black and white. Beneath the photo, Professor Ferndale had written a few more identifying characteristics—six feet tall, about one hundred eighty-five pounds, brown eyes and hair.

So this was the face of a killer. Not that what they had so far on Rosenbaum would get Damon off, but it was a huge opportunity to create reasonable doubt. Damon and his lawyer would be tickled silly. Where was that kid anyway?

Brody stuck the photo and notes from his conversation with Alicia's former supervisor into a manila envelope to show Hallie tomorrow. But he was going to call her *tonight*, whether he woke her up or not, and give her the scoop on this monster. He picked up the phone and stabbed the number keys then drummed his fingers on the desk while the phone rang.

"Hello."

Brody's spine went stick straight. That female voice didn't belong to Hallie. "Detective Millette, what are you doing at Hallie's apartment?"

"Mr. Jordan?"

"Yes, it's Brody. After I dropped Hallie off tonight, I got home and returned a call to a Professor Gladys Ferndale at the University of Washington in Seattle. She told me about Wyatt Rosenbaum. I was just calling to warn her, but I suppose that's why you're there."

"I'm sorry, Mr. Jordan, but we were too late."

"What?" Brody's heart somersaulted.

"There's been an incident."

"She's not—"

"No, but she's unconscious with a head injury and is on the way to Region's Hospital."

Brody swallowed the golf ball-sized lump in his throat. "How bad?"

"No way to tell until a doctor assesses her."

"I'm on my way."

He slammed down the phone and charged to his bedroom for his shoes. He snatched his car keys from the dresser and raced through the kitchen to the attached garage. His car was well up the street before he thought about Damon. He'd just have to call the kid later and tell him where he was. Like that young man would actually waste a second wondering.

Annoyances, major and minor, plucked Hallie toward consciousness. Her head throbbed in rhythm with a beeping noise. No way was that her alarm clock. Her ankle hurt, and something tight squeezed it. And the bed beneath her—too hard. Not hers. What was going on? And what was that smell? Antiseptic? Her apartment was clean, but it didn't smell like a hospital. Hospital?

Her eyes popped open. Pain speared through her brain, and she squeezed them shut against the dim light of, yes, a hospital room. What happened? "Why am I here?" The words mumbled between dry lips.

"What did you say, sweetheart?" Big hands clasped one of hers between them.

She peeked through slitted lids at the man who spoke near her ear. It was Brody, bristly-faced and haggard, but wearing a tentative smile. He leaned over her from a chair beside the bed.

"You're awake!" The smile widened.

"I'm…confused. How…" She swallowed against a dry throat. "How did I get here? Why does my head hurt?" Her eyes closed.

"No! Don't fade away again. They'll want you to stay awake. Here. This might help."

A straw nudged her lips, and she drew in sweet moisture. Sighing, she forced her heavy lids open. "An explanation might help, too."

His brows drew down. "What do you remember about last night?"

"Last night?" She attempted to lift her head, but gave up after battling for an inch. "What time is it?"

He looked at his watch. "It's five o'clock on Saturday morning."

Hallie touched her forehead with the hand that wasn't in Brody's clasp and found that an IV tube came with it. Her fingers landed on a bandage over a very sore spot right behind her hair line. "I don't remember anything after stepping out of the elevator on my floor. Did I trip over my own feet?"

Brody kissed her fingers. "You've had a rough time of it, honey. The doc warned me you might lose a patch of memory. That's normal. According to the report your neighbor gave Detective Millette, he heard a scream and a thud outside his door. When he opened it, he saw some man dressed in a black leather coat and jeans trying to pick you up off the floor. Your head was bleeding. The neighbor hollered to know what was going on, and the guy took off down the stairwell and left you lying there."

"Somebody attacked me? Who?"

"No way to identify him for sure. He was wearing black gloves and had nylon hosiery pulled over his face, but we think we know."

Hallie frowned as Brody told her about an abusive boyfriend of Alicia's from her days at the University of Washington. "So Damon may be innocent after all," she said when he finished. That idea would take some getting used to, but it might not be so bad to be proved wrong.

"I've been trying all night long to call him and give him the good news," Brody said, "but he won't answer either his cell or my home phone."

"Probably scared to pick up after I chewed him out for answering when I called." She tried a chuckle and winced.

"You can be intimidating sometimes." The Brody dimple winked at her. "But no. He's been answering the phone all right. Spoke to that professor at the university around the time I dropped you off at your apartment." His gaze fell. "If I'd only gone up with you…" He blew out a breath. "I'm so glad you're going to be okay."

"Me, too, considering I don't even remember the attack. Have you been sitting here with me all night long?"

"I don't think they had an orderly big enough to toss me out."

A laugh slipped out. "Ouch!" Her hand flew to her head.

Pretty soon a nurse came in, and Brody was shooed out while the woman fussed over vital signs. When she offered oral pain meds and assistance to the bathroom, Hallie didn't turn her down. Then the hospital started to come to life with the clank and creak of cart wheels and the bustle of personnel doing morning rounds. Breakfast arrived, and Hallie nibbled a few bites of hot cereal and drank her juice greedily. She asked for coffee, but the nurse said nothing with caffeine for now. Hallie made a face at the woman's retreating back, and Brody chuckled.

"You should go home and get some rest," she told him. "I'm in good hands here."

"I'll probably take you up on that after the doctor's seen you. I need to check on Damon."

"You're worried about him, huh?"

He shrugged. "I'm sure he's okay. Just indulging a contrary streak."

The words had scarcely left his mouth when a woman with steel-gray hair and a name tag that said Dr. Naylor entered the room, leafing through a chart. She fixed Hallie with a stern stare through a pair of thick, wire-rimmed glasses. "You're a lucky young lady. Either that, or you have a very hard head." She smiled, and her whole face softened. Her gaze moved to Brody. "Are you her young man?"

"Brody Jordan, aspiring to the position." He raised a hand.

Hallie's cheeks warmed, but she awarded him a little smile and a nod. He answered with a grin big enough to eat New York. This man had proved himself faithful too many times for her to fight her heart with her stupid head anymore. Plus, she *did* remember that kiss.

The doctor stepped up beside Hallie's bed. "Well, if you don't mind, Mr. Jordan, step outside and wait with the nice police officer while I examine my patient."

"Police officer?" Hallie's gaze sought Brody's.

He nodded. "You finally rate some official protection." He exited the room.

Doctor Naylor looked at Hallie's head, checked her pupils, listened to her heart and lungs, asked about her level of pain, or if she noticed anything odd about her vision. The doctor seemed satisfied by all she discovered. Then she took a look at Hallie's ankle, which was wrapped in a bandage.

"The sprain may take longer to heal than the head wound," she said.

"I take it I'm going to live. I wasn't so sure the way my head hurt when I woke up." She smiled. "The pain meds are working well, thank you very much."

"Good. You'll probably appreciate those for several days yet. You've got a moderate concussion and ten stitches in a cut on your scalp. You aren't showing any signs of subdural hematoma, but I'm ordering a follow-up CAT scan for this afternoon, and we'll want to keep you another night, to be on the safe side."

Hallie's smile faded. "I don't get to go home today?"

Dr. Naylor's lips thinned. "I'm not sure you'll be allowed into your apartment yet anyway. You'll have to talk to the police about that."

The doctor soon left, and Brody came back in. Hallie gave him the medical report, and he shushed her complaints over staying another day in the hospital. Pouting, she ordered him to go away, and he laughed.

"I am going to check in at home," he said, "but you won't get rid of me for long. I'm sure you'll have other company, too. I called your friend, Jenna, at the restaurant, and she was going to let Sam know." He tapped the tip of her nose with his finger. "See you later, beautiful."

Shortly after Brody left, Detective Millette showed up and plopped Hallie's purse onto the nightstand.

"Oh, thank you," Hallie breathed. "I would have missed that sooner rather than later."

Millette grinned. "I can relate." Notebook in hand, she attempted to take a statement, but Hallie had nothing helpful to offer.

The detective put the notepad away in her pocket. "Good thing your neighbor was home."

"I'll have to send him a whole collection of classical CDs to say thank you." Hallie shifted in the bed, seeking a comfortable position. "Are you going to have my apartment off limits much longer?"

"You can go home any time the doctor says, but I don't recommend it."

"What are you talking about?"

"A couple of reasons." She lifted one slender finger. "Whoever attacked you ransacked your apartment, and I don't think you're in any shape to tackle the job of cleaning things up."

Hallie groaned.

The detective lifted a second finger. "Until we catch Rosenbaum, I would prefer you go someplace for a while where this guy doesn't know where to find you. We won't be able to keep a guard on you after today. Not enough manpower."

The detective left, and a few minutes later, Jenna and Sam walked in, bearing mylar balloons and a big purple teddy bear. They gushed all over Hallie and entertained her until the lunch tray arrived.

"Remember, you're coming to stay at my house after you get out of here tomorrow." Jenna reiterated an agreement they'd come to during their visit.

"I'm grateful."

"No problem." She patted Hallie's arm.

Sam wrinkled her nose. "I'd offer you a place at my apartment, but it's upstairs and no elevator."

"Don't worry." Jenna poked Sam with her elbow. "You and Ryan get to stand your turns at guard duty while I'm at work tomorrow afternoon."

Sam smacked her head. "In all the excitement, I almost forgot. Ryan's got an engagement party booked on his boat tomorrow, and I need to help him." Her fiancé ran a cruise boat rental service on Lake Minnetonka.

"Don't worry about it," Hallie said. "Brody can stay with me. And if not, I'll be perfectly fine. Like Detective Millette said, it's a place this man doesn't know where to find me."

Brody came back a while later, bearing a bouquet of a

dozen peach-colored roses. He'd shaved and slept, but his smile couldn't disguise shadows in his eyes.

"What's up?" Hallie asked. "Everything okay with Damon?"

He shook his head. "He wasn't home." His gaze fixed on the floor, and he tugged his left earlobe. "To tell you the truth, he's been missing since last night. If I didn't know he'd been talking to Professor Ferndale at the time of your attack I'd think…" He cleared his throat and sighed.

Hallie pressed her button to lift the head of the bed. "You don't suppose something's happened to him. That this Rosenbaum—"

"No, I doubt his disappearance has anything to do with Wyatt Rosenbaum. Why would that guy interfere with the man who's about to take the rap in his place? I figure Damon went out, met some friends, and couldn't give up his taste of freedom. He'll show up when he's ready to have me wring his neck."

Hallie frowned. "Shouldn't you tell the police he's gone?"

"It's not against the law for him to leave my house and not check in with me."

"Thoughtless kid."

"No argument from me."

Hallie gestured toward the vase Brody had placed on her nightstand. "Those are gorgeous. Thank you for everything. I love roses. Not like Alicia, who freaked when she saw—" She stopped on a gasp, flesh tingling. "I get it now."

"Get what?"

"Alicia got that white rose a few days before she died. You see?"

Brody shook his head.

"White rose? Wyatt Rosenbaum? I'll bet he used to give her white roses when they were dating. That's just the sort of sappy romance code a couple of college kids would use."

Brody laughed. "I guess that bump on the head didn't knock out any of your smarts. I'll mention it to the detective. If she can verify this history between them, it'll be another nail in Rosenbaum's coffin when they catch him."

The rest of the day passed in Brody's entertaining presence. By the time he left that evening, Hallie was ready to sleep around the clock. Thankfully, the doctor was ready to let her.

The next morning, Sam and Jenna and Brody transported her to Jenna's house. Brody all but carried her up the two steps from Jenna's attached garage into her kitchen. In the doorway, he handed her the pair of crutches the hospital had issued. Their gazes met in a private smile.

"Yoo-hoo, you two," Sam singsonged from behind Brody.

"Yeah, we're waiting here," Jenna added.

Hallie's friends hooted. She made a face at them and crutched away toward the living room with her entourage trailing. Brody clicked on the television and asked what she wanted to watch, while Jenna and Sam fussed about settling her onto the couch with her ankle up. Considering Hallie's limbs felt encased in mud and her head like a throbbing rock atop her neck, she didn't want to move again for a long time.

"It's almost worth the pain for all this attention," she said.

Brody scowled. "You'll excuse me if I don't laugh."

"Lighten up, Jordan. We can't spend every minute worrying. Rosenbaum's bound to get caught any minute, now that the police know who they're looking for."

Jenna patted her shoulder. "Hopefully, he's far away on the run by now."

"You just rest." Sam set a bottle of water on the coffee table within Hallie's reach.

Hallie intercepted conspiratorial looks exchanged between the trio hovering around her. "All right. I get it. You all think I'm loopy from the pain meds. You might be right. That stuff knocks me out." She yawned and snuggled down into the pillow beneath her head.

"Go for it," Brody said. "I'll be right here when you wake up."

Jenna grimaced. "Unfortunately, I have to head to work pretty soon."

"And I have to help Ryan with that event on his boat."

Hallie waved them away. "Don't give it another thought.

Brody and I will be just fine." She took a swig of water, settled in again, and soon the room and the TV noise faded.

After a while, the darkness of oblivion whitened into a dream of a sun-washed field surrounded by dense forest. Ahead of her sat a red and white airplane on a crude runway hacked out of the vegetation.

Her father scooped her up and hugged her. "Stay out of mischief while we're away, peanut."

He set her feet onto the packed earth, and her mother bent and kissed her cheek. "We'll be home before you have a chance to miss us."

A slim man with a freckled face and wide grin stepped up beside them. The smile turned pensive. "Wish I could be saying the same to my little girl right now. But if my wife'll come around to agree we belong on the mission field, maybe you'll meet my daughter soon enough." He squatted in front of Hallie. "I know how good you are with the babies. If we can get mine over here, it'll be Allie and Hallie all the time." He patted her head, and the grin sparkled afresh.

The air-field and the people washed into blackness, but the words echoed. *Allie and Hallie…Allie and Hallie…Allie and Hallie…*

With a gasp, Hallie sat up on her elbow. The room spun then settled. She swallowed against nausea.

From an easy chair across from her, Brody's startled gaze riveted on her. "What is it? Did you dream about the attack?"

"I know who Alicia's father was."

TWENTY

Brody figured he must resemble a beached cod. "Did I hear you right? You dreamed about Alicia's father?"

"Yes and yes. He's Mr. O'Halloran."

"Your parents' pilot?"

"Exactly." She described her dream. "It was more like the surfacing of a buried memory. That conversation really happened."

Brody slumped back in his chair. "So Cheryl Drayton was married to this O'Halloran before she hooked up with James. But why would Cheryl hide that prior relationship?"

"We'll have to ask her. She might be more forthcoming now that we've figured out her secret. But Alicia being Mr. O'Halloran's baby girl at the time of the plane crash explains one thing perfectly."

"And that is?"

"Why Alicia proposed the idea of a Minnesota model story through her agent and asked for me specifically to do her interview. Don't you see?" Hallie struggled into a sitting position. "Alicia must have discovered the truth, and she wanted to check me out, see what sort of person I was, before she let me know who she was and started asking questions about her biological dad."

Brody pursed his lips. There must be some flaw in the logic. This was too simple, too obvious, now that this one relationship was pieced together. For that matter, taking "Allie" to mean Alicia, was a stretch, wasn't it? No, it wasn't. Not in the light of all the crazy happenings in the past two weeks. Not when he could look straight at the bracelet Hallie had found on a dead woman's wrist. He met Hallie's expectant gaze. "That makes complete sense."

"Now if my parents' U.S. sponsor organization can find a copy of O'Halloran's missions application, we can find out where he came from. Then we might be able to unravel the whole sad history of this family, with or without Cheryl Drayton's cooperation."

Brody rose and paced across the room. "There's a question that I have to ask."

"Meaning I'm not going to like it."

He stopped and crossed his arms. "At first, everyone assumed Damon killed Alicia. I knew that wasn't true. Now it's starting to look like this Wyatt Rosenbaum killed Alicia. Neither one of them has any connection to your parents, Nigeria, or that bracelet. But don't you think it's a bit much of a coincidence that Alicia was murdered right on the verge of talking to you?"

Hallie's mouth flopped open then she shut it with a snap. If her glare was a laser beam, he'd just been fried. "Are you implying that my parents could have been involved in something that got them, their pilot, and years later, the pilot's daughter killed?"

Brody spread his hands. "I'm not implying anything. I'm just posing a question that needs to be asked. Aren't you curious, too? Come on! We're reporters."

Hallie screwed up her face like she was chewing on something that tasted nasty. "I—I haven't let myself ask questions like that, not even in my own head." She pressed a hand to her bandage and closed her eyes. "I needed Damon to be guilty. That way, I would never have to look for any other answer."

Brody knelt and touched her cheek. His fingertips traced the wetness of a tear. "I know it rips your heart out even to think such a thing, but isn't it always better to know the truth?"

Her swimming gaze locked with his. "From what will this kind of truth set me free?"

"Perhaps the answer won't set you free *from* something but *to be* something."

"What would that be?"

"Hallie Berglund, daughter of America *and* Nigeria."

A smile trembled on her lips. "You're so smart. No wonder I'm falling in love with you."

Brody leaned toward her, their breath mingled, and... Someone hammered at Jenna's front door. They froze. The knock sounded again, loud and insistent.

Hallie eased away from him. "There's only one thing you need to answer right now."

"What's that?" Whoever was out on that doorstep needed to go away.

"The door, silly."

Brody sat back on his haunches. "We'll pick up where we left off later."

"It's a deal." Her smile teased and promised at the same time. She settled against the couch and closed her eyes.

He rose and stomped toward the vestibule. The rapping resumed. "I'm coming. And it better be important." He put his eye to the peephole. "Damon?" His heart leaped. The kid was all right. He'd been way more worried than he'd admitted even to himself. With fumbling fingers, he twisted the lock and tore the door open.

Damon half lunged, half fell into the house, shoving Brody backward. Brody's back thudded against the closet door. "Wha-a—"

"S-sorry, man! He pushed me." The young man's face glowed sheet-white.

"Shut up!"

The harsh voice drew Brody's gaze to the figure looming behind Damon. A snarl pulled back the lips on a familiar face, but that wasn't the sight that froze all sound in Brody's throat. Heart trip-hammering, he stared down the long, sleek barrel of a Smith and Wesson 500 handgun.

* * *

Hallie sat up stiff, ignoring the protest from her head and ankle. Had Damon finally shown up? Why here? And what was that thud about? "Brody?"

He stepped into the living room, hands raised. Damon appeared right behind him, hands on top of his head. Then the last man on the planet she expected to see limped over the threshold.

"James Drayton? What are you doing here?"

"Protecting my interests." Half-hidden behind Brody and Damon, the man smiled, and Hallie shivered. She liked his grin much less than his scowl. "Everyone please have a seat," he said, "until I figure out exactly how everything must be staged. Mr. Lange, take the ottoman. Mr. Jordan, over there." He motioned with his gun toward the easy chair.

His gun! Hallie squeezed her eyes shut and opened them again. The evil-looking firearm was still there, attached to the end of James's arm. "I don't get it. Are you serious?"

Damon plopped onto the ottoman, hands still up. "He's not kidding. I think he killed some dude last night. Couldn't see anything, just heard stuff. Some guy bragged how he'd ditched parole, picked up his dog and a load of cash from his old man so he could go see Alicia and tell her what his research about James had revealed. Then the conversation went muffled. I heard a fight, a dog barking, shots fired."

"This *dude* have a name?" Brody rumbled from the easy chair.

Hallie glanced toward him. If leashed fury had a face, she was looking at it.

"Rosie-something-or-other, I think," Damon answered.

"You've been with Drayton since the night you disappeared from my house?"

"Yeah. I came back from my walk, and he jumped out of the bushes and clobbered me with something. Next thing I know I'm waking up in the trunk of a car. Been in there mostly ever since."

"Enough talk! I'm thinking." The cannon-sized gun barrel moved from one to the next.

Hallie gulped. She stared at James Drayton. The man stood in the center of the room, eyes narrowed, jaw twitching.

"How did you know where to look for me?" She gripped the edges of the couch cushion.

Drayton lashed her with a look of contempt. "You aren't the only one who can investigate. While you were looking into me, I was studying you—your habits…hangouts…friends. And voila, the first friend's house we drive by, Mr. Jordan's Impala sits outside."

"Pardon me if I don't applaud your cleverness," Brody said.

"I don't require appreciation. I just want my wife and me to be left alone."

"If you already avenged your daughter by killing Wyatt Rosenbaum," Hallie inserted, "why are you coming after us, too?"

Drayton's eyelids flickered. "I avenged my daughter? Is that what you think?"

"We know she wasn't your blood daughter," Brody said. "O'Halloran was her father."

"Then you know why I'm here. Cheryl can never find out what really happened to him."

Hallie's heart fluttered as Drayton's cold gaze studied her. "What really happened? Something other than what I've been told?"

"Ahhh, then you don't know the most delicious detail, either…yet. But you would have figured it out soon enough. You don't have enough sense to know when to quit nosing around, even when I send you a back-off message loud and clear."

"My car!"

James winked. "I rented a nondescript sedan. A parole officer has to be a pro at tailing even paranoid people. But you still didn't quit! I stopped Alicia's mouth, and I'll stop yours, too."

"*You* killed Alicia?" Hallie gasped and half-rose from the couch. "But why?"

"Sit!" The gun stabbed toward her, and she subsided against the cushions, trembling.

"Rosenbaum thought he'd take revenge on me by digging into my life," Drayton continued. "He'd call me, taunt me. A month ago, he started sending anonymous tidbits to Alicia—got her curious. She started asking dangerous questions. Then he told her everything. When I got to her house that day, she threatened to tell you so you could tell the world, but I stopped her."

Hallie pressed her fingers to her mouth. Rosenbaum had played mind games with a madman until it got Alicia killed, and then he switched his attention to another pawn, *her*, until she became a target of the same maniac.

"But you were confirmed at a convention in Moorhead the day Alicia was killed."

Drayton shrugged. "It's easy enough to check into a motel and show up at a registration table before taking off for the rest of the day. They're all a bunch of strangers. Nobody misses you." He chuckled. "Then I just had Rosenbaum to handle. When he called yesterday, I set up a meeting with him in the abandoned dressmaker warehouse where he was hiding out. He had a gun, I didn't, but I played a little trick, and one of us walked off with the firepower." He wagged the small cannon in his hand. "Now I'll put it to good use."

"What did you ever do to Rosenbaum that he needed to go to these lengths to get revenge?" Brody asked the question burning on Hallie's tongue.

Drayton smirked. "Three years ago, Cheryl and I went to Seattle and took Alicia away from him. Then I met with him the next day for a little man-to-man chat and slipped a special gift in his drink. He had an unfortunate accident afterward." He clucked his tongue. "People should know better than to mess with me or mine."

"You're the one who attacked Hallie at her apartment Friday night," Brody growled. "You trashed her apartment first. What were you looking for?" Comprehension flowed over his face. "Something Rosenbaum took from your house in Thief River Falls. Right? You thought he gave it to Hallie."

"Well, since you're so smart and have it all figured out, I don't need to tell you anything." Drayton turned a speculative stare on Hallie. "At first, I thought I had erred by failing to finish Ms. Berglund then, but now I see that this arrangement will work out much better. Here's what's going to happen."

He trained his gun on Damon. "Mr. Lange, the police may now have some suspicions about Wyatt Rosenbaum, but they will never find him. Unfortunately for you, that means you remain the suspect charged with the murder of poor Alicia Drayton. In your rage against the only eye-witness, you came over here to kill her, and succeeded, but when your beloved mentor tried to interfere, you killed him, too. Overcome with remorse, you then turned the gun on yourself. Terrible tragedy, but case closed all the way around."

Chills cascaded down Hallie's body. Her gaze sought Brody's, and she found steel in those gray depths. Neither of them was going down without a fight. She sneaked a glance at Damon. The young man slouched on the ottoman, head down. They couldn't count on help from that direction.

"Ms. Berglund, I need you to get up and come toward me." He motioned with his fingers. "We'll get you situated then position Mr. Jordan, as if he's attempting to protect you. Mr. Lange, your body will be found approximately where I'm standing now, but we'll leave you for last."

Hallie remained stuck to the couch. None of this was really happening. This had to be another one of her dreams. "Answer me one thing first. What did you have to do with my parents' deaths?"

James snorted. "I didn't give two hoots about your mommy and daddy, but Patrick had to go. I thought he was my friend, but he stole Cheryl from me. Then I got work with an oil company, and they stationed me in Nigeria. Paid big money. But I knew that wouldn't lure religious old Paddy-boy over, so I kept writing to him about all the missions opportunities. Finally, he took the bait and came. Then I bided my time. Wasn't too hard to let the right people know the wrong information about who was on that plane. Boom! Paddy was gone, and Cheryl was up for grabs. I told her the accident was his fault—that he strayed into a no-fly zone. She never questioned my word. She was so ashamed she never spoke of him again, just the way I wanted it. Do you think she was going to tell the daughter of the missionary couple who died that her husband was the careless pilot who flew where he wasn't supposed to go and got them all whacked?"

Breath sawed in and out of Hallie's lungs. "You…are… pure…evil."

James grinned. "Don't you know the bad boy always gets the girl?" A sharp click sounded, his gun cocking. "Now get up!"

As if moving through water, she reached for her crutches and struggled to her feet. She took one step toward Drayton then another. An audible growl came from Brody.

"Easy, Mr. Jordan." The gun swiveled toward the easy chair.

Hallie took another step, coming down with her full weight on her injured ankle. Hot pain speared up her leg, but she flung both crutches with all her might toward James Drayton. The man's arms lifted reflexively to protect his face, and the gun blasted. Bits of ceiling tile rained down on Hallie's back as she fell forward. *Umph!* She hit the carpet, palms first.

A large figure shot past her and tackled Drayton. The men went down in a snarling heap. The gun roared again, and Jenna's TV screen shattered. A wild yell sounded from a different direction and a boat-sized, sneaker-clad foot mashed down on James Drayton's wrist. Drayton shrieked and lost his hold on the gun. Brody's arm hauled back then swung. Hallie heard rather than saw the fist connect, and Drayton's thrashing form went still.

"Oh, thank you, Jesus." Hallie put her face into the carpet and sobbed.

"Hey, hey. It's all right now, sweetheart." Strong arms lifted her and wrapped her tight.

She buried her nose in Brody's shoulder, inhaling his scent of spicy cologne mixed with sweat. The pain hammering in her head competed for attention with the throb of her ankle, but nothing else mattered than their hearts beating as one, proof they were alive.

"Open up. Police!" The bellow sounded from outside the door. Hallie gasped and jerked her head up as a crash announced forced entry.

Moments later, the room filled with police officers. A pair of them took custody of a groaning Drayton, who already had his hands bound in front of him with a lamp cord. Damon stood nearby, grinning, the cordless lamp in his hand.

Detective Millette strode in, and her sharp gaze swept the room. "Looks like we caught a killer." She narrowed her eyes at a scowling James Drayton. "Just not the one we expected."

TWENTY-ONE

That evening, Brody cuddled Hallie close on the love seat in the living room of his house. Jenna's place was off-limits until the crime scene people were through gathering evidence. Damon sprawled on a nearby overstuffed chair, and Jenna, Sam and Ryan filled the couch.

Brody finished telling his audience what happened. "So James Drayton killed his adopted daughter to keep his wife from finding out he was responsible for her first husband's death."

Damon sat forward and planted his elbows on his knees. "As far as I'm concerned, Wyatt Rosenbaum was just as guilty of Alicia's murder."

"I agree," Hallie said. "I apologize for thinking you killed the woman you loved."

The young man shrugged. "If I'd walked in on a scene like you did, I would've thought the same thing."

Brody chuckled. "Now you're talking sense, little bro."

"Took me a while, eh?" Damon grimaced. "All those hours around a stone killer and coming that close to biting it myself woke me up to what an idiot I've been, walking around with some kind of stupid chip on my shoulder, figuring folks should put up with my tantrums. I'm on board for some changes, man."

Brody stuck out his fist, and Damon bumped it with his own. Ryan leaned back against the couch and put his arm around his fiancé. "What I don't understand is how the cops got to the scene seconds after the gunshots."

"I asked Detective Millette the same thing," Hallie said. "She fibbed when she told me the police were withdrawing surveillance. They were setting a trap for Rosenbaum. When James and Damon showed up instead, they weren't sure at first that a threat was involved. But, boy, when the first shot was fired, they went into action."

Jenna folded her hands around her knees. "What a miracle you all came out of this alive. I still shake every time I think about it." She gave a demonstrative shudder.

"We're so sorry about your house," Hallie said.

Jenna waved. "Don't give it a second thought. Oh!" She smacked her forehead. "I forgot I picked up your mail like you asked." She rummaged in her oversized handbag, brought out a small stack of envelopes and handed them to Hallie.

Brody patted her arm and got up. "I'm going to call for a truckload of pizza and round up some beverages."

"I'll help." Damon followed him into the kitchen.

"I'm proud of you and those big basketball feet of yours." Brody socked the young man in the shoulder. "Quick thinking."

"Hey, that was no slouch of a tackle, and maybe you should've been a prize fighter, too."

"I hear all that male bonding out there!" Hallie's voice teased from the living room.

"Don't worry," Brody called back. "We're not forgetting the heroine of the hour and her kamikaze crutches."

General laughter floated into the kitchen. Chuckling with his houseguests, he got on the phone for the pizza, while Damon filled a tray with an assortment of bottled soft drinks and water from the fridge. As Brody hung up, a soft shriek prickled the hairs at the base of his neck.

"What's up?" He strode out of the kitchen with Damon on his heels.

Hallie waved a piece of paper. "This was in an envelope with no return address. From Wyatt Rosenbaum, I'll bet. It's Alicia's birth certificate."

Brody bent over the back of the love seat to read over Hallie's shoulder. "There it is in black and white. Parents: Cheryl Anne Gerris O'Halloran and Patrick Rogan O'Halloran from Rainy River, Ontario. Just a second and I'll go get a map so we can look up the location."

Pulse rushing in his ears, Brody loped into his office and retrieved his atlas. A few minutes later they located Rainy River across a river by that name from the small Minnesota town of Baudette. Brody met Hallie's steady gaze. "Are you thinking what I'm thinking?"

"We generally are. Love triangle. North of the border and south of the border boys obsessed with the same beautiful woman. O'Halloran won out until James Drayton murdered him, as well as my innocent parents, to get what he wanted." Tears sheened her eyes. "At last I know all the truth."

"Not quite all."

She blinked up at him. He leaned in and brushed her lips with his. Their audience clapped and cheered. Under the noise, he whispered to Hallie, "I love you, and that's the complete truth."

"I love you, too," she mouthed back, and Brody's heart expanded to fill his whole body.

A month later, Hallie's heart sang as she stood at the front of the church listening to Samantha and Ryan exchange their vows. She glanced a few pews back and spotted Brody, looking distinguished in his suit, with Stan perched beside him, not in a suit or tie, but presenting very nicely in a button-down dress shirt and khaki slacks. Brody winked at her. Stan paid her no attention. His blue gaze zeroed in on Jenna. Hallie didn't blame him. Her friend looked sensational in the emerald-green gown.

She scarcely knew where to start thanking God for His goodness.

Mere days after their deadly brush with James, Hallie received a phone call from the church organization that had sponsored her parents' orphanage in Nigeria. No, they hadn't found the old paper records about Patrick O'Halloran, but they'd found something way better.

After her parents' deaths and the torching of the buildings, the organization had shut down the outreach. However, her inquiries had stirred their curiosity, and they'd checked into what had become of the property.

Iver and Yewande Berglund had planted seeds of the Kingdom of God too well for the harvest to be destroyed by the worst that men could do. A thriving church and orphanage had sprung up on the very spot, completely indigenous to the country. It was run by grown-up orphans who had been raised by Hallie's parents, people Hallie remembered well and fondly. She'd called them, and they were about jumping out of their skins for the daughter of Iver and Yewande to pay them a visit this fall.

Hallie hadn't wasted a moment, and Brody hadn't needed to be asked along twice. A thrill shot through her. If she was picking up on Brody's hints properly, she'd receive a glittering rock for her finger one romantic evening beneath the star-spangled African sky.

* * * * *

Dear Reader,

I so enjoyed telling Hallie's story because I had the chance to mix intriguing tidbits from another culture into a suspenseful adventure, starring an exotic heroine. And Brody wasn't hard on the pen either! Let me know what you thought by visiting my Web site, www.jillelizabethnelson.com.

The neighorhood in St. Paul where Hallie lives and works is based on a real area I visit regularly for my own day job. However, I have taken the fictional license of placing a television studio where none exists. Part of the fun of writing novels.

My personal experience as a short-term missionary in various parts of the world made this story particularly dear to my heart. A slideshow of inspiring photos from my mission trip to Thailand can be found at: www.godtube.com/view_video.php?viewkey=6c8f9eb0bc8c 416f217a. Those who serve on foreign soil deserve all the support we can give them. That's our part in the priceless work they do for the Lord.

Your support, dear readers, of faith-filled fiction is a vital part you play in another important endeavor—insuring that clean, fun and uplifting books continue to be found on store shelves. Thank you for purchasing this book and for telling others about the fine reads that Christian fiction imprints like Steeple Hill Books have to offer.

Excellent blessings to you and yours,

Jill

QUESTIONS FOR DISCUSSION

1. How often have any of us been caught in a predicament because we made assumptions based on appearances—assumptions that turned out not to be correct? Most of the time such situations are humorous or even benign, but they can be hurtful, harmful...or if you're Hallie Berglund, downright deadly. Name a time you jumped to a conclusion. What were the consequences?

2. If you walked into a scene like Hallie did with Damon and the murdered Alicia, would you conclude that you were looking at a killer? Why or why not?

3. Is it reasonable for Brody to insist on Damon's innocence based on his knowledge of the young man's character? What does Brody's unswerving faith in his protégé say about the importance of developing the type of character that others respect?

4. Brody and Hallie have strong opinions about one another at the beginning of the story. What are they, and on what are they based? How do their opinions change over the course of the story, and why do they change? Have you ever changed your mind about someone as you got to know them?

5. Hallie is doing a story about up-and-coming Minnesota models, an industry based on physical appearance. During her investigation into Alicia's possession of her mother's bracelet, she meets a man obsessed with his physical prowess. She discusses the disturbing encounters with Brody. Do you agree with his conclusion that excessive emphasis on the outward is a cover-up for deep insecurities? How can we sometimes fall into the same trap?

6. During a conversation with her two best friends, Hallie mentions that Damon is being ripped apart by the media. Her friend Jenna questions Hallie about fairness in the media. Is the media biased, and if you believe so, do you think the bias is usually deliberate or a natural by-product of the reporters' humanity? Explain.

7. When Hallie came to the United States as a young child, she threw herself into becoming an American girl and lost a vital part of her heritage. What compelled her to leave her past in oblivion?

8. Discuss times you might have left something good behind because of something bad associated with it. How might you overcome the bad in order to reclaim the good?

9. What is Hallie really seeking in her quest for answers about the bracelet her mother made? How might finding the answers affect her ability to commit to a serious relationship with someone she could marry one day?

10. Despite her many character flaws, do you feel compassion for the murdered woman, Alicia? What do you think Damon saw in her that made him love her so much?

11. The real murderer is seriously disturbed and despicable; yet circumstances kept pointing away from him as the killer. Did his guilt take you by surprise? Why or why not?

12. There is a surviving victim in this story. Who is that person, and for what reason was the person victimized, starting well before this story opens? How does that reason relate to one of the themes of the book—obsession with outward appearance?

13. If you were to insert another scene at the end of the story that told about what became of this person after James is out of the picture, what would you like that scene to contain?

14. Office romances can be challenging. Do you think it's difficult to work with someone you love? How can people make it work?

15. Do you think Damon will be able to get over the loss of Alicia? Does time heal all wounds? Have you lost someone important to you? How did you come to grips with the loss?

Dumped via certified letter days before her wedding, Haley Scott sees her dreams of happily ever after crushed. But could it turn out to be the best thing that's ever happened to her?

Turn the page for a sneak preview of
AN UNEXPECTED MATCH
by Dana Corbit,
book 1 in the new
WEDDING BELLS BLESSINGS *trilogy,*
available beginning August 2009 from Love Inspired®

"Is there a Haley Scott here?"

Haley glanced through the storm door at the package carrier before opening the latch and letting in some of the frigid March wind.

"That's me, but not for long."

The blank stare the man gave her as he stood on the porch of her mother's new house only made Haley smile. In fifty-one hours and twenty-nine minutes, her name would be changing. Her life as well, but she couldn't allow herself to think about that now.

She wouldn't attribute her sudden shiver to anything but the cold, either. Not with a bridal fitting to endure, embossed napkins to pick up and a caterer to call. Too many details, too little time and certainly no time for her to entertain her silly cold feet.

"Then this is for you."

Practiced at this procedure after two days back in her Markston, Indiana, hometown, Haley reached out both arms to accept a bridal gift, but the carrier turned and deposited an overnight letter package in just one of her hands. Haley stared down at the Michigan return address of her fiancé, Tom Jeffries.

"Strange way to send a wedding present," she murmured.

The man grunted and shoved an electronic signature device at her, waiting until she scrawled her name.

As soon as she closed the door, Haley returned to the living room and yanked the tab on the paperboard. From it, she withdrew a single sheet of folded notebook paper.

Something inside her suggested that she should sit down to read it, so she lowered herself into a floral side chair. Hesitating, she glanced at the far wall where wedding gifts in pastel-colored paper were stacked, then she unfolded the note. Her stomach tightened as she read each handwritten word.

"Best? He signed it *best?"* Her voice cracked as the paper fluttered to the floor. She was sure she should be sobbing or collapsing in a heap, but she felt only numb as she stared down at the offending piece of paper.

The letter that had changed everything.

"Best what?" Trina Scott asked as she padded into the room with fuzzy striped socks on her feet. "Sweetie?"

Haley lifted her gaze to meet her mother's and could see concern etched between her carefully tweezed brows.

"What's the matter?" Trina shot a glance toward the foyer, her chin-length brown hair swinging past her ear as she did it. "Did I just hear someone at the door?"

Haley tilted her head to indicate the sheet of paper on the floor. "It's from Tom. He called off the wedding."

"What? Why?" Trina began, but then brushed her hand through the air twice as if to erase the question. "That's not the most important thing right now, is it?"

Haley stared at her mother. A little pity wouldn't have been out of place here. Instead of offering any, Trina snapped up the letter and began to read. When she finished, she sat on the cream-colored sofa opposite Haley's chair.

"I don't approve of his methods." She shook the letter to emphasize her point. "And I always thought the boy didn't have enough good sense to come out of the rain, but I have to agree with him on this one. You two aren't right for each other."

Haley couldn't believe her ears. Okay, Tom wouldn't have been the partner Trina Scott would have chosen for her youngest daughter if Trina's grand matchmaking scheme hadn't gone belly-up. Still, Haley hadn't realized how strongly her mother disapproved of her choice.

"No sense being upset about my opinion now," Trina told her. "I kept praying that you'd make the right decision, but I guess Tom made it for you. Now we have to get busy. There are a lot of calls to make. I'll call Amy." Trina dug the cell phone from her purse and hit one of the speed dial numbers.

Haley winced. In any situation, it shouldn't have surprised her that her mother's first reaction was to phone her best friend, but Trina had more than knee-jerk reasons to make this call. Not only had Amy Warren been asked to join them downtown this afternoon for Haley's final bridal fitting, but she also was scheduled to make the wedding cake at her bakery, Amy's Elite Treats.

Haley asked herself again why she'd agreed to plan the wedding in her hometown. Now her humiliation would double as she shared it with family friends. One in particular.

"May I speak to Amy?" Trina began as someone answered the line. "Oh, Matthew, is that you?"

That's the one. Haley squeezed her eyes shut.

* * * * *

*Will her former crush be the one
to mend Haley's broken heart?
Find out in AN UNEXPECTED MATCH,
available in August 2009
only from Love Inspired®.*

REQUEST YOUR FREE BOOKS!

2 FREE RIVETING INSPIRATIONAL NOVELS
PLUS 2 FREE MYSTERY GIFTS

Love Inspired®
SUSPENSE

YES! Please send me 2 FREE Love Inspired® Suspense novels and my 2 FREE mystery gifts (gifts are worth about $10). After receiving them, if I don't wish to receive any more books, I can return the shipping statement marked "cancel". If I don't cancel, I will receive 4 brand-new novels every month and be billed just $4.24 per book in the U.S. or $4.74 per book in Canada. That's a savings of over 20% off the cover price. It's quite a bargain! Shipping and handling is just 50¢ per book.* I understand that accepting the 2 free books and gifts places me under no obligation to buy anything. I can always return a shipment and cancel at any time. Even if I never buy another book, the two free books and gifts are mine to keep forever.

123 IDN EYM2 323 IDN EYNE

Name	(PLEASE PRINT)	
Address		Apt. #
City	State/Prov.	Zip/Postal Code

Signature (if under 18, a parent or guardian must sign)

Mail to Steeple Hill Reader Service:
IN U.S.A.: P.O. Box 1867, Buffalo, NY 14240-1867
IN CANADA: P.O. Box 609, Fort Erie, Ontario L2A 5X3

Not valid to current subscribers of Love Inspired Suspense books.

Want to try two free books from another series?
Call 1-800-873-8635 or visit www.morefreebooks.com

* Terms and prices subject to change without notice. Prices do not include applicable taxes. Sales tax applicable in N.Y. Canadian residents will be charged applicable provincial taxes and GST. Offer not valid in Quebec. This offer is limited to one order per household. All orders subject to approval. Credit or debit balances in a customer's account(s) may be offset by any other outstanding balance owed by or to the customer. Please allow 4 to 6 weeks for delivery. Offer available while quantities last.

LISUS09

Love Inspired
SUSPENSE

TITLES AVAILABLE NEXT MONTH

Available August 11, 2009

SPEED TRAP by Patricia Davids

The fatal crash was no accident. The only mistake was leaving behind a four-month-old survivor. For the boy's sake, Sheriff Mandy Scott *will* see justice served. Yet Mandy finds herself oddly drawn to her prime suspect—the boy's father, Garrett Bowen. If Mandy trusts Garrett, will he shield her from danger, or send her racing into another lethal trap?

FUGITIVE FAMILY by Pamela Tracy

Framed for murder, Alexander Cooke and his daughter fled to start a new life. A life that brings Alex, now Greg Bond, to charming schoolteacher Lisa Jacoby. Then the true killer returns. This time, Alex can't run. Because now he's found a love—a family—he'll face anything to protect.

MOVING TARGET by Stephanie Newton

A dead man on her coffee shop floor. An ex-boyfriend on the case. Sailor Conyers has murder and mayhem knocking at her door. She'll need her unwavering faith and the protection of a man from her past to keep her from becoming the killer's next target.

FINAL WARNING by Sandra Robbins

"Let's play a game..." Those words herald disaster as radio show host C. J. Tanner is dragged into a madman's game. Only by solving his riddles can she stop the murders. And only Mitch Harmon, her ex-fiancé, can help her put an end to the killer's plans.

LISCNMBPA0709